Suzannah Dunn

was born in 1963 and
a novella and short st
title *Darker Days Tha*
novels, *Quite Contrar*
prize in the Betty Tras

ORIGINAL

SUZANNAH DUNN

Past Caring

Flamingo
An Imprint of HarperCollins*Publishers*

| *f l a m i n g o* | The term 'Original' signifies publication direct into paperback with no preceding British hardback edition. |
| **O R I G I N A L** | The Flamingo Original series publishes fine writing at an affordable price at the point of first publication. |

Flamingo
An Imprint of HarperCollins*Publishers*
77–85 Fulham Palace Road,
Hammersmith, London W6 8JB

First published in Great Britain
by Flamingo 1995
9 8 7 6 5 4 3 2 1

Copyright © Suzannah Dunn 1995

Suzannah Dunn asserts the moral right to
be identified as the author of this work

Author photograph by Claire McNamee

A catalogue record for this book
is available from the British Library

ISBN 0 00 654810 5

Typeset in Sabon
at The Spartan Press Ltd,
Lymington, Hants

Printed in Great Britain by
HarperCollinsManufacturing Glasgow

For the memory of Jonathan Warner

Dinah

···········

When September came I thought that I would have all the time in the world, but Zoe is such a slow eater that the days end after lunch. I have to clear away the table and clean Zoe up, and by then it is ten to three and time to leave to fetch Danny from school. It is ten to three now, and she is lurching across the hallway with one welly on and the other held by the thick squashy red stem. Frowning at the floor, she passes me, bumps down onto the bottom stair, and begins to wave the foot ineffectually at the mouth of the boot. Her leg is bound in loose but heavy rolls of beige wool, untight tights. She leans forward, straining the seams of her small blue coat.

I stand over her. 'Zoe, why did you take off your boot?'

Tassel swirling, the hat lifts to reveal her face, an utterly colourless face. (Is she anaemic?) It is a face without distinguishing features, new − a perfect oval held inside the woollen ties of the hat. But the black pupils are burning back into the wet litmus eyeballs. Why? In accusation? shame? irritation? 'There was a thing in it,' her reply bubbles through a pout.

I crouch and take the boot from her. 'A thing? And has this thing gone now?' I shake the boot: nothing. And I run the ball of her foot through my fingertips to check that there is nothing trapped in the tights.

'I think so,' she is saying, happier, to the top of my head.

I place the foot into the neck of the boot. 'Push, Zoe; come on, push against me.' In China, did bound feet mean no shoes or boots for little girls? If so, I can almost understand the attraction.

Zoe is not pushing. She is barely offering resistance to my

I

shoves, so her leg wobbles wildly at the knee. The boot remains dangling from her ankle. 'Come on, Zoe. *Push*.'

She looks back at me, and the expression on her face has nowhere to go, no furrows. So it makes no pattern and leaves no clues. Like the knee, her face merely wobbles under impact.

'Come on, or we'll be late and Danny will be waiting in the playground for us. And it's such a nasty day. We'll have to strip him off and hang all his clothes in the bathroom to dry, like yesterday, remember?'

Down here, I can smell damp. Presumably the carpet by the door is wet. Looking briefly around, I see, to my horror, a few long thin scratches of dried blood on the skirting board. Zoe's nosebleed? I remember that she was standing here – when? two months ago? three? – with blood splashing from her nose onto the back of her hand, and she was shouting, in terror, 'Look, Mummy, look, look!' Perhaps she *is* anaemic. Perhaps I should take her to the doctor. But perhaps he will insinuate that she is being neglected. I must remember to clean here again. (But *how* will I remember?) Thankfully no one is ever here, on the bottom stair, to see.

Zoe is kicking loosely into the palm of my hand. 'Will Danny have a man?'

'A what?'

'A man, a toilet roll man?'

'Oh.' Yesterday, the product of Danny's afternoon was a puppet. 'I don't know. It depends.'

The black centres of her eyes are without light, shadow, shape.

'Depends on what the teacher wants him to do this afternoon.' I squeeze her heel inside the boot to check that it is in place. 'Because sometimes he does a drawing, instead, doesn't he?'

Beside my ear she breathes sharply inwards, before saying, very seriously, 'I do drawings.'

'Yes, I know you do. I see them, remember; I'm your mother.'

I stand. 'Come on, Zo,' I prompt, and she rises and follows me to the door.

I open the door and look out, across our garden, across the road, across the roofs. It is not raining but the air is wet. The bare branches pricking the pathway are wet. My breath, too, is wet, spilling and frothing from the porch. The sky has been sunless all day and will soon be dark. By the time that Danny is home, it will be dark, it will be the end of the day: tea, then telly and bed for the kids, then telly and bed for me and Derek. I reach for my shopping bag with one hand and for Zoe with the other. And then I remember: 'Zoe! You didn't remind me to bring Aunty Maxine's birthday things.'

I hurry back along the hallway and lunge into the kitchen to swipe the parcel and envelope from the table. I enjoy the trip to school in the afternoons because I meet my friend Maxine, if only briefly; and the others, Alison and Georgina, funny Lorna Williams, Alison's squint-eyed sister-in-law, Sarah Reed, and Kitty O'Connor, all fetching their children.

Zoe peers at the package. We bought the box of chocolates and card on the way home from school this morning. 'How old is Aunty Maxine?' she asks, as I shut the door behind us.

'Twenty-eight. A year younger than your old Mummy.'

'How old are you, Mummy?' The small face swivels upwards.

'I'm twenty-*nine*. Aunty Maxine is twenty-*eight*, I'm twenty-*nine*. *Eight*, then *nine*. You can count, Zoe.'

'Danny's five.' She is concentrating now on her fast-moving feet.

'Yes. And how old are you?'

'Three.'

We turn from the Close into the Avenue. Our house sinks distantly behind someone's looming hedge. I can see the broad band of dark stained wood in the middle of the house, and, above, the pair of bedroom windows, awash with nets; and now nothing but the sleek clean roof; and now nothing. It is semi-detached, and of course the twin has gone with it behind the hedge. No doubt one day we will have a detached house, but when we bought this one Derek told me cheerfully that, 'Semi-detached is the best of both worlds.'

'Why?' I asked him.

'One less wall to face the outside world.'

I presume that he was talking about heating bills.

We bought the house two years ago. It is four or five years old. Nearly-new. One-previous-owner. Or, of course, in a sense, *two*: Jonathan and Kay. Or was it Kate, or Katy? A nice couple, according to everyone around here: A-nice-couple. His job moved to Slough. There were no kids, not yet. She was still at work, something in insurance.

'How old is Daddy?' Zoe's question flutters upwards as cold faint steam.

'The same as Mummy. Twenty-nine.'

'The same.' This is said in awe, and with satisfaction. But it is not news to her, I *know* that it is not news to her. I have told her so many times that we are the same age. So why are we going through this again? Why do we go through these things, go over these funny little facts again and again? Which new ritual is this? What is the fascination, this time? I look down at her, for clues, but see the bouncing tassel on the top of her head and the flashing red lights of her boots.

'But I'm two months older than Daddy.' Will this do?

Her wellies continue to punch the pavement in their rapid but regular rhythm.

'I was born first,' I try to explain, 'two months before Daddy.' Will this mean anything to her? 'My birthday is first, every year; two months before Daddy's birthday.' Now she looks up at me. But the look is blank and I suspect that she is simply attending to me. Her face floats beneath the smoky shudders of her breath in the icy air. 'Do you remember?' I urge. 'My birthday, first, this year? When we went shopping in Canterbury? And we bought my present, a new nightie? the blue one?'

'And a new tea strainer,' she shivers.

4

Did we? Why, where, would we have bought a tea strainer in Canterbury?

'Did we?'

She nods glumly.

And I remember. 'Yes, you're right, we did.' I remember that Danny had used the old one – and it *was* an old one, so I was not *too* cross – to lift the goldfish from the tank during cleaning. And I dislike fish, especially wriggling, flipping *live* fish, especially hints of them in my cups of tea. We have goldfish because kids should have pets, but mammals are too dependent. Goldfish are ideal.

'And then for Daddy's birthday, later, we had a picnic in the woods, remember?'

She is nodding gravely. We are turning from the Avenue into the Causeway. On the Causeway the passing cars spit rainwater onto the pavements. I steer Zoe from the kerb, and we follow the Parade of shops, cringing beneath the awnings, clinging to the dry warm shadows beneath their pillars and porches. Zoe squeaks a question but the words are rolled beneath the tense muscular tyres of a nearby car. I crane downwards. She repeats: 'Was he very little?'

'Who?'

'Daddy?'

'When?'

'When he was born.' Her face is dense with concentration.

'Well, I expect so,' I say jauntily. 'Everyone's very little when they're born.'

I glance down. Her expression is lighter, and her face is listing towards me. '*Was* he very little?' She waits expectantly.

'Of *course* he was very little . . .'

Immediately she asks, with great interest, 'Did you take him out in his pram?'

Now I understand. 'I didn't *know* him when we were little, Zo,' I explain, down over my shoulder, to the fluttering tassel.

There is a flash of the eyes – is it possible to have a black flash?

5

—but now they are gone, the face is gone, and she is silent, so I do not know what she is making of her muddle, of the news that I have not always known her father; that, older, I have not always been old; that I have not always been a mother.

'Not far now,' I say, ridiculously, because she knows the route, we walk this route every day.

Nevertheless, she obliges with an appreciative glance into the distance. And she asks, 'Is Aunty Maxine having a party?'

'On Saturday night.'

Zoe twists at the end of my arm. 'Who will baby-sit?' The dusk is daubed and scoured with electric lights, and sloshed with the dregs of rainwater, but her face is still, bright, calm, watchful.

'Maxine says to bring you both.'

Maxine said, 'Bring some blankets and we can bed your two down with my two and Georgina's two, and you can take them with you when you go, or fetch them on Sunday.'

Now I tell Zoe, 'You can sleep upstairs with Maxine's David-and-Robert. And Georgina's Christopher-and-Sarah will be there too.'

No comment from the kitten face.

'Is that okay?'

'Where will we sleep?'

'Upstairs. I don't know. In David's room.'

'In a bed?'

'We'll take some blankets.' Inspiration: 'It'll be like camping.'

She switches to a contemplation of her wellies paddling through the puddles.

'You can play with Sarah.'

'Can I take Rosina?' Rosina the rag doll.

Easy: 'Of *course* you can take Rosina.'

Maxine tells me that she has *Finished her family*. Which, unfortunately, sounds so similar to me to *Finished off her family* that I have to stifle a laugh. She finished before me: her boys are five and seven. She says that she was *Determined to get it all over*

6

with as quickly as possible because I want to be a young mum and then I want some time to myself when I'm still young enough to enjoy it. It does not seem to worry her that she has two boys, no girls. On the contrary, she seems delighted: My boys, she coos, coy. One boy is enough for me: one boy is company, two boys are a mob. But our friend Georgina claims that if her little Sarah had been a boy, then she would have tried again, tried for a girl. I wanted a girl, too, although not enough to try once more, third-time-lucky. Derek assumed, both times, that the baby was a boy: He. I had no experience of boys, no brothers, only a sister. Derek, of course, had been a boy, as well as having brothers, and boy cousins. For Derek, boys were natural. For me, boys meant nothing but damp bathroom carpet and guns for Christmas. I did not want a boy, but when Danny was born, he was not a boy, he was a baby.

As soon as Danny was born, there were rumours among family and friends of another baby: How long will you wait before the next one? Do you want a girl next time, for a change, or a boy, to match? Will you go into St Faith's again, or will you try The Infirmary? As if one baby somehow causes the next. As if there is literal truth in the claim that You-can't-just-have-one. Why have any at all? When I was young, it seemed to me that many women in history, in books and films, had no children. But then I grew up, and I was not a woman in history. I would have been happy with one child, a novelty, but there was no choice. One child is an Only Child, worse than none at all: a deprived but spoiled loner. If I had started, then I must finish, not merely the pregnancy, but the family. I had been a second child, but my sister and I never played together. She made me feel second best.

Sometimes it seems to me that everyone believed so certainly in Zoe that she appeared for them, that everyone spoke so much about a second child that they conjured her. And what would I be doing now, without her? Because as soon as Danny was born, he was growing up, growing away, looking forward to school. What was I going to do when he left home and went to school?

7

Would I go back to work? What work? What work have I ever done? A stint in Reception, waiting to leave. It was easier to have another baby. When Danny was born I had become a homemaker, but without quite enough home. Zoe set the seal on my life.

'Will you and Daddy sleep there, at Aunty Maxine's and Uncle Gerry's house?' Zoe bellows suddenly above the regular sweep of rainwater around tyres.

'No . . .'

'No?' she yelps upwards into my face.

'No, there won't be enough room for us. We'll go home in the middle of the night and take you with us, wrapped up in your blankets, or we'll come and fetch you in the morning.'

'*Late* in the morning,' she complains.

I see that we are approaching some roadworks, some workmen, and immediately I am tense, before I remember that I have Zoe with me. I am safe with Zoe. They will not shout at Zoe. And they are less likely to stare, because, guileless, she will stare back at them. For a while, before the babies, I enjoyed walking, because it was good exercise, and the soothing rhythm and sudden solitary freedom released so many daydreams. But interruptions, intrusions, lay in wait at roadworks, hovered on scaffolding, and flew without warning from passing cars. Each one was a reminder that although I had felt that I was alone, I was being watched.

In front of men I feel naked. I like clothes. I have only ever been without clothes in front of Derek. And, I suppose, doctors, nurses, midwives, who were examining so thoroughly that they did not see me. Without clothes, I like bedclothes, their dark kisses on my skin. I like choosing clothes. In my clothes, I draw my own lines. 'What shall I wear to Aunty Maxine's party?' I ask Zoe.

She shrugs with a flip of her eyebrows and a slump of her bottom lip.

'You don't know?' I rib gently. 'Why did I have a daughter, if not to help me decide on my clothes?'

She looks interested, ponders this question.

'What about my new trousers?' No, too hot.

'The sunflower dress,' she says sharply, seriously.

'No, Zoe, not the sunflower dress,' I exclaim. 'It's an old, old dress, for the summer, for wearing around the house.'

'Will there be fireworks?' she asks immediately.

'No, we've had the fireworks, this year.' Every year we go to Maxine and Gerry's garden on Bonfire Night.

'Is Christmas soon?'

Too soon. 'Five or six weeks.'

'Will I go to Danny's school at Christmas?'

She knows the answer. 'No.'

'A year and a half?'

'Yes.'

'Will my teacher be Mrs Delaney?' The same cheerful tone.

'If she's still there.'

'Will Danny be there?'

'Zoe, we've been through all this.' We halt at the kerbside. The traffic is relentless. I hope that she can learn from example because I am too weary today to explain again about crossing the road. 'The answer is no.' I glance down to see that she is glancing fearfully upwards. 'He will have moved on. Up. To Mrs Petrie's class.' At the faintest twitch in her hand, she leaps with me from the kerb and flies with me across the black spangled road. Momentum hurries us onwards, past the gates of the park. I thrill at this freedom from the park. It is an unforeseen blessing of winter that I cannot spend half an hour each afternoon rotating with Zoe from swing to seesaw to slide.

It amazes me that she adores the park so much: swings, seesaw, slide, so simple. So tedious, for me: hard labour, pushing down on dense planks of wood or against the thrash of chains, or reaching to guide Zoe's shoes on the tuneless xylophone of steps to the summit of the slide. For hours, the planks moult and moan; the rusty chains rustle; and Zoe skims the silver estuary and slams back into my arms. As soon as she is in my arms, she floats upwards and outwards again, blown large and light by her

9

own deep quick breaths. Dodging the breaths are her instructions: *Slide again; Swing; More*. Her gaze, inflamed with excitement, sticks for much of the time to mine, shyly sharing the joy. She never tires of the park; I have sat waiting experimentally – half an hour? an hour? – but she never tires. And so, in the end, I am forced to betray her, to take her away. Now I hear her saying to herself, bravely, 'No park today.'

This afternoon I would have been concentrating even less than usual on the park because I am worrying about Maxine: I owe Maxine and Gerry a meal; so, after the party on Saturday, will I owe them two? Do parties count? Parties with buffets? When Maxine and Gerry come over for an evening, we can discuss the holiday. I do not remember who first suggested that we all go on holiday together this year, but I do remember Derek enthusing that *The kids can play together*. Now, looking down at Zoe, I realise: who will play with little Zoe? No one. Me.

Zoe was listening when Derek and I were talking about the holiday over breakfast on Saturday. During a pause she asked, very concerned, whether there would be a lift in the hotel. Danny was more interested in the possibility of a swimming pool.

'Yes,' Derek was agreeing with Danny, 'you can learn to swim, this year.'

Zoe asked hopefully, 'What about me?'

'You're too small,' Derek replied lightly.

'Daddy!' Her rebuke wheezed with shock, with sheer disbelief.

Maxine and Gerry want more than a holiday. They want to emigrate. Gerry is an electrician; Australia wants skilled workers; electricians are skilled workers. Derek is a cabby, so there is little hope for us. Surprisingly, Danny is old enough to be defensive of his homeland: 'I like it here,' he shouted when we last talked about emigration.

And Zoe echoed frantically, 'Mummy, *I* like it here.'

'You'd like it *there*,' I told them. '*Here* is a *dump*.'

10

Zoe reminded me, 'Danny's school isn't a dump.' She was kneeling on her chair, leaning across the table, elbows nudging toast, eager to emphasise the point.

Derek's newspaper crackled a laugh, and his words soared from behind the grubby pages: 'That's right, Zoe-baby!' Then, quietly, for me, 'Go easy on the kids, Dinah.'

Zoe said, 'Daddy, I'm not a baby.'

Now she wobbles me with a sudden shift of her free arm. She is pointing: 'Can we go down there, soon?' She is pointing beyond the junction, towards Kenwell. Often she uses the name, *Kenwell*. She has always known the name, even before she knew the name of our own area of town. Kenwell has always been a source of fascination for her. I know that children are often drawn, for their own reasons, to the apparently mundane. (Hence Rosina the rag doll, very ragged.) But what are Zoe's reasons for Kenwell? I used to ask her, but she always replied with the same nonsense. In general, Zoe tells me very little. I learn about her by watching. And I learn very little. Usually I watch her whispering over her dolls. She does not talk to them; she describes them, organises them: *You, Jenny you can go to Mrs Delaney's class at Christmas-time, but you, Annette, stay home with Rosina, and, Rosina, you cook sandwiches for lunch; you, Josephine, read to the others when they're in bed; and you, Maria, you're pretty, you're Miss World.*

Now, once again, I glance beyond her stiff quivering arm into the long road full of shuffling cars and lumbering buses. The roving blinkless head lamps are pitted with raindrops. Above the cramped shops, street lamps singe the black sky. But however much light rinses through Kenwell Street, it remains dark. I do not go into Kenwell Street except for items which I cannot find elsewhere: a clothes horse, once; clock repairs, sometimes; or lubricant for locks. And I never go far into the Street. The first stretch is littered with small shops stocking fossilised fashions from the forties and fifties. Fabric shops, too: whenever I look through the windows I see stacks of thin cardboard skeletons bound thickly in frills, sequins, even towelling – enough towelling to make the biggest bath towel in the world. These shops are Bargain Basements without the basements. There is one small, suspiciously nameless supermarket at this near end of Kenwell Street, the windows stuck with hand-written posters, the porch strewn with boxes, big booming shells of cardboard.

There is a pawnbroker, too, in Kenwell Street. I have seen the telltale sign peeking from a wall in the distance: the golden globes so oddly high, clean, neat. I was surprised when I first saw them; no, I am still surprised to see them, every time, because surely pawnbrokers belong to the past, to my childhood. Although not to my *own* childhood.

'Zoe,' I start, 'how many more times? There is nothing down there.'

Her lips bud – anger? embarrassment? – and her gaze slots downwards.

'Kenwell is horrid.' I would say that nothing in Kenwell has changed for fifty years, but fifty years is meaningless to Zoe.

Her tiny hot windpipe, opening, hisses at the cold touch of air: 'I used to live there.' She throws a glance hard into my eyes.

This is the answer that she has always given to my questions. But we have never lived in Kenwell.

'Well, if you *did* live there, then you didn't live there with *me*. Or Daddy. Or Daniel.' I increase the pull on her arm. I want to hurry past Kenwell. I want to hurry. Her wellies churn puddles.

The words struggle out among her crowded breaths: 'I lived there with Mama.'

Usually she tells me that she lived there with *My other mummy*. I turn and dip slightly to glimpse her face, which is straining with seriousness. *Mama* is new. Which telly programme is responsible for *Mama*?

'Mama?' I whoop.

'And Papa.'

'Papa?'

Her up-turning face is lit with pity for me. Perhaps she thinks that I was too loud. I quell an urge to remind her that not so long ago she used to enjoy a good scream in the street. And, anyway, there is no one here, no one in particular to hear us, merely the flickers of a crowd of shoppers.

'And anyone else, Zoe? Did you live with anyone else apart from your *Mama* and *Papa*?'

She gazes calmly at me. 'My little sister.' Momentarily, absently, she staples her lower lip with a row of teeth.

I hope that this is not a hint. I have been waiting for the request for another baby. 'I didn't know that you had a little sister,' I exclaim pleasantly.

Zoe performs another of her elaborate shrugs. 'She was only a baby,' she says uncertainly.

'Oh. Well, then.' I smile carefully. And then ask politely, 'What was the name of this sister of yours?'

Her expression flattens beneath intense concentration. Eventually she says, 'I can't remember.'

Looking ahead, I can see the school, the glowing windows, glass-filled arches. 'That's a turn up for the books, Zo: you, unable to remember.'

'Eileen,' she says quickly; but immediately, quietly, 'No, not Eileen.'

'I should hope not. Because what kind of name is Eileen for a little girl?' I can see Danny in the darkening distance, swinging very ineffectually on the stiff school gate, his limbs threaded through the white steel bars.

'Look!' I urge Zoe: 'It's Danny-boy.'

Caddy

·················

Like almost everything else, the power of digestion decreases
with age. Every day I spend an hour digesting my lunch. I sit in
an armchair and let the radio run, and then at half past two, I
turn everything off, shut the house down for a while, make
myself go out. At three o'clock this afternoon, as usual, I reached
the supermarket. I do not like the supermarket – poor choice and
high prices – but I buy tins of cat food there, nothing else. The
daily trip provides me with exercise and fresh air, although I
suspect that the air in Kenwell Street is not particularly fresh.

Through the glass doors I could see fruit and vegetables, *Fresh
Produce*, lying in boxes frilly with plastic grass: Clue, plastic
grass, answer, *Fresh Produce*. In each box there are always very
few examples of a particular species, never good examples, never
Fresh. I was wondering who ever buys fruit and veg from a
supermarket. A few moments previously, I had been wondering
whether to go to a cafe for a cup of tea: something which I
contemplate every day, before telling myself that I have tea at
home, which costs less, and that I would feel awkward walking
alone into a cafe. My mother, like all good mothers in the old
days, brought up her daughters to avoid going alone into tea-
rooms, and it is difficult for me to shake the habit of a lifetime.
But it was particularly cold this afternoon and, in retrospect, I
was closer than ever to changing my mind and going somewhere
for a cup of tea. If I had done so, I would have missed the
reflection on the doors.

A little girl walked in front of the glass. I turned. She was
walking across the top of the street, and she was pointing at me.
The tiny finger woke my heart. It was my heart that recognised

her, my huge clamouring heart. The tiny finger whipped my heart. She was with a woman, and as they walked away I saw that she was not pointing at me, but pointing past me, down Kenwell Street. What did it matter? Not once during the past forty-three years have I seen her. However much I have wanted to see her, my wish has never come true, she has never appeared, not even momentarily in the corner of my eye. Yet suddenly she was there, at the top of Kenwell Street. And she was walking away. So I followed. Usually I like to be home before dark, but I followed, walked behind them from Kenwell into darkness. They were fast, much faster than me. I was kept at a suitable, spy-worthy distance. I do not know what I was thinking. Nothing. Everything.

Ahead of me, they fetched a child from school, a boy, and then the three of them came back along the road, came back to me, past me, and now they are going into a Co-op. I did not know of this small Co-op, so close to Kenwell. I follow. Inside, a wire basket is hanging from the crook of the woman's arm, occasionally bumping the little girl's head. In the basket there is a coconut sponge cake, a jar of treacle, and a packet of crispbreads. I am following them to the till. The woman snatches a packet of sweets, at the last moment, from one of the shelves; and the little girl's gaze rips an arc above herself in the fizzing yellow light, her mouth dropping open. 'Wait,' commands the woman. I can focus firmly on the little girl. I know the tiny face, know every radial stitch of gold in the irises, every swirl of fur in the eyebrows. We have reached the till. I turn back to the end of the shelves to pick something, anything: a bottle of lemonade. I'm-a-secret-lemonade-drinker.

There is no queue, so they are moving through and moving away from the till. The woman breaks neatly into the packet of sweets: 'I said wait.' Both children are shifting anxiously around her legs. She takes one sweet daintily from the packet for the little girl, before turning to the boy. The little girl is wide-eyed and breathless with chewing. My legs are shaking, I have never been so aware of my legs, but I manage to smile at the little girl and say, 'Mmmm, you like that, don't you?' Not a proper question, but something to hold us together for a moment longer. Unsure, she nods in reply. There is no jangle of recognition in her face. But, of course, I look very different. Forty-three years different. The woman, chewing, is looking at me because I am holding a bottle of lemonade and it is not lemonade weather.

'Is she yours?' I force myself to ask, quickly, pleasantly. The woman smiles in reply, and her sweetless hand lands very softly and briefly on my little girl's head. But the boy is bleating, so she turns away and throws a few words at him. I do not hear the words, just the crack of them in the air; and I see the shape of him shrink away into a sulk. I am looking at the little girl and she is looking at me. Where has she been, for forty-three years, since 1922? How can a child go away when she is six and then reappear forty-three years later, as a toddler? *Don't ask questions.* I have never believed in anything, religion or superstition, but I know that this is my little girl.

I have heard it said that all children look the same; and they do, until the child is your own. That is the trick.

'You have a scar on your lip,' I say, bending to trap it gently beneath my fingertip, but stopping short. The skin on her face is translucent, untouched. Milk teeth, milk skin.

The woman bends between us.

'Where? That? No, that's not a scar. That's just a mark. From birth, or something.'

A birthmark?

'No,' squeaks the little girl, suddenly interested, and indignant, 'I fell over.'

'Did you?' I encourage, flaring inside with fear. I do not move my smiling face away from her.

'No you didn't,' whines the woman. 'Well, yes, you fell over, but you knocked your *nose*, do you remember? Do you remember the nosebleed?' She bends again, taps the scar with an orange fingernail: 'But you didn't get this from falling over.'

'Where did you fall?' I ask.

Her eyes are lively with their own special dark sparks. How do eyes, cold orbs, light up, shine, dance? Pleased to be believed, she sings out, 'The doorstep.'

I hear the woman's harsh sigh. 'No, you didn't.'

But, yes, she did. I remember the rush of air as she flew from the doorstep, and the simultaneous scraping of my own breath in my gaping mouth; the bounce – yes, bounce – of her head on the floor, then the rich blood, so much, from someone so small, and finally the siren of terror and pain.

'Oh dear.' I straighten. But such a small scar, in the end.

Walking now towards the exit, the woman dispenses another sweet to each of the two children. 'Say good-bye to the lady,' she prompts the little girl.

And she obliges, on cue; her attention focused inwards on the sweet.

I follow them into the street. 'Cold,' I whisper to the woman, wincing.

She nods sadly.

'Far to go?' *Where do you live?*

She shakes her head, frowns at the dripping dusk. 'Harts-bridge.'

'I'm out beyond Kenwell.' And hastily I add: 'This is the nearest Co-op.'

She flicks a faint smile down at the little girl. 'Did you hear that? Your favourite place. Kenwell.'

The little girl's night-light face twists towards mine, a throatful of frosty air tipping into her open mouth. 'I used to live there,' she steams.

'In Kenwell? So did I.' When most of the little terraced houses were for the families of workers at the brewery. Before the brewery sold them and young couples bought them. Before I was moved out, four years ago, onto the Westerbury Estate.

'Yes,' drawls the woman to the little girl, patting her towards the kerb, 'and I used to be Enid Blyton.'

And they halt momentarily on the kerbside, one little mitten rising blindly into a bigger hand.

Realistically, what could I have done? They have now crossed the road and she is gone. But she is not gone; she is found. Because I know that they will come back to the school every day for the little boy. And I know that they live in Hartsbridge, which is a small area. I can find her. Every day, any day.

So I did not follow. I came home. Shouldn't I be drinking Champagne? Instead of tea. I am taking the photograph from the pile of old documents in my top drawer. There is solely this one photograph. Of Evie. Over the years I collected more and more photos, but by then Evie was gone. My other, later children fill the two albums beneath the coffee table.

I lift the photograph very carefully from the drawer. But why carefully? It is tough, leathery, very different from the tiny, flimsy, slippery photos of today. I saved for a long time from my housekeeping money for this portrait. By the time that I could afford to go to the studio, there was not only Evie but Iris. Two for the price of one? In the photograph they are cosy with each other, and trusting and adoring of the photographer, like puppies. Forty-three years ago, I took down this portrait from its place on top of the old chest of drawers. I was afraid of being morbid, I was afraid for Iris. No one ever remarked that it was gone. Ever. Iris was too young to know. Forty-three years later, I am creeping back across the room with it, this time to the sideboard, where I can prop it against the fruit bowl until I buy a frame. After all, it is mine. I saved long and hard, I made the appointment with the photographer, Alfred Donnelly. It is his name, not the children's, which is printed on the bottom of the photograph. Is he still alive? Forty-three years ago, he was in his twenties. Like me. A few years older than me, if I remember correctly. So, yes, it is possible that he is still alive. How many people did he photograph during his working life? And always at their own instigation: their births, birthdays, engagements, weddings, anniversaries. So many, many successful moments: laid end to end they would stretch to . . . where?

This photograph is mine because I was the one who laid it in the bone-dry darkness of a drawer and kept it safe for forty-three years. Kept it, and kept it safe. Now I stroke my fingertip very gently across the smooth surface; which I did not dare to do when I was so concerned that it should last. But how much longer will I last? Ten more years? A fraction of the time that it has already survived. And why do I need it? To remind me of Evie? I do not need reminding. And, anyway, she looked nothing like this photographer's moll. I stroke the warm rusty rosehip surface, very softly. Each shade has been pitched perfectly against the others, has been melted to an exactly correct consistency. Photographs are made from light and dark, yet this portrait is conspicuously free of shadow. Even the faces, especially the faces, two little lanterns, are free from shadow. A friendly fading lifts the edges of the whole portrait so that it becomes a face with a smile. I prop it up on the sideboard and it smiles softly at me.

Caddy

I have become much fitter during the past two years because I walk so far during the afternoons. Or perhaps not, perhaps this is not good for old ladies, perhaps unknowingly I am wearing myself away, but who cares? The Co-op is too far for my own shopping. I cannot carry too much, but I buy sweets, or crisps, or creations which seem to be related to crisps, *Wickers, Twists, Puffs and Frazzles*. I will buy anything to secure Zoe's dappled gaze, however briefly, for myself. She is five years old now, and seems tall for her age. Is this tallness due to genes or vitamins? I have read that children are taller nowadays. Certainly my children never grew tall. At the moment Zoe is crouched on the narrow foot-plate of the roundabout, pedalling the warm spongy tarmac with one sturdy sole. I am sitting on a bench. The woman – Mrs Fox, her *Mummy* – is in the chemist. She left me to look over Zoe – 'Five minutes, thanks a million,' – before crossing the Causeway, slinging her hips from side to side in her hot pants. I could have been anyone. For all Mrs Fox knows, I *am* anyone. In one sense, though, she knows me well enough because, for two years, we have been coming across each other several times a week, in the street: she, fetching Zoe from school; me, on bogus shopping trips to the Co-op. Then we walk together for a while, quite often coming in here, into this park.

I cannot risk telling her who I really am; who her Zoe really is; who she, Mrs Fox, is not. In the beginning, I was nameless, a nameless friend: Mrs Fox encouraged Zoe to know me as *Your Friend*. She stage-whispered, *Here's Your Friend*, or *Say goodbye to Your Friend*. Each time, before I could protest (*No, call me . . .*) she was talking again, or gone. And call me what? But I did not like *Your Friend*. It was too impersonal. Like *Good Samaritan*. It was indiscriminate. Which I am not. I knew Zoe's name from the beginning because I had asked, bending, doting: 'And what's your name?'

'Zoe.' Very trusting, awaiting praise.

'Zoe!' I repeated, to give myself time. It seemed such a ludicrous name, to me, that I was afraid that it had come somehow wrongly from my mouth: *Sew-y; Zowie*. But, then, nothing could replace *Evie* for me. Or so I felt. I was wrong: *Zoe* has had to replace *Evie*. 'Sounds very modern,' I added, splashing my words with enthusiasm.

'It's Greek,' interrupted the woman, flatly. I glanced at her, and she shrugged in reply. 'Or so it says in my book.' Then she tensed with a sudden realisation: 'Ancient, I mean. Ancient Greek. Not . . .' and she shrugged again . . . 'well, not modern, I suppose.'

I learned the surname, Fox, by continuing, 'Zoe what?'

They did not know my name until much later, months later, when Mrs Fox — and I have never been invited to know her as anything else — snapped around to me, mid-sentence, and asked, 'What *is* your name?' as if I had been secretive.

'Dutton,' I said, loudly, clearly, 'Mrs Dutton.'

But there was no blink of recognition from Zoe, who was staring at me and chewing with determination on a sweet I had given her.

So then I said, more quietly, 'Caddy, my name's Caddy.' I had not heard this name spoken aloud for a long time. It was my name when I was young. All I hear nowadays is the bus pass form of address, *Mrs Dutton*; and *Mum*, which is not a name, not even a proper word, but a mere sound, a whine. And *Granny* and *Grandma*, of course, but rarely.

'Caddy?' yelped the young woman, disbelieving. 'Caddy? As in tea caddy?'

No. '*Caddy*,' I urged, confused. 'Short for Caroline.'

21

'Oh.' A big, arcing, satisfied Oh. Then one final blip of doubt: 'Not *Carrie*?'

'No. *Caddy*.'

'Short for Caroline,' she repeated, apparently accepting, but explaining it to herself, committing it to memory. Retaining doubt, seeking confirmation.

'Perhaps it's old-fashioned,' I suggested desperately, miserably.

By now I have had whole conversations about Zoe with this young Mrs Fox (and how old is she? mid-twenties?). I know where Zoe was born, and when. Or, I *knew*, because I have forgotten, because the details are arbitrary, they do not tally with Evie, there are no clues, no coincidences, just a clatter of numbers and words. I remember the new birthday, though, for Zoe's sake. And I remember that Mr Fox is a taxi driver. Because, for some reason, I like this. Perhaps because he is self-employed; or self-employed *more so* than most other people who are self-employed, he is *supremely* free, sealed into his own big black car, forever on the move. And of course there is something very grand about such a big black car, about the daily trips to London, to the very centre of London. It is nice for Zoe that her father goes so far each day to work because then he comes a long way away from work to come home.

I remember their address, too, of course, the fragment of Fox address that I was inadvertently given: McAllister Close, in the Hartsbridge area.

The first school holiday was awful – suddenly, day after day, all Co-op and no Zoe – so I found McAllister Close. And now, often during the holidays, I walk into Hartsbridge and to the end of the Close – the *opening* of the Close? – and watch, and wait, until I see her. I do not let her see me. Because I do not know what I would say, how I would explain myself. I simply need to know that she is still around.

Now, with a few loosely strung steps, she is moving from the roundabout to the climbing frame. I shift forward on my bench: pointlessly, because how can I reach her any more easily? I must either go and stand guard, or stay still, here. Mrs Fox stays, but bellows warnings: *Hold-on-tight*, as if this would not otherwise occur to Zoe, and *Don't-mess-about*, as if there is anything else to do on a climbing frame. Zoe, who, a fraction of a moment ago, was sitting on a bar, now falls, swinging suddenly backwards, the bar held in the crook of her knees. I lurch from the bench. She laughs, leaves me standing, her upside-down eyes fixed firmly on me. She stretches to pat the tarmac with her palms.

'How will you get down?' I protest.

Holding the bar again, she slowly swings her crooked legs away and drops them over her head to the ground, which winds her body upright. Smiling only with her eyes because she is still biting her lip, she chucks her arms wide, bobs a curtsey – 'Thank-you, fans,' – and then turns again to the frame. Her four limbs harden among the hot steel bars, but her hair and skirt are fluffy from the spin. I sit back down reluctantly on the bench, suddenly resentful of the splinters straining for my skirt.

'Why don't you come and sit for a while with me?' I yell. And now, tantalisingly, 'I'm good at stories.' Our first opportunity to sit and talk together without Mrs Fox.

But she is pretending to be unable to hear me through the hum of her activity. I remember that I learned to tell stories when I had my own children: Anything-for-a-quiet-life. Lies, damn lies, and lullabies. Usually my conversations with Zoe – no, they are *her* conversations *with me* – tinkle with references which, sadly, mean nothing to me: school and school friends, and the various doings of her older brother Daniel. I smile and nod and murmur, lying in wait for clues, sinking into the shifting sprinkle of light in each dark eye. I have less trouble with her many references to telly programmes: I manage to trace Darren and Samantha to *Bewitched*, The Jackson Five to *Top Of The Pops*, Daleks to *Doctor Who*, and the Cookie Bear to *The Andy Williams Show*. Zoe watches too much television. When I was young I wanted more than anything to go to the Picture House. Now I would like to go one afternoon with Zoe.

23

Last week I asked her what she wants to be when she grows up. She replied, 'A pop singer. What did you want to be?'

'Nothing like a pop singer,' I laughed. 'Except, perhaps, a Queen, I suppose.' And if not a Queen, then the power behind the perfect household. Spick and span: why *spick and span*? Why *spick*, why *span*? My own house, my own children. I served a long apprenticeship under my mother. For streets and streets around, she was famous for homemaking. Our house glimmered among the others: from the front step to the upstairs windows. My mother defied dirt. And there was so much dirt in those days, chimneys in the skies and horses on the streets. And we had nothing, she worked magic with nothing. Every Monday morning my father's suit went in its neat package to the pawnbroker and stayed there until Friday afternoon, and he never knew.

When Zoe has gone, and I am alone again, *I* have conversations *with her*, or rehearsals for conversations with her, in which, at last, I tell her who she is, and who I am, and we wonder together, and make sense of it all. Perhaps she has the answer, perhaps she will have the answer when she is older, when she has the words. Her current life makes no more sense to me. The Fox family is a tiny satellite, Mrs Fox's mother living a hundred and fifty miles or so away, Mr Fox's people less far away but in a neighbouring county. It seems to me that the Fox family has no reason to be here rather than anywhere else. When I was a young woman, I lived half a mile from my mother (half a mile too far, when my children were small). I come from this town, and, within this town, from Kenwell. My husband came from a nearby village. He left home for a town, for work, and the first place that he found was Kenwell. Apart from that one adventure, my husband was a stayer; yes, a stayer, I think, rather than an optimist. But never despise a stayer: my mother liked to say that he would *Make a good provider*; and he did, eventually.

Now Zoe is turning head-over-heels over the same bar. The bar is turning inside her fists, probably burning her palms. What is the attraction? And from where does all the energy come? Was

I ever like Zoe? Of course there was no climbing frame for me when I was a child. But Zoe tells me that this climbing frame, here, is new, a late addition to the set of wooden swings, see-saw, roundabout. It seems that this park was previously a cemetery because the boundary wall is lined inside with broken gravestones. They are ripped, rootless. Surely there is a law against this? Or perhaps I am thinking of plague pits. But surely it is wrong to walk on a grave? Yet I remember walking all over dead bishops when I went on a visit to Canterbury Cathedral: there was no choice, because they were sunk into the floor of the aisles. No doubt bishops know what to expect. But these poor lost souls, beneath my bench, beneath Zoe's orbit? Voiceless against the local council. Even in death. Surely this is grave-robbery? Gravestones are so very expensive. *Of course* they are expensive: there is so much work on them. Presumably these ones will stay slapped against the wall, here yet not here, in limbo, because there is nowhere else for them to go. The local tip would be useless because they will not burn.

When I was a child, where did I play, what did I play? I did not play. Or, only rarely, and briefly. I helped my mother in the house. And I did not complain, because I wanted to help my mother. She had so much, too much, to do. Our house, like all houses, was full of children. All children, everywhere, helped their mothers. There were no machines in those days, not even to heat water. In our houses, heat and light were messy, singeing walls and ceilings, and falling, silting every surface. All children had their own household jobs, everything was done by hand, our hands, the hands of mothers and children. No: in our case, mother and daughters. And I remember that when my brothers went to work, they paid a proportion of their earnings to my mother – true, it was a large proportion – but she took all mine and gave me pocket money in return, always, from the day I started work when I was fourteen years old, until I left home to marry.

Zoe is working upwards on the frame, on lever-limbs. At the

top, she looks beyond the wall of graves towards the Causeway, over the Causeway, for Mrs Fox. When I was a girl I was told, at school, with all the other girls, that it was my job to populate the world. And that there could be no higher calling. What do they tell girls now that the population is too big? *You might like a kid or two, they go nicely with a new suite.* I do not like the expression population *explosion*. It implies mess.

Looking at Zoe, who is pushing hard against the bars to hold herself above them, I can see the difference between her five-year-old body and the bodies of my friends in Kenwell when I was a child, and even the bodies of my own children. It is not simply a matter of height. Zoe is thin, but slim; streamlined, a modern version of thin. I remember rickets, the drastic kinks in little limbs. Tuberculosis was worse, the insides rotting unseen, the bones dissolving. My own father died of TB, but not, of course, the childhood version, the bony version. When I was a child, many children in Kenwell were marked by a brutal bristle on their heads: lice. Others showed, in their glittering rashes and sores, the failure of their skin to hold and soothe their busy bodies. There were no antibiotics, so eyes and ears popped with pus. Ears, in particular, were to be feared, cradling poison in secret before spilling it into the soft clean folds of the brain. Faces were different, too, because they were blocked: we were told again and again, in class, by our teachers, to force each breath through our sticky noses because otherwise our mouths would stay open, slack, and cold air would crack our teeth, and dirt would sweep down our throats. But worst of all, and fairly common even when my own children were born: the strange unstoppable wasting away of a baby, leaking milkily from its orifices. So died my mother's first baby, and another between Connie and me. Unlike nowadays, there was no technology for doctors and nurses to use against the wills of sick babies – to feed them, to breathe them.

Zoe's face, turning to me from The Causeway, is all frown.

'Chemist,' I shout to her, in explanation.

The frown merely hardens. 'What for?'

'*I* don't know,' I protest. And now, softer, 'Why don't you come down and have a little sit with me here?'

'In a minute,' she asserts loftily, turning away and rolling herself slowly headfirst over a bar.

Dinah

Guiltily, looking across the kitchen at Derek, I remember my flush of relief this afternoon when I returned to the park and found Zoe with the old lady. What would I have said to Derek if she had disappeared? Derek, who provides so well for me, only for me to lose his daughter on the way home from school. I had told myself, when I left them, that I could trust an old lady. Or, at least, that I could trust an old lady to be unable to go very far. From the chemist, I had been able to see Zoe bobbing on the roundabout and flopping on the climbing frame, but then I was jolted by the sudden disappearance of the tell-tale turquoise cardigan, the sudden lowering of Zoe's bright flag, somewhere in the corner of my till-busy eye. With one huge burning heartbeat I re-focused on her little apple-green T-shirt, and realised that she had merely discarded a layer.

When I came through the gateway, I was surprised to see that she was sitting on a bench with the old lady. That she was sitting properly, sensibly, soles barely skimming the ground. The cardigan was slumped in the old lady's lap. The lady turned her smile on me, and Zoe's head followed.

'Zoe has been telling me all about life in Kenwell,' she called to me.

Again? How many times have I had to listen to the Kenwell story as I try to hurry Zoe home? Mrs Dutton has been encouraging her.

'Her Mama and Papa and little sister, and the house with the yard.' One hand rose from the cardigan and dropped over Zoe's knee. Zoe's knee was hidden entirely by the hand, and her lower leg wobbled feebly in the air.

'Oh, that,' I said. And then, more buoyantly, because there was nothing more to say: 'What an imagination! She takes after her mother.' But it seems to me that Zoe's imagination is unique. It is strange, hard. Unlike her brother's imagination, which swoops, settles briefly, and soars again, forever dropping and finding, finding and dropping. Zoe seems to have been born with a set of imaginings which do not change, and they weigh heavily on her.

'We've cooked up a little plan between us,' the lady was purring. 'I'm inviting you both to my house for tea.'

I glanced rapidly at Zoe. If she had been a grown-up, she would have been able to tell me more, without words, but her eyes were black and blank. 'What, *now*?' I yelped. My life – or, my life as it should have been for the next two or three hours – was passing before me: a browse in the boutique, with a fresh consideration of the cheesecloth halter-neck top; a detour to the bakery to buy a scone ring; then home for a pot of tea on the patio. I stood still in front of them, the smell of an old lady's house closing in on me: cat food, gas fire, old carpet. I was brought up in such a house; I have had enough of old ladies' houses for one lifetime.

'No, not now,' she was wheezing. 'How about tomorrow?'

And so here I am, explaining and complaining to Derek. Although I have not told him that both Zoe and I have been invited. I want to send Zoe alone.

'Perhaps she's lonely,' he counters good-naturedly. He has begun drying the dishes whilst I am washing.

'Well, I'm sure she *is*, but that's not *my* problem.'

He glances at me wide-eyed over the swirling cloth.

'I *mean* . . .' And *what* do I mean . . . 'Why Zoe?' People do not usually fall for Zoe, dark little po-faced Zoe. But perhaps that is the explanation: she is somehow so unlike the brash kids of today, horrible Jackie Moore whom she calls her friend, and the rest of the merry little gang, Tina Livesey, Gaynor Beckett, Linda Someone.

Derek is replacing a glass with great precision on the shelf in the cupboard. The glasses are his responsibility. The kids and I prefer plastic beakers.

'As I said, perhaps she's lonely.'

I pause, press my weight onto my palms on the bed of the sink, savour the sting of the hot water on my forearms. Why do I feel that Derek is answering a different question from the one that I am asking? 'No . . .' I breathe aloud; then, trying again, 'But do you think it's *all right*?'

In the corner of my eye, the cupboard door blinks.

'I mean, do you think it's . . .' and there is no other word, '*healthy*?'

Strolling into view, he flicks the tea towel over his shoulder, something only men do. 'Do I think *what's* healthy?'

'To be so . . .' *obsessed* would beg the question . . . 'taken with her?'

Derek takes a handful of cutlery and shakes it vigorously above the sink. I glance at the lace of bubbles which remains crackling quietly around the prongs of the forks, and then I slide this disapproving glance to Derek. Nevertheless, he drops them wet into the drawer, and I am too tired to stop him. 'Could be a good thing,' he chirps above the crash. 'I wish *I* had a sugar grandmummy.'

'No,' I correct him hastily, 'I don't think Zoe will make any money out of this old dear.'

'You-never-know,' he continues. I see him glancing surreptitiously at the clock; he is stalking the *Nine O'clock News*.

'Well, I *do* know,' I say, simply to tweak his attention.

'Oh, you *do* know, do you?' he says, delighted. He rests back against the draining board; he is delighted because he thinks that he has finished the drying, that he is merely passing the time until nine o'clock.

'Plates.' I nod towards them.

'They're draining,' he says.

'They've drained.'

Cheekily, he extends a fingertip towards them, to indicate residual moisture.

'They've drained, Derek.'

'A lot of people store all sorts inside their mattresses,' he says cheerfully, as he relents and begins the plates.

'*All Sorts*?' I have a brief vision of colourful pieces of liquorice.

'All, sorts,' he corrects. 'Money, really, I mean.'

'Oh.' I tug the plug from the hole. 'That. No, I've told you.' I turn to him and try again: 'So, is it all right?'

'Is what all right?'

'For Zoe to go to this old lady's house?'

'Of course it's all right.' But now, suddenly: 'Does she have any grandchildren?'

'I don't know.' I dry my warm wrinkly hands.

'It's not like you not to know something like that about someone.' For the first time during this conversation, his tone is almost serious.

'I don't like to ask. Something stops me.'

'Nooo!' Derek brays, sliding the cupboard door triumphantly shut on the neat stack of dry plates. 'She probably has seventy-three grandchildren! All in Australia!' Then he nudges me: 'Came here to escape them.'

'I just get a feeling,' I try. And I shrug to fill the space which is empty of words.

'Oh, a *feeling*,' he says, and touches my nose with his lips.

'Are you coming to watch *The News*, then?' I reach for the light switch.

'A *feeling*,' he is proclaiming, following me into the living room. 'Feminine intuition.'

Feminine intuition? I never know how to feel about this. Probably because whenever Derek says the phrase, it seems to ring with ridicule.

Zoe

Mrs Petrie's voice knocks through everyone else from the other side of the room: 'Zoe! Zoe Fox!'

I look away from my friend Jackie to distant Mrs Petrie. She is pausing, peering over everyone else and down onto me. She is standing with a small group of mums (Peter Ainsley's mum, Sarah's mum with sticky orange lips, Tammy's huge mum, *Here-comes-the-bride-forty-inches-wide*). The mums flick their eyes towards me.

'Zoe, I haven't had a note yet from your mum to say that you can come on the trip next week. Can you ask her?'

I nod.

'*Don't* forget,' she smiles, and turns back to the mums.

I return to Jackie. 'It's my turn to come to yours.'

Jackie says, 'If you come to my house tomorrow, then I can come to yours on Friday.'

'Can we see the guinea pigs?' Jackie's guinea pig, Tabitha, has had babies.

Jackie nods. 'My favourite is black and white, I'll show you, she's lovely. I want Mummy to let us keep her, and I'm going to call her Minnie.'

'Do they bite?'

Jackie squeaks: 'No!' Then, slower, lower, 'No . . .'

'But they do have teeth?' I check.

Jackie huffs, 'Of course they have teeth. How else could they eat?'

I am fairly sure that my fish have no teeth, yet they eat. I feed them a pinch each day from the small tub which I buy on Saturdays from the pet shop. The food is in flakes; the flakes

32

look tiny to me, but presumably not to Peter Pan and Wendy, my two fish.

Jackie frowns into my face. 'Would your mummy let you have a guinea pig?'

I shrug hopefully, she might let me have one for my birthday, I'm going to be seven in two weeks and two days. 'Well, they're not very big . . .'

'Tabitha's quite big,' Jackie interrupts crossly.

'But not as big as a dog.' I glance around and realise that, although we started well, clearing-up time is ending and our friends are leaving, and our table remains covered in a mess of painty newspaper. 'Come on,' I tell Jackie. As the sheets of paper hiss and scatter into balls under our grabs, I explain: 'Mummy says that dogs are too big. And they make a mess.' I do not explain *mess*, but add, 'In the garden.'

Together we drop our grimy bundles of newspaper into the bin. I tell Jackie, 'Granny and Gramps have a dog, called Bryn.'

'*My* Grandma and Grandpa,' Jackie begins, as we go to the sink to wash our hands, 'have a setter, called Lady Monday. Lady, for short.' She swings around to lean back on the sink, folds her arms to show off a bracelet.

I turn on the tap. 'Why?'

'Why what?'

'Why is their dog called Lady Monday?'

'She *just is*,' Jackie snaps. 'Why are *your goldfish* called Peter Pan and Wendy?'

Why *did* I call my fish Peter Pan and Wendy? Mummy says that they are Danny's fish, too; he calls them Stingray and Goldfin. Around my hands, water is coiling from tap to plug hole. I think hard of Peter Pan and Wendy, the real Peter Pan and Wendy, not my fish. 'Because they'll never grow up,' I explain to Jackie, 'because fish don't live for long.'

Jackie is staring at me.

'And because fish sort-of fly.'

'No they don't!'

33

'Well, they don't *walk*, do they?'

'Zoe!' Mrs Petrie pipes, 'Goodness!' Her shoes slap across the tiles towards me. I turn, but she is already here, above me, leaning over me. A soft beige sleeve brushes my cheek, and beads click close to my ear. One of her hands, built of so many bones, comes down onto the cold metal daisy of the other tap. Water clatters into the basin. '*Hot* water, Zoe.' She turns off my tap. 'You won't shift any of that paint from your fingers under a dribble of cold water. And I can't send you home with hands like that, can I? What would your mother say . . .' She takes one of my hands inside her own into the tower of warm water. 'Goodness,' she sings again, fishing behind the taps for the soap. She begins to rub everything together: her bones and rings, my fingers, the tumbling hot water, the frothing soap.

Suddenly I say, 'We didn't have a hot water tap in my old house.' I do not know why I said this. I wait to find out.

'Is that so?' Mrs Petrie hums.

'In Kenwell,' I add.

'Zoe Fox, you fibber!' She swops my hands. 'You lived in Brillington before you moved to Hartsbridge; and I know, because you lived very near me. You lived in one of the Shenfield Hill flats, your mummy told me; and I happen to know that those flats are very nice,' she says, smiles. She lets my hand drop.

'Not *that* flat,' I start.

'Dry them.' A stiff green paper towel appears in front of me. 'Properly.' Two taps of her heels on the tiles and suddenly, somehow, I am on the other side of her. 'Jackie,' she is saying, turning her back to me, 'let's have your hands, quickly.'

My old house opened onto a yard. The fence around our yard was tall but there were cracks and holes; through the cracks and holes I could see a muddy alley. In one corner of our yard there was a privy. Whenever I went into the privy, I did not close the door. I looked out onto the cat-daubed yard and the distant house, and held onto Mama with my eyes. She was always in the house, inside the windows. The sink, where she was so often

34

standing, was the same as the one here in our classroom, a huge deep box of stone. The tap was crooked, high above the basin.

Water was warmed on the stove. I remember that when it is cooking, water has its own smell. But I cannot remember the smell. Mama had a smell, too, the smell of powders stirred into her clothes and creams soaked into her skin. I remember coming through the door from the yard, and seeing Mama working, at the sink or stove, her arms white but her hands like red crabs. Between her eyes the skin was so thin on her nose that I could see the bone underneath.

I remember that she was frightened of spiders; that she waited, watching, behind her broom for spiders. But she was frightened of nothing else, no one else; except the baby, when the baby came. I remember when the baby came. Mama was screaming in the bedroom as if someone was trying to kill her. But there was no one else there but the old lady who had come to bring the baby, and she did not look as if she would kill anyone. Papa would not go to help, and would not let me go either. He kept me wrapped in a blanket in his chair whilst he squatted in front of the hearth, his eyes hot with the fire.

Apart from the night of the baby, I did not often see Papa, although his smell was always in the house; and his smell was the smell of *him*, unlike Mama's. Whenever I woke in the middle of the night, though, Papa's breathing was in the bedroom, swishing in the big bed, the creaking wooden bed above and beyond my own little bed, its white sails flicking in the darkness.

'Zoe?' says Mummy.

She is standing above me, holding my painting high up.

'Mrs Fox,' says Mrs Petrie, beside me, 'I'm afraid these two have been rather slow.'

'So I see.'

I can see up into her nostrils but not into her eyes. 'Mummy, can I go to Jackie's house tomorrow?'

Mummy says, 'And what does Jackie's mummy say?' This is a question for Jackie.

Mrs Petrie walks away with our damp paper towels.

Jackie replies, 'I have to ask, but she'll say yes.'

'Come on, then,' Mummy sing-songs.

We follow Mummy into the cloakroom. She turns to tell us, 'I'm popping next door to catch Mrs Borden when Danny's class comes out.'

Jackie and I sit down on the long low bench and feel underneath for our outdoor shoes. 'Let's speak Spanish,' I tell her. On holiday, Daddy said that my accent was very good. Jackie went to Spain, too, last year, so she knows how Spanish sounds.

Flipping off a plimsoll, she shrugs and says something.

I reply, in my perfect accent.

Turning her laces around her fast-moving fingertips, without looking down, she begins another stream of Spanish.

Suddenly Mummy's head swings through the swing doors. 'Come on.'

I follow Jackie across the tiles, with one untied shoe.

When I reach the main porch, I stop to see to my crumpled shoe. Jackie continues onwards, behind Mummy. Drawing the lace into the skin of my forefinger, I look ahead, across the playground, to watch Mummy talking to Jackie's mum. Jackie flits around them, and then stops to loll on the fence. I check the bow on my shoe, and hear the hum of their voices becoming louder, higher. When I look up, I see that they are stepping apart, backwards, nodding.

'Good,' hoots Jackie's mummy, turning towards me. 'See you tomorrow, then, Zoe.'

'Yes,' I shout back.

'Come *on*,' Mummy calls to me.

I run across the playground towards her.

'Have you managed that shoe?' she is asking.

'Where's Danny?' I ask.

'Gone home with Mark Robinson. Have you done that shoe?'

We both look down at the shoe, at the bow. 'Yes,' I tell her. And now I look around for Danny or Mark, peer into the cars along the kerb.

'No need to shout,' shouts Mummy, walking away. 'I was checking because I don't want to stop again, two yards down the road, for you to fuss with your lace.'

'It's *metres*.'

'What?'

'It's metres, not yards.'

Her eyes flip, her tongue clicks: 'Christ. Does it matter?' Then she says, 'It's yards, as far as I'm concerned.'

After a few more steps, still ahead of me, she calls, 'As Danny has gone to Mark's, there'll be extra tea tonight for you, me, and Daddy.'

'What is it?'

'Chops.'

Yuk.

'*And* baked potatoes. Before you pull a face.' Stopping, turning, waiting for me, she frowns. '*You* try planning a meal for every day of the week, then.'

I start to think.

'And I said *every* day, of *every* week,' she shouts, turning away.

'Macaroni cheese.'

'Every day?' she wails.

'No . . .'

'Well.'

She stomps onward. Would she notice if I stopped? And if I stopped, and she stomped onwards without me, where would I go? Could I join some gypsies? 'What about a rota?' I shout to her. My teacher, Mrs Petrie, likes rotas.

Her head turns. 'What?'

'A rota: macaroni cheese on Monday; something else on Tuesday . . .'

'Oh.' She wrinkles her nose. 'No.'

'I'll have half of Danny's potato, tonight,' I tell her.

'A third,' she says. 'If you're lucky. A small third.'

When we stop to cross the road, I say, 'I wish we could go home in a car.' Everyone else goes home in a car.

'Zoe! Walking is good for you.'

Like chops.

'Walking keeps you fit, keeps you trim.' She straightens on the kerb beside me. 'These-legs-were-made-for-walking. Walking is good for your figure.'

My friends' mummies have thighs inside their skirts, and bottoms, and bosoms coming out of their blouses. Mummy's figure is lost inside her little dress. Where the dress stops, the legs start. With each step, the legs shake the chain belt, the chain of papery golden coins slung around the dress. Mummy wears no bra. In wintertime, she wears a vest like mine.

Mummy makes her figure invisible by doing exercises; or *sexercises*, as she calls them, laughing. She saves them for the evenings when, she says, *The house is empty*: empty of Daddy, but not empty of Danny and me. I go with my toys to my bedroom, and she fills the living room with her stretching, swinging legs.

Now she is saying, 'Look at your friend Jackie's mum if you want to see what a car does to a figure.'

Jackie will be home by now, stroking the guinea pigs.

'I don't know why you have to pick Jackie Moore as your friend. I do *not* like her mother.'

Could a baby guinea pig hide inside my pocket?

'A snooty piece of work. She looks at me as if I come from Mars.'

She runs her eyes over the Parade on the other side of the road. 'Whenever she sees me coming, she can't wait to escape into that car of hers. Have you noticed?'

Daddy likes animals; surely he will not allow Mummy to send my furry piglet back to the Moores.

'Snooty moo. It doesn't hurt to make an effort. Does it?'

I look up, stroke my gaze over her eyes.

'No,' she replies to herself. 'But she looks at me from behind those silly sunglasses. Mind you, if she smiles, she runs the risk of cracking her face.' She is pleased with this one. Beside me, the chain belt swings widely. 'Whenever someone is wearing that much make-up,' she chirps, 'always ask yourself, What is she trying to hide?'

She stops so suddenly that the little coins crash into her dress. I look ahead. Uncle Gerry – Aunty Maxine's Uncle Gerry – is standing in the middle of the pavement, facing us, hands up and open; his face pulled between wide eyes and saggy smile.

'Gerry!' squeaks Mummy. She walks towards him, and he drops his arms heavily to his sides. 'What are you doing here?'

'You want the truth?' He folds his sparkly eyes into wrinkles: 'Nah. Truth is, Maxey's laid up this afternoon so I've been sent to fetch the boys from school.'

Mummy stops in front of him. 'With what?' she asks. 'Maxey's laid up with what?'

I circle behind Uncle Gerry.

'Oh, you know.'

'Oh,' says Mummy, much more slowly than Uncle Gerry's Oh. Then, 'Women, eh?!' And this was quick, with a laugh.

'Yes,' joins in Uncle Gerry.

I step away, towards the window of the book shop.

'Well,' Mummy says, 'that's rotten for her. Send her my love.'

I scan the pictures on the books in the window. Mummy's reflection scatters them. She is hugging herself. I cannot see the two bones which stretch from the base of her throat to her shoulders, but I know that they are there: thin wings, they rise in her skin whenever she hugs herself. Once I ran a fingertip along the length of one, and she told me that men like them.

Mummy is laughing. 'It's nice to see you out of your van in the daytime.' One foot is flopped in front of the other, rocking to and fro inside its sandal. 'It's nice to know that you don't just exist from the waist upwards.'

In time to the beats of her laughter, Uncle Gerry is swinging his hips from side to side beneath his huge hands. 'I'll wear my shorts next time,' he laughs.

There are not many books in the window. On one of the books, there is a picture of a pink blancmange.

'You men spend too much time shut away from the world,' Mum is saying.

'And not enough time on the streets, like you women?' chirps Uncle Gerry.

'Oh you are awful.'

Suddenly Mummy says, 'Go on, then. Off you go. Go and do your fatherly bit.'

I return from the window.

'And tell Maxey to give me a ring if she needs anything.'

One of Uncle Gerry's hands is high, wide and flat in the air, like a man guiding a plane from the end of a runway. 'Will do.' Then he winks at me with the whole of one side of his face.

Mummy and I walk for a moment before she says in a low voice, 'Maxine has period pains.' She looks down at me. 'You'll have to face all that, someday.'

'Mummy,' I try, 'can I have a guinea pig for my birthday?'

Her gaze is very heavy on mine. 'Why would you want a guinea pig?'

'A little tiny one.'

She sweeps her hair up through her fingers. 'Your fish will be jealous,' she warns.

'I won't let them know,' I plead.

'We'll ask Daddy,' she mutters.

But Daddy is not the problem, the problem is you. 'Did Daddy ever have a guinea pig?'

Mummy breathes through her nostrils. 'They'll be no more talk of guinea pigs until you clear up that mess in your bedroom.'

What mess? It is a camping site for my dolls, and not yet finished.

Zoe

....

Every time I come here to Mrs Dutton's house, I go for the magazines. We do not have magazines at home because Mummy says that they are a waste of money. Mrs Dutton has lots. I like to read the stories about animals: one lady's cat bit a burglar; one little boy fell into the elephants' cage at the zoo but was lifted up by a trunk and returned to his family. Mrs Dutton has a cat, Oliver. As well as Oliver and the magazines, there are lots of other things in this house which we do not have at home. Mrs Dutton keeps the cream at the top of the milk, which Mummy shakes through the whole bottle, *share-and-share-alike*. Mrs Dutton has cushions on her sofa. We do not have cushions because Mummy says that they are messy. Like ornaments, which Mrs Dutton has everywhere, music boxes with lids of little shells or shiny pictures of the Eiffel Tower. We do not have ornaments because Mummy says that they collect dust and make work. Mrs Dutton's cups have saucers, and she uses proper glasses even for milk or lemonade, not beakers. Her telephone is in her living room; ours, at home, is out in the hallway, on a glass tabletop held by ivy leaves which are metal but painted white. But, then, Mrs Dutton has no hallway. Her front door opens into her living room.

Mrs Dutton's telephone never rings; not like ours. Mummy spends her evenings with our phone, in the hallway, humming into the receiver and looking into the mirror on the wall, looking over her face, and sometimes over her teeth, if she has just eaten. And Mrs Dutton has no Danny, which is good. But her house is not like my old Kenwell house. My old house was dark but there was a fireplace. I could see that there were people who lived in the fire, little people who danced in the cave of the chimney. There is no fireplace in Mrs Dutton's house, only the gas fire with its small squares of bright clean flame, one, two or three. So there are no sudden angry bangs, no popping of dry hot twigs. There is no smell of smoke. Her house smells of things wiped down, perhaps the shiny brown tiles around the gas fire which look like huge cool chunks of milky chocolate. It smells like the inside of a newly washed cup. This living room is very bright, and the big green lampshade on the tall brown stem reminds me of the palm trees on holiday. There are photographs, too, of old-fashioned people, in frames. When I asked Mummy why there are no photos of us in frames at home, she said that they collect dust and then she said, 'And I see you all day every day, so why on earth would I want to see a photo of you as well?'

Here, Mrs Dutton looks at me when she talks to me. At home, Mummy talks to me all the time, but usually without looking. Usually she is moving crockery around in the kitchen; sometimes she is standing at the living room window and peeking out of the net curtain. She says, *You will clear that up, won't you?* I wonder what would happen if I said no. Or she says, *Don't make a mess, will you?* What if I said yes? Sometimes she tells me what she is going to do: *I'll wash these things through, and stick them out on the line before the rain.* Sometimes she tells me what we are going to do together: *We'll leave at two and pop into the library.* Often she complains: *Your Granny is being awkward about Boxing Day, and of course it's just an excuse to be awkward, and what gets me is that I've spent this last year trying very hard, but, well, no, I have never been good enough, have I, which is a laugh, coming from that old hag*; or, *This tap is leaking again and I've TOLD your father.* Sometimes I do not know if and how I should answer. Like when she asks, *Did you SEE Eliza Roache? she's even BIGGER, she seems to be bigger whenever I see her, which is every day, and it can't be healthy, surely, to carry all that weight around, and what do you reckon, is it lack of willpower?* Sometimes I know that her comments are not for me: listening to the radio, she often calls out, *I like this one!* And whenever she is dressing, or sewing a hem, or shopping for clothes, she says, or laughs, *If you've got it, flaunt it*, to herself. She also says, *You're only young once*, although she does not seem very young to me.

Mrs Dutton is looking at me now, and saying, 'Guess what I have for you!'

I widen my eyes in return, which means *What?*

'Tizer!' Her smile stretches and sticks, waits.

She thinks that I am waiting for the Tizer. In fact, I am not keen on Tizer. I prefer Fanta, which I have on holiday.

'Shall I get you some?' she checks.

'Yes please.'

She turns and creaks towards the kitchen. Mum often says to me, *I really do not know how you can spend all your time stuck in that old dear's house.* And she is right: she really does not know how. For her, these magazines, my favourites, are *Silly chit-chat about curtains*, even though I have tried to tell her about the animals. And whenever she comes here to fetch me, she sits on the armchair nearest the door, not in it but on the arm of the armchair; tapping her feet, missing her radio.

But I do not spend all my time here. I spend time in other people's houses too. I am more often at Jackie's house. *I don't know how you can spend all your time with that awful Jackie Moore*: but although Mummy does not like Jackie, she likes Jackie's *house*. Whenever she comes to fetch me from Jackie's house, she stands inside the doorway and smiles very wide to cover her nosiness as she looks around. In Jackie's house there are no armchairs, only a long black velvet sofa on the lower level of the split-level room, and three beanbags, although they are much bigger than the beanbags that we have at school and are for sitting on, not for throwing around in Music And Movement. The floor is wooden, smooth and shiny, and the stairs, too, which float without banisters from the middle of the floor. I have never been upstairs. Upstairs, apparently, is private. When

Jackie came to my house I decided to make my own bedroom private but I forgot and we went there to make a camp beneath the bed.

Children's shoes are banned from Jackie's house by Jackie's Mum. If it is not dark or raining, we are shut out, in the garden, with the guinea pigs. The first time that I went to play with Jackie, she wanted to play Dare, but I refused. Because I felt that she would go too far. Jackie is afraid of nothing. When I said no, her face stiffened: 'Oh go on. Just a little dare.'

But how little? I said no.

'Just . . .' she shrugged . . . 'go and switch on the oven.'

But I knew: a tiny dare, this time, but eventually..? And I did not want to risk meeting her mother alone, in her kitchen, especially not if I was fiddling with her oven, and especially if I was wearing shoes. And worse: there is the brother. Jackie's brother is ten, nearly eleven. Jackie says that Lindy Richards is his girlfriend. Lindy Richards is the leader of the girls in the senior class. She is a model; her mother puts her into adverts.

'No,' I said.

'Just go and open the fridge, then,' she wailed. Then: 'Tina and Gaynor would.'

'That's their look-out,' I said, copying a phrase from Mummy. 'Let's play horses. Mine's called Star.'

For tea, at Jackie's house, we have lovely Saturday lunch time food: scrambled eggs on toast, or alphabet spaghetti with grated cheese. And when I come home, Mummy frowns because it was not a *proper hot meal*. Mummy has a rule: A proper hot meal every day. If I say that scrambled eggs and spaghetti *are* hot, she replies, *I SAID PROPER*. School dinners do not count, either. She says, *Sod school dinners, mash and custard*. I do not dare to tell her pudding at Jackie's house is an ice lolly each from the ice cream van and that Jackie melts hers in a mug to make a drink.

I have told Jackie about my other home, in Kenwell. She said, 'I've a twin sister, in Spain.'

'What's her name?' I asked.

44

'Natasha.' She was balancing above me on the low knobbly wall which surrounds her patio; one leg stretched stiff, and the foot, too: she was doing ballet.

'Why is she there, and you here?'

'I'm adopted.'

'Oh.' I looked down and squeezed one of my feet into a point. But Jackie's face was burning the insides of my eyelids. She looks so like her mum. 'It's lucky that you look so much like your mum, *this* mum,' I said helpfully. They both have blonde hair with an even blonder streak in the front. Everything about their faces is big. Especially the freckles on their noses. No, not the noses, the noses are not big, but Sindy-doll size. But the eyes are big, and everything about the eyes, the lids and lashes. Their lips are swollen as if they are surprised, although I know that Jackie is surprised by nothing.

Mummy says that with two inches of make-up, anyone can look like Jackie's mum. She also says, *Her figure must be a disappointment to her*, and then adds, as a tip for me, *Always check a woman's thighs*. I know that I look nothing like Mummy. We are different colours, even: eyes, hair. Granny frowns at me through her glasses whenever we visit, and says *She reminds me of Stella* or *She has Donald's eyes* or *There's a little of Lillian in her*, but no one else seems to remember any Stella or Donald or Lillian or whoever.

Earlier this afternoon, Mrs Dutton took down a photo to show me. 'Do these two remind you of anyone?' she asked, bending beside me.

'No.' Two little girls from the olden days.

Often she likes me to talk to her about my old home, in Kenwell. Sometimes she asks me about my mama: what was she like, what do I remember about her? I tell her that she was different from the mummy that I have nowadays, she was quieter. At home, she wore a long white apron over a long grey dress. Whenever she went out, she pinned a hat onto her hair. If I close my eyes I can see the slippery grey skirt, the apron, the row

45

of hat pins in her mouth. A couple of times, Mrs Dutton has asked me about the baby. Once, she asked me the baby's name.

'Eileen, or something,' I said. 'Eye-something.'

'Iris?'

'Yes, Iris.' Of course Iris. How silly to have thought that it was Eileen. 'And Mummy *said* it wasn't Eileen!'

'She did?' Mrs Dutton sounded surprised.

'She said that Eileen wasn't a baby's name.'

Mrs Dutton's mouth was open, but the breath stayed inside her chest for a moment. Then she said, simply, 'Oh.'

Now I remember that the baby was not a baby at all, or not always, because it was Iris who wanted to stay awake one night to see if there were any ghosts in the bedroom. Mrs Dutton is coming back into the room with a glass of Tizer. She lowers it carefully in front of me: 'There.'

'Thank you.' I take a sip.

She sits down in the armchair opposite me.

'Aren't you having any?'

She frowns at me and then at the glass. 'Ooooh, no. I don't like bubbles. I only keep a bottle in the house for you.'

Without realising, I have been busy sipping, because when I look up I see that she is staring at me, her bottom lip tucked beneath her front teeth. I lower the glass in both hands into my lap.

'Just one thing,' she says, very quietly, and very slowly. Her lip slips dented and wet from her teeth.

'What?' I ask her.

She clamps shut her crinkly eyelids for a moment longer than a blink. And then she says, 'Where were you, in-between? I mean, in-between your Kenwell home and the home where you live now?'

This is new to me. 'I don't know. Nowhere.'

'Nowhere?' Her lips move but everything else on her face stays very still.

I try: 'I lived there then, and now I live here.' I listen carefully to my own words, because I do not know if they make sense.

Before I can decide, she says, 'So how did you come here?'

'I don't know, I don't remember.'

'I mean, why are you not there any more?'

Whenever I try to remember, there is nothing but blackness. I shrug, carefully because of the glass of Tizer. 'Perhaps my mummy and daddy had to go away.'

'Oh no,' she says suddenly, sadly, 'no, I'm sure not. Why on earth would they leave you?'

Another careful shrug. 'Perhaps they were being chased, or something.'

'Chased?'

By a wicked witch. 'Or perhaps I got lost. And was too young to remember my address.' Because I am certain of something: I was only little.

Her face is stiff but her eyes sparkle with sadness. 'Don't you think that your mama would come and look for you?'

'Perhaps she couldn't find me.'

'And your *new* mummy *did* find you?' She frowns.

'No. I probably went to an orphanage.'

I do not remember any orphanage. But I have seen on television that, in the olden days, children often went to orphanages. In stories of olden days, almost everyone is an orphan. I do not know any orphans. Is an orphanage the same as a Home? Mummy talks sometimes about children in Homes. Children in Homes do not seem to be orphans. It seems, from what Mummy says, that they are in Homes because their mums and dads have been bad to them. But sometimes it seems that the children are bad, because Mummy tells me, *If you don't stop this, I'll be on the phone to that Home and they'll come round to take you away*. The Home is near my school: it is big with a tree-house in the garden, and a wooden sign above the hedge. Mummy says that it is a Children's Home, but I have never seen or heard any children in the garden.

Mrs Dutton leans forwards and rests her folded arms on her knees. Her eyes are level with mine. I have never noticed, before,

47

the green edge around each pale brown middle. 'Wouldn't your mummy have told you if she had found you in an orphanage?'

One of Mummy's favourite sayings is, *There are no secrets in this house.* But it seems to me that there are secrets and *secrets*, and the secrets that do not exist in our house are mine: *What did you do at school today? What did you do at Jackie's house? What did you wish when you blew out the candles?* Any secrets of Mummy's which she tells me are the boring ones: how much weight she has gained, or what argument she is having with Granny. But I know that Mummy would never adopt a baby. I remember when we went to see Auntie Theresa's new adopted baby, tiny Gary, flat on his back in his Moses basket, wriggling with his eyes and mouth wide open. Afterwards, Mummy said to me, 'She knows nothing about that baby, nothing at all, and I couldn't take a chance like that.' And I know that Mummy was pregnant before I was born: there is an old cine-film – Daddy shows old films when he shows the new ones of holidays or birthday parties – where Danny is so very small, falling all over our toys on a patch of grass, and then Mummy comes onto the screen, with a huge smile and a huge dress, and moves slowly, strangely, towards baby Danny, as if she is ill or old. 'And there's you,' Daddy laughed once: 'Zoe Fox, you were a film star even before you were born.'

'She was pregnant,' I tell Mrs Dutton, 'I've seen pictures. But perhaps it wasn't *me*.'

Mrs Dutton frowns.

'Perhaps the baby died, and they gave her me.'

'Oh Zoe,' says Mrs Dutton, and the voice is lower than I have ever heard from her.

'Perhaps the baby died, or went into a Home because there was something wrong, because Mummy is sad when something is wrong with someone.' Like Lucy Hartley's little sister, who is four but comes with their mum to school, strapped into a special pushchair, to fetch Lucy, and Mummy says to me *It's a shame*, and *It isn't right to keep someone alive like that*. Like what?

With thin legs? 'Perhaps she took me because I came from poor people.' Mummy talks a lot about poor people and their poor children: they live in dirty houses, and never go on holiday. I do not know if we ever went on holiday from Kenwell, I do not remember any holiday. But I do remember that Mama was always cleaning: floors and windows, places where my new Mummy never cleans. Whenever Mummy is cleaning when Daddy is home, he calls out from behind his newspaper or in front of the football, *Just RELAX, will you?*

'So where is Iris?' I wonder. Mummy says that *Two is quite enough*. Danny plus me makes two, and no room for Iris. 'Should I go and look for Iris?' Iris, who never goes on holiday and so probably has not learned to swim yet. I need to teach Iris to swim. It is easy, and she will love it. 'But will they come and take me back, the poor people? Has Mummy made a plan with them?'

'Zoe, please.'

I think she means *Please shut up for a moment*. She has never asked me do anything; not even to shut up, especially not to shut up. She looks scared, but surely she is not scared of me. But she is looking at me. 'Zoe,' she says very quietly, 'it wasn't like that.'

'Like what?'

Her face shrugs. 'There was no orphanage.'

I take a slow sip of the Tizer and then place the glass on the little table which is below the arm of the sofa. 'What, then?' Has Mummy told her?

Her face is like Daddy's face when he is telling Danny or me, *You really mustn't ever say that word again, regardless of the other kids at school.* Serious. But she says, 'I . . . was . . . your Mama.'

But she looks nothing like Mama. There is no long grey dress, and never has been a long grey dress. Mrs Dutton's dress, opposite me, is on top of her two big knees, slightly above a slithery silvery slip; and it is not grey, it has tiny red bits, not insects, but flowers, on a yellow background. And her hands, in a ball in her lap, are not Mama's hands, which were huge and bony. And there is no diamond of nose bone between her eyes. But there is, was, I did see, I do remember, the green ring inside each eye. But she is much too old to be my Mama. She even smells old, like Granny. She is older, even, than my friend Dawn Greg's mummy.

'Are you going to take me back?' I ask her. Will I have to leave my bedroom? And Mummy and Daddy? Do they know, or, what will they say? Will I be able to come back to see them? Will I have to change schools? And if I do not change schools, what will everyone say when they find out? And if I do change schools, will I ever see Jackie again?

She pulls a row of fingertips across one eye and then the other. 'Zoe,' she says, 'it was a long time ago.'

'Did you give me to Mummy?' Should I have mentioned Mummy?

'No, Zoe, I didn't give you to your Mummy.' There was a tiny laugh inside these words, behind the swishing fingertips, but I can see that she is crying. I have never seen a grown-up cry, not even Mummy, who is so often shouting and screaming.

'So..?'

She leans towards me, waves the fingertips in front of my face, whispers, 'You'll hurt yourself.' And I know what she means, because Mummy often complains to me, *You were born biting that lip of yours and if you're not careful you'll die biting it.* I let the lip go from my teeth, and tighten my hands in my lap around each other.

'Zoe,' she starts again, 'this is very hard to explain.' And now she is staring at me. 'You became very sick.'

So, she *was* a poor person: no money for proper food; no heating in the bedroom; no holiday in the sun; perhaps no bus fare, even, to come and visit me in hospital. 'And you couldn't take care of me,' I finish for her, helpfully.

She surprises me with a small laugh. 'No, I *could* take care of you, I *would* have taken care of you, for*ever*, but . . .'

Her gaze bounces off mine.

'This will sound very odd,' she says, 'but, you died.'

Died means Heaven and angels with smirks and pyramids of praying fingers; and Gramps going away; and Grandma's cat, Jeffrey, run over by a car and taken to the vet.

'And somehow,' she is continuing, 'you're back.'

Like my favourite telly programme: the olden-days children come back to play in their garden. But they wear knickerbockers, and I do not. And they are secret, and there is nothing secret about me: I have a Mummy and a Daddy and I go to school.

'You had a different name,' she is saying, slowly. 'You were Evelina.'

I open my mouth, but I cannot repeat the name: I have never heard it before and now it is gone. Was it foreign?

'Evie, for short,' she says. 'Always Evie.'

'We had a cat,' a white cat, on the wall around our yard, four silent feet the size, shape, of pennies. 'Not Oliver.'

Her face flutters with a smile. 'Not our cat: you mean the white one?'

I nod.

'The shop's cat. The shop near our house. Milly. Minnie. A wonderful mouse-catcher.'

'Mimi.'

Her face loosens again, pleased. 'Mimi, yes, you're right.' Then she turns sad again: 'I don't think that you should tell your mummy.'

'About Mimi?'

'No, about us. Because I think she would be very upset. So I think this should be our secret.'

So I *am* secret.

But not yet. First, I need to know: 'Where did Papa go?'

She is looking at me as if she is waiting for me to go on, to say more. But that is all: *Where did Papa go?*

'Go?'

Still there is nothing from her, so I reach out sideways for the

51

glass of Tizer, moving my hand until it is tickled by the cold rim. Then I watch her through the bottom of my glass, as she says, 'It was a long time ago.'

'Iris?' I hurry, 'Where is Iris?'

'Zoe,' she says, 'it was a long time ago, and I am the only one left here.' She heaves herself from the armchair. 'Let's get you cleaned up, before your Mummy comes to fetch you.'

Caddy

Zoe has been here for an hour or more, kneeling by the coffee table, working on a jigsaw. So why have I not noticed this distinctive sound until now, this piping of breath through narrow tubes? 'Zoe?'

She looks up from the jigsaw, very attentive.

'Zoe, you're wheezing.'

No response. I realise that she is not attentive, but blank.

'Your chest,' I urge, explain, leaning towards her from my armchair. 'The noise in your chest, listen.'

Faintly, she says, 'It's a cough.' And she coughs, obligingly, once; a fake cough which dislodges nothing. As the tubes fill again with air, they whine loudly.

I am balanced, but barely, on the edge of my chair. 'How long have you had this . . . cough?'

She shrugs, unconcerned, but nevertheless she is thoughtful for a moment before deciding, 'A few minutes.' And now her next breath hisses from her lungs.

Alarmed, I stand, without any notion of what I can do, but happen to glance down onto Oliver, who is asleep on the rug in front of the fire. 'Is it Oliver?' I ask Zoe, quickly. 'Are you allergic? To cats?' Oliver prefers the outdoors; it is unusual for him to spend much time in here with us.

Zoe is frowning doubtfully.

'It *is* Oliver,' I tell her, because I am remembering: 'You *are* allergic, you *were* allergic.' How can I have forgotten this? Where has this memory been, for more than forty years? It comes back to me, comes home to me, fits flush with all my other memories. As I bend to haul Oliver from the rug, I remember how long I took to realise that Evie's wheezes coincided with visits of the white cat to our fireside. 'We had to make a rule,' I puff. 'No cats in the house.' Zoe cranes, interested. Oliver is dripping from my hands, so I hurry with him to the door. 'It was difficult,' I continue, calling back over my shoulder to Zoe, 'because you loved cats. You were too young to understand.' Gently I deposit Oliver on the cold kitchen tiles and retreat to close the door.

Zoe watches me return. Her hands are in her lap, below the table, the jigsaw untouched. I ease myself down into my arm-chair and tell her, 'We used to have a terrible time with you in Grandma's house, until we realised, because she had three cats.'

She lifts an unplaced jigsaw piece and taps the tabletop, slowly, quietly. 'Grandma has a dog,' she says, uncertainly. Uncertain of me. Certain of the dog, certain of the absence of cats. 'Called Bryn,' she adds, but no more boldly.

'No,' I start to help, 'not . . .' And I stop. 'Your other . . .' I start, stop, again. 'My mother,' I say finally, meaninglessly to Zoe.

She seems to notice that she is holding the jigsaw piece. She focuses on the fragment and shuffles it around on her fingertips; turning it so carefully, under such scrutiny, that it could be a cut gem.

'Do you remember her?' I ask, and I am surprised by my tender tone. The tone, this tenderness, is for my mother. The tenderness is no surprise to me because I know that I still miss my mother. I suppose that I will never stop missing her, not now. But the tone? I was sure that I had learned to live with this feeling, this missing, to keep it to myself.

Zoe switches her puzzlement from the jigsaw piece to me.

I try, 'An old lady with a hat?'

'An olden-days lady with a hat,' Zoe mulls over these words. 'Yes,' she says carefully, 'I remember.'

Her serious black gaze causes a spark in my chest. Suddenly the cold dark surface of her eyes is a soft warm home for me. She is with me, no longer opposite me, so much smaller on the far side of the coffee table. Those eyes have slotted over mine and we can see together. 'What do you remember?' *Bring her back for me.*

Her gaze is empty, turned inwards. Eventually she replies, 'Long pins to hold the hat.' The hand with the jigsaw piece rises again, but vaguely this time, untracked. I detect a twitch of her fingers to the side and the back of her head.

'Hatpins.' I tell her. 'Your grandma was a lovely lady.' For whom do I say this? For Zoe? Or for my mother, until now lost and forgotten? 'She was heartbroken when we lost you.' *Believe in her.* 'You were her first grandchild,' I explain, 'and first grandchildren are very special. Her own children were grown, but suddenly there was a baby again. *You.*'

Her smile, coming in reply to mine, is unsteady, and falls away.

'You were everything, to her.' *Take her, Zoe, take the memory of her.* 'When we lost you, I was very worried about her.'

Zoe's eyes have not moved from mine but she wraps a corner of her lower lip over her teeth and holds it down with an eye-tooth.

I shrug, suddenly exhausted. 'I was very worried about all of us.'

Zoe looks down onto the jigsaw, a flat wooden island on the tabletop, and slips her stray piece towards the coastline. Beneath her fingertip the piece bobs from bay to bay.

I tell her, 'That'll be why you don't have a cat at home.'

She looks up, her face forming a question mark from the wide sweep of eyes down to the tiny mouth.

'Because you have an allergy.'

'No,' she says, timidly but definitely, 'it's because Mummy doesn't like cats.'

'She doesn't?' What kind of woman dislikes cats?

'She says that they're for old ladies.'

'And they . . .' she wrinkles her nose to summon the word or expression, '. . . go around your legs.' To illustrate, she stirs the air with an index finger.

'Your mummy doesn't like that?'

Zoe resumes the hunt for a dock for the stray piece. 'No,' she confirms, uninterested. But she stops sharp, apparently remembering something else: 'And they take advantage.'

Someone else's words in Zoe's mouth, I do not know if this is funny or sad. 'That's what your mummy says?'

Busy with the jigsaw, she does not bother to reply.

'Zoe,' I say softly over her bowed head, 'cats don't take advantage. We're useful to them and they're useful to us. We feed them and they catch mice.' I laugh to myself: 'But *I* like them because they catch spiders, too.'

Briefly her face lifts and her eyes swipe mine. 'You were frightened of spiders,' she says, rather grimly, perhaps reproachfully. Having been successful with the stray piece, she turns to the pile and corkscrews her attention down onto another one.

'Yes,' I manage, through my inward breath, 'I was. I am.'

'Very,' she mumbles, doing her diamond dealer act on the new piece. Swiftly satisfied, she lowers the piece into a specific bare area of the jigsaw, and pauses. Much more brightly, she says to me, 'You used to push things, our clothes, your shoes, to see if any spiders came running from inside.'

'I still do.'

'Once,' she begins excitedly, completely discarding the jigsaw piece, 'a spider was on you, on your arm . . .'

I laugh quickly. 'Oh no, Zoe.' Never.

'And you couldn't brush it off,' she leans forward onto the coffee table, her forearms narrowly missing the jigsaw, 'but it wasn't big, or not *very* big, but its legs were hooks . . .'

'Zoe.'

She withdraws from the table and drops her gaze onto the bare patch of the jigsaw.

I try to laugh again, explain, 'I think I'd remember if I'd had a spider on me.'

The piece of jigsaw slides straight home beneath her fingertip, rasping briefly on the shiny surface of the tabletop. The fingertip selects another piece and moves more slowly this time, and silently. I say cheerfully to the top of her bent head, 'Sometimes you're confused.'

She glances up, her face snub with surprise, as if she had forgotten that I am here.

'Listen to you,' I tell her, softly. 'You're still wheezing.'

Her gaze drifts nowhere as she listens to herself.

'What will your mother say?' These words shuffle uneasily inside my laugh. Now I dare to ask, 'What does she say about you coming here to see me?' Not that I care what Mrs Fox says, or thinks. What concerns me is that she will try to stop Zoe from coming to see me. I must never, ever give her any excuse to stop or limit these visits. Even if Oliver has to go.

Zoe's reply comes muffled from beneath the downturned focus. 'It's nice to get me off her hands for a while.' Said blankly, a faithful repetition. Part of Zoe's lower lip disappears again, although I cannot see the predatory tooth. The index finger switches rigidly to another piece.

'So what does she do, when she has you off her hands?' I continue probing, jauntily.

Zoe looks up with welcome relief from the two stray pieces. 'She goes to see Aunty Maxine, I think.'

'You have an aunty?'

'Not real,' she replies thoughtfully. 'She's just Mummy's best friend.'

The woman has a best friend?

'She's not a real aunty like Aunty Antonia.' The jigsaw piece fidgets to and fro beneath her fingertip, huffing and puffing. 'Aunty Antonia was Mummy's sister.'

'Was? Has she died?'

No response.

Gently, I prompt, 'Where is she now?'

'Peterborough.'

I do not allow a smile to creep across my face; I receive the reply with the seriousness with which it was delivered. 'And do you go to see her, very often?'

'No.'

'Why not?'

Her brisk, hard little shrug; an exaggerated, pantomime shrug. 'Don't know.'

There is so much to learn about her life, the life with which she has come, and I know that I have to know. 'Do you have cousins?'

A faint, dismissive wrinkle of her nose. 'Boys. Grown up.'

I decide to return to my original line of enquiry. 'So, what does your mummy do, when she goes to see Aunty Maxine?'

Confidently, Zoe replies, 'She talks a lot.' And adds, 'She laughs a lot.'

Difficult for me to imagine.

'She has known Aunty Maxine for a long time,' Zoe begins to elaborate comfortably, 'since before I was born.' She is ready with her mother's story.

Quickly but politely I ask, 'Does Aunty Maxine have children?'

'Boys.'

I try to tickle her with a smirk. 'And you don't like boys.'

'No.' She returns her attention, business-like, to the piece of jigsaw in hand. 'And, anyway, they don't like me; they want to play with Danny, not me.'

She tries the piece along a frayed edge.

'But you have your own friends, don't you?' I soothe. 'You go to play with your own friends.'

She twists the piece around, to fit, and says brightly, 'I like coming here, too.'

My heart flashes: is there more to this apparently innocent statement? Is this something which she says, which she has to say to Mrs Fox? 'Do you?' I utter, feebly.

She flickers with surprise, checks with me. 'Yes.'

So I dare to ask, 'Why?'

Her gaze drifts vacantly around the room. 'I like it here,' she decides.

Here? I follow her eyes over the dark shine of the green three-piece suite and the tall, tasselled lampshade. Across the dull dry lid of the raffia needlework basket. Along the endless track of pictureless picture rail. I want to tell her that *here* seems to have so little to do with *me*. Instead, I breathe the low empty *Oh* which swells inside me.

And she says, 'I like having a talk.'

I look at her.

She smiles. 'You tell me some good stories.'

It occurs to me that she does not often smile.

She is asking, 'Do you remember my friend Sarah?'

'Sarah . . .' I repeat hopefully, giving myself time, trying to do my best.

'She had very curly hair.'

'Sarah . . .' I try harder.

'White hair.'

I have to admit, 'No, I don't.'

She is undaunted: 'Yes, you do.'

I try again: 'White curly hair?'

Her face darkens with doubt. 'Well, *almost* white.'

Briefly I shut my eyes: a few little girls in my memory, china dolls, but none with fair curly hair. None with fair hair, none with curly hair. 'No, Zoe,' I say kindly but firmly, 'I'm afraid not.'

'You *do*, she was my *very best* friend.' As if this will persuade me.

So now I have to do this: 'Are you sure that Sarah was from the old days?' *Old days* is new: before the words came, I did not know how I would say this.

'Sure.' Her mouth closes tight.

This is hopeless, *I* am hopeless. Her black eyes press hard and heavy on me. Busy inside with the unanswered *Sarah, Sarah, Sarah*, I cast around differently: 'Why do you ask?'

'Because she went away and I don't remember why or where.' The eyes drop to the jigsaw, but unseeing. Unsettling. 'It was a long time ago,' she speaks down onto the jigsaw, 'so I thought you might know.'

I am sitting so still in my armchair that my ears are filling with the chunks which the second hand shears from the clock. And the gas fire is far too loud: an endless, breathless sigh. Carefully light, I ask, 'What do you mean, *She went away?*'

Her eyes come back to me, flat and calm. 'I don't know,' she says, matter-of-fact, 'I was very small.' But suddenly she squeezes a plea, 'You don't remember?' And just as suddenly, but definitely, 'You don't remember.'

Before I can stop myself, I am saying, 'I do. I'm sure I do. I will.'

Her eyes hold fractionally too long onto mine, treacly with suspicion, before returning to the jigsaw.

Leaving me to the murmur of the clock and the shuddering fire.

Talk to me, Zoe.

We do not have long.

She joins two pieces and works with these twins on the jigsaw.

'Zoe,' I start, without knowing how I will continue.

She is curled over the tabletop. 'What?'

I watch the tough yellow hoop of lamplight stretching and contracting around her cold, clean parting. 'Do you remember your Aunt Connie?'

Momentarily she glances up; a reflex, a twitch.

'*She* was *my* sister.' I smile, but down onto nothing, no one. 'She taught you to play conkers.'

Her eyes return, this time for a little longer and warm with interest.

'Do you remember?' I laugh, 'Aunt Connie was a bit of a tomboy when she was young.'

Zoe enthuses, 'I love conkers. I'd like a necklace of conkers.'

She asks, 'What happened to Aunt Connie?' Less a question, more a happy hum whilst she continues to work on the jigsaw.

'She went to work in a big house in the countryside. For a lady.'

Zoe sweeps a piece all around the jigsaw and into place. 'A lady in a long dress?'

'Yes.'

'Was she a nice lady?'

'Oh yes. She was called Adelaide. Adelaide St Clair.' Silvery hair, silvery skin, silvery pearls: I never saw her, but I heard the stories, first-hand, from my sister. 'Isn't that a grand name?'

'Mmmm.' Another grand sweep. 'Adelaide is in Australia.'

'Yes. It was a name for ladies, too, though, in those days.'

A chain of four pieces hooks onto the bottom of the jigsaw.

'And it was a grand house, too. A mansion, in a huge park.'

Zoe shoots a frown at me. 'In a park?'

'Grounds. Fields and forest. Acres and acres. Full of deer and horses.'

Surveying the jigsaw with satisfaction, Zoe asks me, 'Did your sister go horse-riding?'

I laugh quietly to myself. 'Oh no. But no doubt the lady did.'

'What were the names of the lady's horses?'

The tips of my laugh remain, tickling me. 'I don't know.'

'Star,' she says directly to me, decisively. 'Sky. Storm. And a foal called Snowflake.' And now, 'Did she ride side-saddle?'

'Why Star and Sky and Snowflake? Are these the names that you'd like to call *your* horses?'

After a second of hesitation, she nods shyly. 'Star,' she emphasises, but in a whisper. 'And Snowflake for the foal.' Her tooth creeps briefly onto her lower lip. 'I want a foal, too,' she confides.

I am nodding slowly, appreciatively, in reply.

We lower our gazes together to the jigsaw: two horses and the thin back legs of a third, a foal. Zoe sighs wearily. 'Was the lady a princess?'

'No,' I reply kindly, 'not a princess.' But there were plenty of princesses in those days, obscure European princesses. 'I'm fairly sure that she wasn't a princess.'

'But you had princesses in those days.' Her upturned face is muddy with worry.

I try to ease this worry with my smile. '*You* have princesses *nowadays*.'

'Princess Anne,' she says, doubtfully, despondently. 'But she's not a *real* princess.'

I am considering how to counter this confusion when Zoe asks, 'Was she an Arab?'

Which loses me, utterly. 'Who?'

'The lady, the rich lady.'

'Was she an *Arab*?'

She repeats, urges, 'The rich lady.'

'No, she wasn't an Arab.' Unsurely, I add, 'We didn't have Arabs in those days.'

Expressionlessly, Zoe looks down onto the jigsaw. 'This horse is an Arab,' she says, placing a finger on one of the two horses. 'Did you know?'

I smile. 'No, I didn't know. How do *you* know?'

'You can tell because . . .' My doorbell showers noise into the room. Followed by the slump of silence. We hold each other very still with our wide eyes. And I say, 'Your mother.'

As I rise from my chair, Zoe rises over her jigsaw. 'Can I finish this?'

'No, Zoe, leave it.'

'But I want to finish it.' Panic beats about in her words. 'It's so nearly . . .'

'I'll *keep* it.' I have reached the door. Pausing, hanging on the handle, I check back with her: 'I'll *keep* it, okay?'

'Leave it?' A delayed echo. '*Here*?'

'*Yes, there*. Now, hurry with your coat,' I gabble, 'because you know your mummy, you know how she hates to have to wait for you.'

Zoe

....

Mrs Dutton opens the door, and Mummy is standing on the doorstep. And something about Mummy is different from usual. Against the darkness of the garden, she shines white, she seems lit up like when she is caught in the flash of Daddy's camera. Her smile glides past Mrs Dutton to me. 'Ah!' She seems pleased.

Ah? I brace myself for the rest: *There*-you-are; or, worse, Come-*on*-Get-a-*move*-on. My coat is only half on, and I am jabbing my arm down into the empty sleeve.

Mummy turns away, flicks the smile back to Mrs Dutton to check brightly, 'Everything all right?' She seems to expect so.

And sure enough Mrs Dutton replies with a happy murmur: 'Oh, yes, fine, thank you.'

'Thursday?' suggests Mummy.

Mrs Dutton's mouth opens, shuts, and opens again. Because usually she has to ask Mummy for the next visit. Now she answers simply, 'Lovely.' Her smile is held down for a second before springing so wide that her cheeks puff like the big soft loops of a bow.

As soon as I reach the doorway Mummy places both her hands on my shoulders to steer me over the step onto the path, although I do not need steering. Then I feel one hand float away, presumably into a wave because she is calling cheerfully over my head to Mrs Dutton: 'Thanks, bye.' We are walking towards a big white van which is grunting warm grey fumes into the damp black air. 'Come on,' Mummy starts, as we go through the gate, 'because Uncle Gerry is giving us a lift home.' When she opens the door, when Uncle Gerry can hear her, she adds, 'Isn't that nice?'

She pushes me up onto the seat, and Uncle Gerry smiles, says, 'Hi, Zo.'

My smile, in reply, is small. Uncle Gerry's smile is always the same, always big. He grabs the shaking bobble of the gear-stick. Next to my knee, his shaky hand is huge and heavy.

Squeezing next to me, Mummy asks, 'Did you have a nice time?' Even her voice is glittery.

'Yes.'

'What did you do, today?'

She never usually wants to know what I have done. I look around, up, at her. She is not looking at me; she is looking ahead, through the windscreen, far beyond the windscreen, her eyelids low, she is smiling. She looks as if she has had a long but nice day.

I tell her, 'I did a jigsaw.'

'Oh. Nice.'

No one says anything for a while, so eventually I try, 'Mummy?'

'Mmm?' She shifts around but stays far above me, her face on a level with Uncle Gerry's face.

'Do you remember my friend Sarah? With curly hair?'

She replies, 'Mmm.'

'No, but *do* you?'

'*Yes*,' she says, annoyed with me. 'Sarah who lived around the corner.'

'Where did she go?'

Her face tips down towards the top of my head. 'I told you, don't you remember?' This was said with surprise. 'Her family moved to Devon.' Far above me again, she adds, 'Thank God.'

Uncle Gerry's voice slides sideways over my head towards her. 'Why *Thank God*?'

Her reply slides back, lazy, mostly a sigh: 'Because hers was a mother-and-a-half. Religious freak. You should watch your Maxine,' she adds suddenly, 'because you wouldn't catch me sending any kid of mine to Sunday school, not even for the chance of a lie-in.'

Uncle Gerry's happy murmurs stay low with the sound of the engine.

'You don't get any of that from Mrs Dutton, do you?' Mum's question hooks down onto me.

'What?' I twist towards her, for clues, but she has settled too close for me to see.

'Religion. Baby Jesus.'

It is obvious from the way she says his name that she does not like Baby Jesus. I twist so hard that I can see her mouth from below. It is so firm that the corners are squeezed downwards. 'No,' I reply.

'Good.'

'But in school, we do.'

'Never mind about school,' she yawns, 'I can't do anything about what they teach you in school.'

Caddy

I do not go regularly to Evelina's grave. For the first few years I had a routine, visiting on Monday and Friday mornings. On Mondays I could check that she was all right to start the week; and on Fridays, that she had survived the week and was ready to start the weekend. That her flowers were alive, that she was free from weeds. I do not know when, or how, I lost my weekly routine. But for years now I have been going only when I want to go. A long Sunday, perhaps, or yet another Monday, when the rest of the world has nothing or everything to do. I have been in sunshine and snow and all the in-betweens.

For the past ten years I have not gone to the church solely to visit Evie. Her father, my husband, Clem, is buried there too, although he is in a different part of the churchyard. Churchyard? No, he is not buried in a churchyard; he is buried across the road, in a special park for graves which was built when there was no more space around the church. I know that it is north of the church, and I have an inkling that the north was once an unlucky place for burial – left to criminals, suicides – but obviously not nowadays, or not in the opinion of these new graves: big sparkling flesh-pink headstones with black lettering, their plots of quartz rubble bounded by plastic chain, strung low between stubby white posts. There was no choice for me, for my husband: north or nowhere. But I am not a believer so I was not particular.

Evie is in the churchyard because I did not want a cremation, and where can a coffin go but into a churchyard? And where else would I have wanted Evie to go? No one walks in the new park unless they are visiting a grave of their own, but Evie is in the churchyard, so people walk past her, perhaps even over her, on their way at Easter and Christmas, drumming gentle rhythms with their feet into the soil. I have seen children giggling on their way over Evie into weekly choir practice.

Evie was one of the last to go into the children's corner. There is a seventeen-year-old girl near Clem, four or five down. I wonder whether she was too old for the children's corner, or whether the children's corner is full now. Presumably no provision was made for children in the new cemetery because dead children are a dying breed. The inscription on the headstone records that the seventeen-year-old died on a Christmas Eve. Why should this seem especially awful? Why more awful than Evie's ordinary date? Christmas Eve is somehow suspicious, linked inextricably to Christmas: an accident on the way home from a party, or on a journey somewhere for the holiday. Or suspicious but not sudden: it could have been an illness rather than an accident, because people try to survive for Christmas, and perhaps she tried so hard that she nearly succeeded. If someone is ill before Christmas, I imagine that it is important, increasingly important, to buy presents for him or her. So what happened to the seventeen-year-old girl's presents? Were they wrapped? And then unwrapped? Whenever I pause in front of the teenager's grave, I try to tell myself that the date is insignificant: if people die every day, some will die on Christmas Eve.

I do not visit regularly but I would not want to move away from here. Families which move away leave their old bones, which seems wrong. In one sense Evie has stayed with me, all through my life, when everyone else moved away. My father is buried at the sanatorium where he died. Ten or fifteen years before my mother died, she went to live with my sister Kitty, and she is buried with Kitty and Kitty's husband Tom in their local churchyard. It is not far away, two or three miles, and I visit there, too, irregularly, to check, to take flowers; clear old flowers away. I am not bothered that my husband was not buried with

Evie, that I will not be buried with her. I am not sentimental. I do not want Evie to be disturbed, not even for me.

Thankfully there is no gross grassy mound beneath Evie's headstone. The headstone was bought by my mother. Clem and I had no savings. Clem's work mates had a collection, for the funeral. The local pub, too. Where, of course, I had never been. My mother was furious. She told me that, in her day, all families, however poor, especially the poor, insured the lives of their children, saved for their funerals. She told me that when she married, she began to save. Because a pauper's burial was no burial at all. But I did not expect Evie to die. Not then, in the nineteen-twenties. Not when she was six years old, supple and never sick. Not even after her first few weeks, or perhaps her first few days, or hours. I remember when I first shakily held her to me, I was startled by the punches of a heart which I assumed was mine before I realised that it was her own.

My discovery of Zoe makes no difference to my visits to Evie's grave. Because something of Evie remains there, pressed firmly into the ground, if only the tiny threads, borrowed from me and Clem, with which her cells were spun.

I am not on my way to visit Evie today; I am walking to Zoe's house. I am close now, in the quiet streets of Hartsbridge. Streets? Streets without people, cars, shops? This one is a canal of tarmac, lined with low new houses which have been planted at regular intervals. The houses have grown differently, sprouted garages, gables, porches, and often an encrustation of leaded lights. The front gardens are moats; the driveways, trusting drawbridges. Today is a lifeless spring day, with stringy sunshine. Spring is so often a lie, the only difference from winter is a smattering of cold snowdrops and daffodils. It is not until May and the flowering of the trees and grass that I am sure of the summer.

I suspect that there is something wrong with Zoe. I do not go and wait for her every day, of course; and before the weekend I did not go for several days, and on Monday there was nothing, no one, no Zoe, no Mrs Fox, no Danny. It was not a half-term or holiday because the playground was shot through with the blue and white of other schoolchildren in their insubstantial blazers and socks. I went home. The next day, I went to the corner of the road again and waited, which was unwise because then there was no time to go into the playground to look for them, to ask after them. The next day I went to the gate. As I approached the busy building, which was spilling schoolchildren, I became heavy with panic: what was I going to do? should I ask some-one? and who? And then I saw Danny gusting in his unfastened duffel coat towards a group of women and children, and into a car. The car jerked from the kerbside and was gone. The follow-ing day, yesterday, despite an effort, I was no quicker, and he went again, unseeing behind glass. My walk home was long and painful. Today I am equipped with corn pads.

Danny is still at school, so the Fox family has not gone away. Presumably Zoe is ill. But if so, would Danny be allowed to bring the germs to school? I cannot remember the details of the childhood diseases, incubation and isolation. Or perhaps Zoe has had an accident. Danny seemed happy when he crossed the playground, but this could have been due to the prospect of the car. A little boy's four o'clock face is no reliable indicator of calamity at home. What will I say to whoever opens the Foxs' front door? But the young are told to watch for the unexplained absence of the old, so why not vice versa?

Now I can see the house. The damp wooden midriff is tickled by short spring sunrays. In front of the identical house next door – Spot The Difference – there is a pram, complete with cat net, parked next to the porch. What do I do if no one opens the door? What do I do if I wake next door's baby? Perhaps there is no one at home, perhaps Danny is staying with the people with the car. I could leave a note. But what if no one ever comes home again? No, someone will come, because, if nothing else, there are curtains to collect; lime green and lemon up-stairs, orange and brown downstairs, a large leaf pattern. I could ask the neighbours. I am an old woman, surely I look innocent enough.

I have never been so close to the house. I stop by the hedge. I did not expect the doorstep to be so secluded by the small hedge. What kind of hedge is it? Old people are supposed to be good at gardens, nothing else, just gardens. I never had a garden until I moved to my current house. My garden is a patch of grass, cut by the council. Young people assume that old people come from a time before towns. But I came from a time *of* towns. And young people say that it is important for children to have a garden; but I am not sure that the local park is not more fun. And further from the road. There is no evidence that this front garden is used for anything at all. It is gardened, but barely. The grass is longer than the grass next door.

Next door's baby is asleep, lying on its front, deep inside the navy-blue pram. Its head is turned sideways for air, one little fist a seashell on the hem of the soft yellow blanket. What do babies dream? There are no clues on this tightly buttoned face. I turn back to the house and I know that it is not empty. It does not *feel* empty, although the windows are bleary cataracts of net curtain. I find the buzzer, which is hanging slightly loose, and press, briefly, once. I strain to hear the steady flow of footsteps to the other side of the door, but there is nothing. Suddenly the door snaps open, and there is Mrs Fox.

'Caddy,' she says, to convey surprise, but the tone is fractionally too flat. She is not surprised. She saw me coming. She saw me looking, and thinking. She is not pleased to see me. But, then, she is never pleased to see me, and I suspect that she is never pleased to see anyone, or not completely.

Her eyes are wide and bright. Unusually, she has eyes which are so pale that they are wider and brighter without make-up. Standing inside her own doorway she is more substantial than usual. She has a modern type of thinness, confined to her selling points: her face is full, healthy, strong, and her hands, too. I have never noticed until this moment that she is so very fair: usually she wears colours so strong that she steams the insides of my eyes. But today, under the limescale of a man's white shirt, she is as cool and colourless as the lady in the Cameo soap adverts.

'Fancy . . .' she begins, but I press a forefinger to my lips and then point to the sleeping baby. She frowns at the pram, clamps shut her lips, and folds her arms. Gazing up at her on the doorstep, I suddenly know exactly what I will say. Or, I know that I want to be clear, direct.

'Mrs Fox,' I start, 'it's Zoe, I've come about Zoe.'

'Really?' She slaps down this muttered sarcasm in my path.

'Is she all right?' I continue nobly.

'She has tonsillitis,' she answers immediately, conclusively, shifting from one leg to the other.

'Oh. Are you sure?' I did not mean to say this. This is not what I meant to say. But a sore throat is a sign of so many serious diseases.

She splutters her exasperation. 'Of course I'm sure.' One gold-graced hand spreads speedily through her hair. 'At least, Dr Wentworth is sure.'

'Well, how is she?' I begin to realise that my breathing is failing to return to a more gentle rhythm after my long walk. I realise that the air seems increasingly scarce, sparse. It is losing its sheen, becoming rusted with darkness. And my head is tightening, and my legs are loosening. And she is peering at me.

'Mrs Dutton?'

I know that I must lie down.

'You'd better come in.' She has taken my arm and she is hauling me over the doorstep. I can feel with my feet that the doorstep is high and slippery. I am shaking so badly that nothing of me will move. My eyes are open but I cannot see. I am trying to locate the doormat with the soles of my boots, to wipe them. But she is pulling me onward.

'I must lie down,' I say, or think that I say, mean to say.

She has stopped pulling me, and now she is pressing down on my shoulders. I am resisting, because if I relax my rigid legs I will fall; and I can still see nothing, so I do not know where I am going, how far I will fall. But somehow she wins, and suddenly I am sitting on a soft chair or sofa. I lower my heavy icy head into my hands.

'Are you all right?' she is saying, hushed. 'Are you all right?'

I can hear the blood rushing back into the veins in my brain, swishing through the coils closest to the insides of my ears. It is reaching my eyes because the pattern of the carpet is twinkling through the darkness: more large orange leaves. I want to tell her that, yes, I am all right; but for the moment I cannot because there is too much happening.

'I'm going to get you some water,' she says.

She is so quick, I marvel at how quickly she is back here again, the hand back on my shoulder again. This time there are two loud cracks of bone to warn me that she is bending down, and a simultaneous lightening of the hand on my shoulder. She is nudging something into the small space between my knees and my head. 'Come on,' she says: 'drink.'

How will water help me? But I oblige, lift my head, take the cup, take a sip. And it is so smooth that it is immediately everywhere in my mouth and gone.

'All right?' This is confident, almost kindly, not requiring an answer. She swings around me, perches beside me on the arm of the sofa, chirps a laugh of relief. 'I thought you were going to die on me.'

And if I was, a glass of water would have saved me? 'Oh no,' I manage in a similarly cheerful tone. 'I think I've probably been overdoing things lately, that's all.' I am still not looking at her; I am still assembling the world in little pieces (the orange wooden leg of a sideboard, the smoked glass top of a coffee table) because I am afraid to test my regained eyesight too far.

'I wouldn't have known what to do with you,' she is saying, and I can hear the smile of relief skipping along with the words.

'No, really,' I say. 'It was nothing, I'm fine.' Finer by the minute. I glance around me. The room is a little bigger than my

72

own front room. The back wall is glass, two huge sliding panels of glass. So how does she manage to keep the room warm?

'Zoe's upstairs, asleep,' she says in the new friendly tone. 'She is much better now, but you know how these infections can knock them out. I decided that she should stay at home for a few more days. Better to be safe than sorry.'

'I do worry about her,' I try to explain, glancing up at Mrs Fox, glimpsing the many colours in the apparently colourless skin which glides down from the temple over the cheekbone. Freckles; a mole no bigger and no darker than a few grains of damp sand; and a blue lace of veins. On the temple, on the hairline, there is something less than hair. And I am looking at the bristle of eyelashes from the underside.

'No, she's fine,' she says. My look has bumped her from the arm of the sofa, and she strides across the room to another chair. There is a word these days for her way of walking: rangy? Except that she is too short for rangy.

'You see,' I try, 'if anything happened to her, I might not ever know.'

She is sitting forward in the chair, elbows on knees, chin in hands. 'Well, no, I suppose not.' She lowers her pearly eyelids. Neither of us speaks for a moment. Then she asks, 'Did you have children?'

Did? Did is unusual. Did is easy. Usually people ask, Do you have children? meaning *And if so, how many?* And then how do I answer? Do I disown the dead? I nod: 'Four. My first daughter died when she was six.' I cannot say eldest; there was nothing old about Evelina. I raise the beaker of water, and drink.

Her face is stiff with fear. 'Oh, I'm sorry.'

I cannot resist: 'It wasn't your fault.' But I relent immediately: 'It wasn't anyone's fault.' And I add, 'Children died more often in those days.'

I remember my recent lie to her, that I have no grandchildren. White lie, half lie, because I have no grandchildren *nearby*, and I wanted very much to take Zoe to the cinema. It had worked, we went to see *Bambi*. Now I reach into my pocket for the photograph of Evie and Iris. I cannot pretend that I carry this photo always with me, because it is hardly a handy size for a purse. Now it is sliding easily from my large square pocket. And I want to see it, too, now; now that I can feel the warm dense grain of the card. So I look for a moment before I pass it across the room. Because it is much more to me than a voucher, I-claim-my-child.

'That's her on the left, that's Evie.'

She glances soberly at the soft brown surface. 'Eve?' she confirms respectfully.

'Evelina, actually,' I answer, looking firmly at the photo in her limp, polite hands. Then I look up and laugh my despair: 'Girls named Eve are supposed to live for a long time, did you know that?'

She drops her gaze down onto the photograph.

'An old wives' tale,' I explain.

Her gaze springs back to me and I realise that in her eyes I *am* an old wife. Rapidly I return us both to the photo. 'Now do you see?' I urge.

She looks down into her hands with a frown. Eventually, reluctantly, she mutters, 'She's an awful lot like Zoe.' Leaning forward to hand the photo back to me, she checks, 'Is that what you mean?'

I leave the photo in the air between us. 'She *is* her.'

Mrs Fox's eyes become very still, but slowly she rolls her lips inwards. She has lowered her arm to rest across her knees so that she is both holding and yet not holding the photo. She is holding it away from her.

'No, I'm not mad,' I anticipate. '*Look* at the photo.'

Obediently she dips her head, shifts her wrist, but I can see that she is not looking. She is confident that she does not need to look. She thinks that I am mad. The inwardly rolled lips tell me that she is thinking about what to say to me. She surprises me by looking up again so soon, shifting the arm again so soon in my direction. 'Yes, I can understand *why* . . .'

'Look, I don't understand this any better than you, but she *is* her.'

'*Caddy*,' she says slowly, to slow everything down, the photograph limp on her knees, 'I don't like to be *rude*, but I *was there* when she was *born* . . .'

'I *know* all that,' I counter. And, of course, I *do* know all that, but unexpectedly her reference to birth, pain, the pelvis cranking open hour by hour, reminds me that the little girl is not solely mine, not simply because she was first mine. How would I have felt if someone had come to claim her away from me? My eyes fill briefly with the huge warped leaves of the curtains, capturing the afternoon sunshine.

'I know all that, and I don't know *how* this has happened, but it *has* happened.' I splay my hands in a gesture of helplessness: Don't-shoot-*me*. . . It is a gesture of reasonableness, too, of course. Mad old women do not pause to appeal to reason, to offer sympathy. 'I'm sorry,' I conclude, shrugging my hands back into place on my lap.

Mrs Fox firmly returns the photograph. 'She looks very like her,' she stresses confidently.

'It's not the photograph,' I explain hurriedly, slipping it back into my pocket. 'She remembers everything.'

Mrs Fox twitches to attention.

I insist, 'You *know* that. She has *always* remembered: the Kenwell house, me, her little sister.'

Wide-eyed again, she nods towards the photo. 'Does she know all this, does Zoe know all this?'

'She has told me so much.'

Her eyes narrow. 'I'll kill her,' she mutters.

And, firmly, I remind myself that I did not come here for this. 'My Evie died suddenly,' I am starting, before I realise. Suddenly? No, I cannot imagine a slower death. 'That's a laugh,' I correct angrily, and try again: 'What I mean is, she became so ill so quickly.'

Mrs Fox is frozen, watchful, *listen*ful.

'There had never been much wrong with her, only the usual kiddie stuff, snuffles, a day or so of sickness.'

She nods.

'Peter was much more frail,' I admit, 'when he was little.' But Peter was not yet born when Evie died, so I stop. I do not want confusion. 'Evie went down with something.' Down and down. Heavier and heavier, so that, in the end, her mouth was full of her own sticky water and her little lungs sank under the dead weight of her own dead muscles. 'It started with the usual kiddie stuff, aches, tiredness, and she went to bed.'

Mrs Fox does not move.

'But she didn't get better, she got worse, she couldn't move.'

I know that I will have to explain: 'Doctors, I dreaded doctors, everyone dreaded doctors, they cost money, a lot of money, we had no money.'

She makes no attempt to interrupt me.

'But the doctor came, he was very nice, a lovely local man, we were very lucky.' Rapidly I wave in an aside: 'They weren't all like that.'

'No,' she says expressionlessly.

'And he didn't want any payment. But he did want her to go into hospital.' How can I possibly convey the horror of this to an antiseptic young woman who knows nothing but the wide open ambulance-whizzing sweep of the driveway in front of a new Casualty Department, and the obliging automatic doors of a Maternity Wing? 'Which was complicated,' I try. 'Because hospitals wanted payment, or a letter of recommendation, sponsorship.' There is no sign that she understands, nor that she misunderstands. 'But, anyway, he did manage to get Evie a bed.'

'I was there when she died,' I stress, 'I was there.' I shrug. 'The Sister was very nice to me, she let me stay.'

I knew that Evie was going to die. She was growing old in front of my eyes, growing hard somehow, split in half by her hard little frown.

I explain: 'She couldn't breathe; or, not without an effort.' *An* effort? *Every* breath required an effort, no, two efforts perhaps, an effort for in and an effort for out. 'Imagine, every breath, every second.'

'Yes,' murmurs Mrs Fox, and a fingernail strays between her teeth. And now she flicks a glance onto the blind white window, in response to a sudden recognisable sound. 'Next door's baby,' she informs me quietly, unnecessarily.

'Yes.'

We sit listening; or, rather, we sit without speaking, so we can do nothing but listen. It is a forlorn rather than an angry cry. After a moment there is another sound outside the window, the shuffling and snuffling of an adult, and then the crying falters and ceases.

'I'm sorry,' Mrs Fox says slowly, 'I interrupted you.'

'No – ' I divert a forgiving smile towards the window.

Unsurely, she manages her own smile.

'It's just that . . .' But I must continue because I have left Evie hauling open and pushing shut her lungs. 'She tried so hard, she never stopped.'

A ridiculous embarrassment prickles me: if I say that she did not want to die, am I implying that she did not want to be born here again?

'She was so brave.' And once again it strikes me: 'So much braver than me.'

Evie wanted nothing but air. Whenever I leaned with a glass towards her dry lips, she tightened against the confusion of water. Eventually I learned to dip a fingertip into the water and dab her lips. After I had wiped away the spittle which was swelling there. And then her eyes would focus on me in gratitude. 'She couldn't swallow,' I tell Mrs Fox.

Mrs Fox frowns.

Evie could speak but she did not want to speak because the words blew away her diminishing breath. So any words from her were short, sharp, so unlike the usual careless babble of a child. Her most frequent word was *No*. (Perhaps not so unlike a child after all.) No to the heavy hands of the doctors on her hand-cranked chest. No to me, too, whenever I moved *in*, let alone *from*, my chair beside her bed. 'Quite late, Clem – my husband – came to the hospital,' I tell Mrs Fox. 'After he had come home from work and found that we were gone.' I remember that his eyes were dusty from the day at work. 'I sent him back to my mother; to fetch Iris from my mother, to take Iris home, stay with her.' For once, my place was not at home.

'Iris,' repeats Mrs Fox.

Evie and I stayed alone through the night, the half-baked hospital darkness pinpricked with movements, noises, voices.

I left her once only, briefly, when I could wait no longer to go to the toilet. Out in the corridor, I saw through a door, through the porthole of glass in the door, into the neighbouring ward. People – six or seven of them, nurses, doctors, others – were standing around a bed. No, they were standing around and yet not around a bed. It seemed to me to be an unnatural distance to stand from the bed. On the bed there was a child, lying uncovered, on its back. From the porthole I could see little of the child except the feet, two little feet, naked soles. In between the group of people and the child, the people and the bed, there was a woman. She was turning from the bystanders to the bed, but in the same instant she turned back from the bed to the bystanders. She tried to return from the people to the child, then from the child to the people, but failed to reach either destination. She was trapped. She began to scream, to wail, the scream was made from words. The words were strange, full of song but, for me, without meaning. She looked foreign; I do not remember how, now, but I knew that she was foreign, even without the song I would have known.

She screamed the same words, over and over again, and they came with her steps, to match the steps towards the bed and away, towards and away. No one else was moving; not the people, nor the child. Nor me, I suppose. Once, the woman reached the tiny toes, touched them, but recoiled, ripped away by the scream in time for the rapid but regular steps back from the bed. She was beside herself, literally beside herself, turning and turning beside herself. I stood and wondered if I would be the same, when my moment came. Wondered what I must look like, to the nurses, as I sat so still and quiet and obedient at the bedside of my dying child.

I returned to Evie, and as it became later and later, then probably very early, she became more and more sleepy, and although she stayed awake for the yanking open of her lungs, her thoughts periodically lost focus, and it was then that the nurses in their uniforms, their tall white hats, were frightening for her.

'She became so white,' I remember now for Mrs Fox: so white, like – what? – those fragments of shell which have been blasted for years and years onto rocks? I had never been to a beach, when Evie died. She had never been to beach. And, yes, she was so very wet. If I had tried to hold her, she would have slithered from my hands. But I did not try to hold her. 'I should have rocked her,' I tell Mrs Fox. I should have picked her up and rocked her, not to tip her gently over into sleep, because by then she was already sleeping, but to squeeze the air into and out of her body. 'But for some reason I was afraid, I could only sit there, squeezing her hand.' Afraid of what? What could have been worse than her death?

Does Mrs Fox know that there is truly a death rattle when, at last, the lungs empty of air? Because they do empty.

'Presumably it was morning when she died because, although it was dark still for hours, Evie was tidied away by a new shift of nurses. I was sitting outside the ward on a wooden bench when Clem came blazing with morning air. I said, "She's gone, Clem." And, would you believe, he said, "Gone where?"'

I look up at Mrs Fox, who has not moved. Her hands are threaded together in her lap.

'You see?' I tell her: 'However long it takes, it is still sudden. So sudden that it does not seem to happen at all.' I stand, pass the glass back to her. She stands to receive it. I can go as soon as I have asked what I came to ask. 'This is all I want: will you – and will you *promise* me that you will? – tell me if anything happens to Zoe?'

She is standing stiffly in front of me, clutching her glass of water.

'Then I can go.'

'Okay,' she says.

Dinah

....

As I came back down the stairs from Zoe, I saw through the doorway into the living room, saw where Mrs Dutton had been sitting when she told me the story of her long-ago little girl. Saw the hollow which had been left by her in my settee. I hurried from the stairs into here, into my kitchen, for a cup of tea. She was so calm, when she was telling her story; no, more than calm: *compelling*. I was held there by her. I was aware of her hands, open yet closed. Around the photograph. Aware of her face, suddenly surprisingly smooth. And her voice, perilously smooth.

When she said what she said about Zoe, I remembered myself, experienced a vague version of the feeling more usually brought on by Jehovah's Witnesses: *how do I get away, get them away?* But that was all. *This is going too far*, that's all. Because many people have odd beliefs. Ordinary people. People who are otherwise clever. So many people believe in the Bible: why is it normal to believe the Bible but not to believe that your dead daughter is alive again? To me, all beliefs are irrational.

I do not know how I would survive the loss of a child. I have only known the loss of my father. But I know that Mrs Dutton was brave to talk of her daughter. No one mentioned my father, his death. Not at school, where I had been called from my classroom by the Headmistress and told to go home. Nor at home. So, for many years, I did not know the details. Perhaps I still do not know the details: *Heart* and *He was in the garden*, are these details? Because I still cannot talk of him to my mother and my sister. No, not talk, but ask: I cannot ask questions, *How did he look, What did he say?* They have the answers, have always had the answers; they are older than me, and, more importantly, they were there. Of course I know the reason for their conspiratorial silence: it is, was, accepted wisdom, *Better left unsaid, Easier to forget*.

After my father died, I was convinced that I had lost someone who would have stood up for me. Perhaps I was wrong, though, because now I cannot remember him ever having done so. Caddy Dutton's situation is the opposite: a child is someone to stand up for. So, how would I feel if I failed, if I could do nothing and one of my children died? I cannot know how Caddy Dutton feels. I cannot blame her.

But I can blame Zoe. She should have told me, I should have been told. She should have known better than to keep this to herself. But she is not a sensible child. She is a daydreamer. Now that I know, do *I* tell *Derek*? I suspect that he will think me mad, think me mad by association. More importantly, will he stop Zoe from spending time with Caddy? Not *physically* stop her, because he is not here during the daytime; but will he tell me to stop her? Will he *stop me* from sending her to spend time with Mrs Dutton? And why? What harm has Caddy Dutton ever done to Zoe? She has been seeing her for years and there has never been any problem. Caddy gives her the sort of attention that, for some reason, I have never been able to give her. And me? Caddy has given me freedom, free babysitting. No, there is nothing wrong with Caddy Dutton.

I remember that, sometimes, my grandma spoke about my dead grandfather as if he were alive. And she was always harmless, cheerful, kind. Is this so very different? And for a long time after my father died, I spoke to him every night before I went to sleep. This notion of Mrs Dutton's will pass. As long as we do not encourage her. As long as we ignore what she has said. Zoe and I can keep this little friendship going, we can keep Mrs Dutton under control. As long as Zoe keeps me informed. I must impress upon her to keep me informed. Yes, this is up to Zoe. Down to Zoe.

Zoe

I have been ill for a long time; or, so Mum says: *You're ill.* She says this whenever I ask whether I can go back to school. I *was* ill, but I am not sure that I am ill *now*. I do not feel ill; but, then, I do not feel very much at all, because I am usually asleep. I do still feel my throat whenever I eat. Mum has been saying that I can go back to school *Soon*, although suddenly this has become *Next week*. We seem to be still stuck somewhere in *this* week. The long days end with *Jackanory* and *Blue Peter*, when I know that for everyone else it is hometime, that for me it is teatime, then time for bath and bed.

Where does Jackie think that I am, every day? Does she know that I am ill? Mum says that *Of course she knows* because *Where else do you think that she thinks you are, on safari?* But does she think of me at all? There is not much time at school for thinking. When I am there, I never think of home. I am sure that I would notice, though, at the very beginning of each day, the bare peg among the coats around the cloakroom wall. And if I was Jackie I would notice at playtime, too, because she needs two to play horses, one to be the horse and one to be the rider.

On the first day that I was home, Dr Wentworth came to see me. I was asleep but I woke to hear a stranger climbing the stairs. Mum tweaks the floorboards when she moves around the house. And Dad moves fast, two stairs at a time; this house is too small for him. But the stranger on the stairs was slow and heavy, in shoes. And then there was the voice. It was not the type of voice that I hear very often in this house, perhaps only on *The News*. After a moment I realised that it was Dr Wentworth's voice. His

83

voice had never seemed strange to me before, in the surgery, but it was strange on our stairs.

He came into my bedroom, bringing very different smells with him: the smell of the inside of a car, and the smell of cold air, the cold air of schooldays and shopping trips. Different sounds, too: the scratch of his sleeves when he reached for my wrist, and the two clicks when he opened his briefcase. His touch is softer than anyone else's touch. I saw his cufflinks, two small square beads of shiny black stone. I fell asleep again, and when I woke he was gone, there was no sound of him, simply the radio in the kitchen below.

Early every morning, from the kitchen, there is the sound of knives on pieces of toast. This is the time when the house is noisy around my bedroom – doors, footsteps – and the taps sing. The front door slams into its frame and the taxi begins to growl in the driveway. Everywhere smells of toast and hot radiators. And then suddenly everything is quiet again; and the radiators go cold again, creaking like Dad's knees. Yesterday morning Dr Wentworth came to see me again. I was in Mum's and Dad's bedroom, at the dressing table, with Mum's make-up. I have given each piece – bottle, tube, jar – a name, and together they are a class, and I am their teacher. I have learned a lot from my own Mrs Borden about how to be a teacher. My class was sitting in lines, ready to start, when Dr Wentworth arrived. Mum called me downstairs. This time I was not lying in bed, listening, so I did not notice his voice. And when I went downstairs I was thinking about the three nail polish bottles – are they triplets, can they be triplets if they are not exactly the same size? – so I forgot to look for the cufflinks. I noticed his smile, though. He is a very smiley doctor. Why?

He liked my throat, and left quickly, before I had decided about the triplets. Usually he does not come here to see us, but we go to see him. Once I heard Mum telling Aunty Maxine that *Dr Wentworth is the nicest man in the world, I never knew they made them like that, no one ever told me.* Nicer even than Mr

Bennett, the chemist? Before I went to school, I went with Mum whenever she went to see Dr Wentworth. She would dress in front of the long mirror and turn from side to side with her hands on her stomach. I always wondered if she was going to have another baby. Then she would put on her make-up, singing so much to the radio that she made a mess of her lipstick.

The Health Centre is new, made of bumpy orange brick. It reminds me of Hansel and Gretel, the gingerbread house. There is brick inside as well as outside, whole walls of brick, scratchy and bumpy whenever I forget and lean back on the bench in the waiting room. The walls that are not brick are glass. The glass front door of the Centre has a long runway which Mum says is for prams and wheelchairs. But I have never seen any wheelchairs at the Health Centre. Perhaps wheelchairs go straight to hospital.

We would read magazines in the waiting room until one of the team of ladies would call *Mrs Fox* through the hatch to tell Mum that Dr Wentworth was free. Mum would grab my magazine from me, throw it back onto the table, and hurry me to the ladies' open door. *Just sit in here*, she would tell me, under the frowns of the busy ladies, *so that the ladies can keep an eye on you*. And then, bangles jangling, she was away, down the corridor of closed doors.

This morning, a little while ago, she came up the stairs, two stairs at once: one step, two, three, four, five, and then she was here, swinging through the doorway. I was in her bedroom again, at the dressing table, with my class. Luckily it was playtime for the class.

'God,' she puffed, 'it's Caddy Dutton. Outside. Up the road. I've just seen her. Coming here.' Her forehead snapped into a frown. 'You stay up here, and – I'm warning you – don't make a sound, and I'll get rid of her.' Then she said, 'Don't look at me like that. You can play with her any other time. Next week. But not now. Not here. I don't want her coming around here all the time.'

But she does not come around here all the time, she has never been here before.

But in the end she was here – downstairs, with Mum – for a long time. Perhaps they decided to have a Coffee Morning. Jackie's mum has Coffee Mornings. But I remembered Mum's warning, and I did not dare to go downstairs. After a while, I felt cold, packed away the class, tiptoed back to my bedroom and sat in my bed with a book from the mobile library. A moment ago I heard feet on the hallway carpet and then their voices, especially high and clear for farewells. Now the hallway is silent again but the stairs are tweaked one by one by Mum's tread. I can hear her hand thumping the banister. I close the book and put it down beside me. Now Mum is in the doorway, one hand slapped onto the door frame. On her face there is the look that she has when she wants to ask questions. 'Zoe,' she says, although there is no one else here, 'what have you been telling Mrs Dutton?'

'Nothing.' What does she mean?

'Did you know that she had a little girl who died?'

Well, *yes, of course*. How could I *not* know? She talks about her all the time.

'Her firstborn. She's very vulnerable. You can't go around preying on old ladies.'

Praying? What does she mean?

'I realise that you are an imaginative child, but you must realise that you cannot go around telling old ladies whatever you like.'

Whatever I *like*? 'It's the *truth*.'

'Zoe, when I was a little girl I was sure that I had been Mary Queen of Scots, but I didn't go around telling her mother.' She turns away but looks back over her shoulder: 'It's *cruel*, Zoe.'

Cruel? But Mrs Dutton *likes* me to talk about my old home. And whenever I do, I am not telling her anything that she does not already know. *She* tells me. She told me about Iris: I was not the only one to die, there was Iris too. She told me because I wanted to find Iris, I wanted to invite Iris to my birthday party last summer. I had told Jackie that I had a little sister, living somewhere else.

'What's her name?' Jackie had asked me, and I could tell that she did not believe me.

'Iris.'

'Iris?' She still did not believe me.

I wondered how *Iris* would be spelled. Jackie and I had been trying the dictionary earlier to find *prostitute* because Dominic Turner has been going around school saying *Don't you know what prostitute means?* I had asked Mum, whose eyes sparkled with her Can't-wait-to-tell-Dad smile when she said that a prostitute was a naughty lady.

This was not what the dictionary said. The dictionary said, *Woman who offers sexual intercourse for payment.* Jackie and I know all about sexual intercourse. We have seen it on television at school, *The Miracle Of Life*, a programme about elephants and their babies, but with a diagram of a man and a lady lying down together with no clothes, the lady beneath the man, a tube slipped down into her tummy. And I already knew because Mum had told me that Dad planted the egg in her tummy which grew to become me. To me, a prostitute seems not so much naughty as horrid. But, on the other hand, why not get paid? Do prostitutes have a lot of babies? And do they sell their babies too?

When, finally, I asked Mrs Dutton about Iris, she smiled, but the smile was for me and not my questions. She did not answer until I told her about the birthday party. Then she said, 'Zoe, Iris died a few years ago, seven years ago.'

Iris? Dead? Little Iris? 'How?' I asked. Did she die, ill, with me? Or was she run over by a car, like all the children in the adverts on telly?

Mrs Dutton was frowning; worrying about me, I felt, and not Iris. 'It was a cancer,' she said.

Cancer? Like Gramps?

'Some difficult cancer,' she said. 'Of the glands.' And she leaned from her chair and tapped my armpits with her fingertips.

'Gramps died of cancer,' I told her.

Back in her chair, she nodded slowly. 'Did he?'

Poor Iris.

'Iris had been ill for a long time,' she added, still nodding. 'For some years. No children.'

'Did she live with you?' I did not mean *Unlike me*.

Mrs Dutton's nod turned slowly from Yes to No. 'She's buried down there in Plymouth. Her husband has stayed down there; I don't see anything of the poor chap, these days.'

Jackie did not seem to remember Iris, never mentioned her again, not even when Iris did not come to my party. She does not often remember very much, she never remembers the name of my horse, Star. I will not tell Mum about Iris. I will not even tell Mrs Dutton any more about Iris, or about me.

Caddy

·················

The heat from our cups of tea is breathing life back into us. Such a startling effect from something so barely visible, so nearly non-existent. Nothing but a puff of steam. But so thin, this steam is sharp, slides everywhere. I am tracking its route through Zoe, who is sitting across the table from me. It started from her fingertips, which were pressed to the warm cup, and flew immediately into her face. Pinked her face, pricked lights into her cold eyes, drew a smile of shiny teeth from her iced up mouth. Now the heat is elsewhere in Zoe, everywhere, because she is moving around on her chair, settling, melting into the chair. But not *fidgeting*: the wrong word, inaccurate, insulting, a clumsy swipe of a word when it comes to Zoe. Children fidget, but there is not much of the child in Zoe. Not now that she is ten, into double figures. Not ever, perhaps.

As usual, she is behaving herself impeccably, here, with me, in this cafe. But this is an odd expression, *behaving herself*, because who else could she behave? It implies two halves, one half in control, the other half under control, and this is not true of Zoe; there are no halves to Zoe. It seems to me that there is nothing of Zoe which is not under her control. I have never known her to misbehave, she never does anything but behave. Unlike Mrs Fox. There is none of Mrs Fox in Zoe. When she came to my house today to leave Zoe, she was so inappropriately dressed for this weather. But she is always inappropriately dressed, whatever the weather. Shiny plastic and loopy crochet. Inappropriately dressed for anything. Short skirts and skimpy tops. What I remember of the girls and women from my own childhood and girlhood are necks, wrists, ankles: the turning points of their bodies, mysteriously both tender and tough. Ever since, the trend has been for fewer clothes, more body. I would have liked to have had more clothes, when I was younger; to have been less close to the surface of the world. Today, Mrs Fox wore a thin suede jacket. She was defying the weather. She is always bared, she confronts the world. So unlike Zoe, whose way in the world, like mine, is to slip by.

This is our favourite place. We have tried every cafe in town over the past year or so, on our Thursday afternoons, now that Zoe is too old to be fetched from school and taken to the park. Certainly this is the warmest one. Why is it always so cold, nowadays? Why is the past always warm? The *deep* past: it is *childhoods* which were warm, *my* childhood. Except, of course, for a few spectacular occasions of snow. Perhaps I did not feel the cold when I was a child, or not enough to brand me with memories. Or perhaps it was during the summer warmth that most of my childhood took place: long afternoons and evenings of games in the street with hoops and skipping ropes. Yes, perhaps there was more to remember of the warm days. Unfortunately it is the cold which I remember from when my children were small. It was always cold, I was always battling to keep the cold from them.

As usual, we have chosen tea, and a bun to share. Zoe chose one of the big buns from the sugar-bright pile inside the perspex dome on the counter. This dome reminds me of the toy, the tiny wintry watery world in the see-through hand-held chamber which is shaken to stir the snow from the ground, to whirl the snow in the air, through the water, to make the snow fall again. Our bun is in the middle of the table between us, and, as usual, I have sliced it into six fingers, soldiers, which we can take one by one from the plate. Zoe copes well with the paraphernalia on the table: the cup with its pinch of handle, the saucer with its central circular slot and clutter of teaspoon. Whenever she moves these pieces, she does so with concentration, as if she is playing a board game. Sometimes she licks her lips, but quickly, the tip of her tongue hooking the few stray sparkles of sugar. Shy-eyed, her gaze is sweeping slow and shiny around the room. Like me, she is not merely relishing the tea and bun, but the whole cafe.

'So,' I start, now that we have caught our breath after the cold air and these first few mouthfuls of tea and bun, 'What have you been doing, this week? What did you do yesterday?'

She looks across at me, tilts her gaze upwards and open. Below, she is slowly squeezing the handle of her cup between forefinger and thumb in preparation for the next move. 'I went to Martina Cole's house,' she replies, helpfully, cheerfully.

'Who's Martina Cole?'

'She's new,' she frowns, considers, corrects, 'well, quite new: new last term; she came from London.' The cup rises; cups her face, the rim aligned with her lower eyelids.

'Is she nice?' I coo, rather stupidly, into those thirsty and bottomless eyes.

Lowering the cup, she focuses on her aim, the saucer. 'Well,' she says firmly to the saucer, *my mum* doesn't like her.' A mere, brisk appraisal of the fact. 'Or,' she starts to qualify, and I do not know if this is backtrack or further explanation, 'my mum doesn't like *her* mum.'

My mum, my mum, my mum. 'But do *you* like her?'

She files her hands below the tabletop into her lap. 'Oh, yes,' she says, surprised that I should ask; and *of course* she is surprised that I should ask. It was a stupid question. Sometimes I still talk to her as if she is six years old.

Her muddy gaze is taken up by the people who are squeezing past our table to the counter: a new crowd of people, coming through the door and bringing with them the smell of the street, the smell of raw air. Zoe's eyes are fired up by the sparks of their flicked scarves and the switching of buttons in their buttonholes. She sits higher in her chair, drawn upwards, ears swelling with their conversation.

I ask her, 'What did you do?'

Her eyes leave them and return emptily to me. 'Do?'

'When you went to Martina's house.'

A pincer of fingers rises from her lap and comes low over the tabletop to the plate of bun. 'Played horses.' Rising, the pincer pauses; a tiny daisy of sugar falls silently, softly, from the slice back onto the plate. 'Well,' she admits, 'not for long, because Martina's not keen on horses.'

'So, what else?' I press the stray sugar into my fingertip, press my fingertip onto the tip of my tongue.

Through a mouthful, Zoe replies, 'We sang.'

'What did you sing?'

'Records,' she chews this word, but now shuts her mouth to turn and look around the room again, to hook her gaze back onto the new people and the busy crockery with which they are leaving the counter. 'Hot chocolate,' she says.

She wants hot chocolate? I follow her gaze to the crowd, crane surreptitiously towards their cups but cannot focus on the contents. Nor, from here, can I read the menu which is hand-written on several sheets of paper on the wall behind the counter. I do not want to disappoint her, to ruin this treat of ours, but I do not know if hot chocolate is available, I do not remember it from the menu. And if it *is* available, is it expensive? How much money do I have left?

But I turn back to a knowing, grin. 'I meant, Hot Chocolate *the pop group*,' she laughs, but kindly. '*You know*,' she coaxes.

Does she really think that I know?

'They're one of Mum's favourites, so we have their records and I know the words.'

This time, when she tips her nose down into her rising cup, her eyes drift free along the rim, off to the next table. I lean over the table to catch them, bring them back. Now I speak into them: 'Do you miss having a sister?'

Dutifully she lowers the cup but her lips remain busy, tracing the taste of the swallowed tea. When she has finished, she considers helpfully, 'I think I'd like a little sister.'

I settle back down into my chair, gathering my words.

But she continues, 'I don't want to be the youngest for ever and ever.' Turning sharply to the crash of keys on the till, she reaches vaguely into the middle of the table for another slice of bun; opens her mouth wide, without focus.

Now I can tell her, 'You liked Iris.'

'Iris,' she repeats, thoughtfully, before the first bite.

'You won't remember, of course, but you loved to play with Iris. When you both began to talk, I heard a lot of your funny little conversations.' Which I do not remember, now. Not the contents. Because the contents were nonsense, *Let's pretend*. They bore no relation to the real world. Of no consequence, they would evaporate when spoken. Barely spoken. Breathed.

If I wanted to hear them, I would have to stop whatever I was doing. Something would halt me; I would sense that I should stop. I was always doing something, there was always something to do, there was never time to listen. But suddenly I *would* stop, and listen, and then I would hear them. And it is the tone that I remember: those whispers, daring, conspiratorial, confident. Those breezes around a tiny world, a snug world. 'Iris was so quiet, once you were gone.' *Weren't we all.*

Zoe is glancing around the room, a turn of her eyes for every turn of her jaw.

Iris stayed quiet. And Peter, too, for the whole of his childhood. Peter was born quiet because he came too soon afterwards, eight months afterwards, when no one had much to say. I wrench a paper napkin from the dispenser, to wipe my sugary fingers. 'It wasn't until Ruthie,' I say, determinedly cheerful, 'that there was chatter in my house again.' A whole generation later. I force myself to smile for Zoe: 'And *she* didn't have a sister *or* a brother, they'd both left home; no, she'd chat to me, or to your Dad . . .' I stop, laugh, and stop the laugh to explain, 'Usually to *herself*.' Or to anyone: Ruthie took chances on people, so many and so often that perhaps they should not be called chances. Ruthie was, is, a natural; a natural at life.

'Perhaps you should meet her,' I enthuse, over the *tsk tsk* of the ball of paper on the sudden cleanliness of my hand.

'I can't,' Zoe tells me, widening her eyes to mine, but, below, scraping the core of her cup around aimlessly in the centre of her saucer. 'I have homework now.'

'Homework?' I hoot from the shudder which is my laugh of dismay. 'Not *now*, Zoe; I didn't mean *now*,' I start to explain. 'Because Ruthie doesn't live around here, she lives in London.'

But Zoe continues, 'I have lots of homework now.' Suddenly spun tall and thin in her chair by her tornado of distress, she hurries, 'Mum makes me stay in to do my homework.'

Gently, kindly, I say something that I never expected to say: 'Well, she's quite right.'

For a moment Zoe is frozen, seems to be listening for more, before she sinks, tentatively, turning her attention down onto the hands in her lap. Hands which are invisible to me. I wait, but for nothing, there is no change, no movement from her. The plate, and our cups, are empty. 'Do you want to go, now?' I check with her.

She simply nods, without lifting her head: three or four jabs of her silver parting down her dark hair.

'Where shall we go next week?' I enthuse. 'Here, again? Or should we try the tea shop on Dane Street once more?'

Rising, she pauses, and decides, 'Here.'

As we walk to the door, bowing over our buttons, hurrying to fasten them, I tell her, 'Oliver needs to go back to the vet on Tuesday afternoon. A check-up.' Holding the door open for her, I ask, 'Have you ever seen a vet at work?' I suspect not.

Ducking below my outstretched arm, she looks up for my eyes. 'No.'

'Do you want to come along? Oliver hates his basket, he plays me up; perhaps you could help me with him.'

'Yes,' she breathes; the breath freezes and floats away.

'Four-thirty, then? Usual place, bus stop, corner of the High Street?'

She lowers her mouth behind her scarf, nods her reply.

Dinah

....

Now that Danny is eighteen and Zoe sixteen, they are no longer children. Why is there no word for grown-up-children? Now Christmas is as much a worry for them as for me. Zoe has been working overtime at her Saturday job so that she can afford to buy presents and to go to her endless end-of-term parties. Danny has been saying that he does not believe in Christmas. In my experience, denial solves nothing. For me, as ever, Christmas is wet, cold and dark on the outside, but full of hot, gaudy shops. Tonight is Late Night shopping. I have hurried through the old Arcade, which, I remember, was new, modern, when Danny and Zoe were small: pale blue, the colour of public toilets. Then I slipped into the new indoor shopping centre, which, from the street, is indistinct from its huge multi-storey car park. I did not come by car, of course, so eventually I had to leave the warm warren and now I am hurrying back along black slimy pavements to the bus stop. I have no idea of the time. It has been dark for hours, but although it feels late, it is probably no later than five or six o'clock. If this were summertime, I would be somewhere between lunch time and the remainder of the day. Winter shortens lives.

It seems to me that there are shops everywhere: the whole world has become one huge shopping centre, although unfortunately not the indoor version. I suppose that they have always been here, but now, at Christmas, they no longer blend into the landscape. Bristling with fairy lights and tinsel, they are twice as bright as usual in this winter darkness. The tinsel is everywhere; even in the window of our local chemist where it tickles a Beatrix Potter baby bowl-and-spoon set, a hot water bottle dressed as a penguin, and a Ladyshave: all of them presents without homes for Christmas. But tinsel cannot prompt me to buy. And who would go Christmas shopping to a local chemist? Well, I suppose that I did, for several years when Zoe was younger, when she wanted little gifts to give to her friends. No, when she was *frantic* for little gifts to give to her friends, when she had no time or money to spare: I went to the chemist to buy toiletry bags, manicure sets, pretty tins of travel sweets, all of them ideal in my opinion but later blessed with Zoe's black frown. I suppose that Christmas is easier nowadays, now that I do not have to buy for Zoe's friends or even for Zoe, who is happy to be given money. As for any other presents, I do not need tinsel to show me what to buy. Or perhaps I do – why am I pacing presentless to the bus stop?

Nine days to go: Countdown To Christmas. Even the air around me is tense. Even when I am away from all this, in my own home, whenever I turn on the radio there are Christmas records, quips about Christmas, checklists for Christmas. Everywhere the focus is firmly on The Day. My stomach is stiff and I know that it will not now breathe with me again before The Day. Whenever I see Zoe around the house, I see her brittle frown, and I can hear that she, too, is barely breathing. She is exhausted by pre-Christmas celebrations at school, work, with friends. Why *pre*-Christmas? Why does everyone pretend that these mid-December days are normal, non-Christmas days? that Christmas comes later, for a mere forty-eight hours? Zoe is still struggling with homework in the early evenings, between shopping and parties. Why not stop, and resign ourselves to a month of fiesta, like foreigners?

I cannot remember everything that I must do before The Day, everything that I must buy, everything that I must send. I lose lists. And do I – and do I *remember to* – write cards for the families of Danny's girlfriend and Zoe's boyfriend? Because they are not on my list of last year's cards. Glancing into the big black sky for momentary relief from these worries, I can see no further than the illuminated Santas-and-sleighs strung across the street. Lucky Santas, suspended above the bustle. Down here, on the pavement, it seems that nothing is moving yet everything is moving very fast. I cannot keep up, nor can I escape.

I am passing, in the window of a newsagent, a hand-scrawled notice boasting of stocks of the Christmas editions of the *Radio* and *TV Times*. On telly there have been previews of the various Christmas Specials, hints that these are the ripened fruits of the year even though everyone knows that they are the stale ingredients in the usual stew. Newspapers have been listing the events of the past year: some of which seem to me to have happened two or three years ago: and some, last week. I feel that the world is poised for an extravagant send-off to Christmas but I know from experience that it will begin and end with a whimper, the shops sneaking shut one by one during the afternoon of Christmas Eve and leaving everyone marooned with cold turkey and *Morecambe and Wise*. And then, two days later, everything will return to normal again, as if nothing has happened. We will continue with the winter. January, February: if Christmas is supposed to lessen the misery of mid-winter, then why is it so early in the season, leaving us with the worst to come?

Does no one else notice that nothing ever changes? All these people, in this one little town. All these lives. On my blunt horizon there are crowds on the old stone bridge, crossing the small, motionless, useless river: all of them coming from somewhere, all of them going somewhere. How do they cope, continue so busily with their changeless lives? Even my own children, complete now with a set each of mock in-laws, seem to be happy with their changeless lives. But for them, of course, change will come, in time. What change will ever come, now, for me?

Whatever did I think would happen to me? But I did not think, when I was young. Because how could I know? What did I know about grown-up life? It would happen to me, just as it seemed to happen to everyone else. One day, I would be a different person with a complete life: grown up. Of course I had hopes, fantasies, daydreams of a big house in the countryside with stables and a swimming pool, but these were the details. The details did not alter the sweep of the story, which was everyone else's story: I was me, and sometimes later, in the future, I would be someone else, a grown-up. But here I am, older, still waiting for the future, still waiting to be different, to be grown up and complete. No, I *am* different, nowadays, because I am *less*, because I have learned to live my life without the prospect of a future. Will I become less and less, as I grow older and older?

When I was young I knew the details of the life that I did not want in my future. I did not want a big old cold house like the house in which I lived with my parents. It was left to my father by my grandfather. Because leaving such a house was the sensible course of action. My grandmother moved out into a cosy flat. My parents were not wealthy enough for a big old cold house, so lodgers moved in with us, one into the attic and another into the spare bedroom, which was not spare because it should have been mine. My sister Antonia and I shared a room; it had two windows, we had our one each. I never stopped being scared of going upstairs, of meeting those strange men on the stairs. What else did I not want? I did not want the silence of my parents on Sundays, or the hush of their front room, not a word out of place. Nor did I want Antonia's hand-me-downs. I did not want to raise my own children as I had been raised. I knew how *not* to raise my children. My children would be smiley and successful, like the children in stories and adverts. But I have ended up with Danny, who tells me that he believes in nothing; and Zoe, who gives nothing away.

Derek made my life. Before Derek, I had no life of my own; my life was those hand-me-downs and the overhead tread of lodgers. This life – the life that Derek made for me – is warm and snug. He is pleased with it, himself. He likes to enthuse about how it has All Turned Out. As if he is pleasantly surprised, as if he was expecting an ordeal. When we met, Derek liked me: it was as simple, and, of course, as wonderfully complex, as Derek liking me. He was kind to me, is still kind to me. My parents had always regarded me as someone who was taking up space: a space-taker; a problem, always, with which they should deal. Never a pleasure. To Derek, I was a pleasure.

Derek says that I was different from everyone else. It seems to me that everyone says this about his or her own choice, so I doubt that it is true, I doubt that everyone can be different from everyone else. Unless, of course, we are all differently different. And perhaps some of us similarly so, two-by-two. Derek says that he fell in love with me because I was in love with freedom. But now I know that freedom, to Derek, meant freedom *from* the world, rather than *in* the world: freedom to be inside his own four walls, or, more particularly in his case, his own four wheels. And me, what did I love about Derek? I loved Derek for his kindness. And still do. He saved my life, saved a life for me.

Will I never have another love affair? Never? Never, ever, and then I will be dead? I have seen and heard all those pep-talks in magazines and on television, How-To-Spice-Up-Your-Marriage: they are lies. Because a marriage is not a love affair. There is nothing wrong with Derek. Sex with Derek is warm, soothing, even strengthening. But I know that there is more to sex than intimacy. I know that there is excitement.

When I was young I excelled at *turning heads, winning hearts, sweeping boys off their feet*: these are the expressions which my mother liked to use. Was she aware of the emphasis of these expressions on the physical, on bits of bodies and their rapid reorientation towards me? She liked the expression *Sweet on you*. My friends and I preferred – still prefer – *Fancies you*. A-little-of-what-you-fancy. My mother liked *Sweetheart*, and nowadays Zoe and her friends describe their favoured boys as *Sweet*: quaint, come full circle. In the middle, my friends and I preferred *Dishy, Tasty, Juicy*. I enjoyed turning heads. I enjoyed choosing: the little black book in the back of my head. Little black brain cells. Stealthily, I collected information. My choices were usually realistic, but with a few outside chances thrown in for good measure. For inspiration, too. And all the time the tingling inside my skin, and the swish of daydreamed conversation through my mind. Then there was the necessity of making myself known to my choices. This, too, required fine control: how to be stunning but not too stunning, striking but not too striking. Practically an impossibility. But I never failed.

Perhaps life should have changed for me when my children were born. But they have not even taken twenty years of my life, and now I am forty-two and they are no longer children, and soon they will be gone again. And, in a sense, what have they been but repositories for thrice-daily meals and lots of television? Danny is the image of his father, and Zoe resembles none of us, so how different would they have been if I had not been their mother? One day soon, I suppose, I shall be a grandmother. I never wanted to be anyone's mother, and I want even less to be a grandmother, but this time I shall have even less choice. When my children were born, my life did not change, I did not change. Except that, for years, it has been my own head which turns, the head which I turn is my own.

Zoe

....

'We should go downstairs,' I tell Mickey, via the mirror. 'Mum's *late* night shopping, not *all* night shopping. She'll be back soon.' I am jabbing my comb into my hair, concentrating on the most badly tangled areas. Behind me, Mickey is still lying on my bed, and I can tell, without looking, that he is making no effort to move.

'You wore me out,' he says, and in these slow words I can hear the slow stretch of a smile.

My comb momentarily misses the worst tangle as my gaze skids across the mirror. His eyes are there on the mirror to meet mine, hold them, and I watch the dark blue ripples of the smile. The warm back of his head is resting in his hands on my pillow.

'I mean it,' I say half-heartedly.

'Oh you do, do you?' he chimes pleasantly, resignedly, swinging up and around so that he is sitting up on the bed, feet on the floor.

'Shoes,' I remind him, pointing to them. In desperation I give up on my hair, start to fluff out the straight bits rather than try to straighten the tangles. But suddenly he reaches for me, across the gap between the bed and the dressing table, and lays a hand on my arm. His grip becomes firmer, to steady himself, stretched out, swaying very slightly. Now it softens and drifts on my arm. I look back into his eyes, open my mouth, but no words come. Instead, there are the words from the stereo, downstairs, whirring indistinctly over the rhythm of the music, Danny's music. The beat bumps the room softly, tickles the soles of my feet. Sometimes I wish that Mickey would not look at me like this, with his wonderful, spooky eyes. Does he know, can he see the strange sensations that come so quickly to me with one of his slow looks?

I flinch, and my attention drifts from his eyes to his hair. I know that it is exactly the same colour as mine: *non*-colour, blotter of all other colours, black. Together we soak up the sun, and lose no light. If we have children they will be the same, presumably, because there is no relief, no pinprick, in our black genes. But whenever I lay a strand of my hair onto his, match mine so perfectly to his, I cannot fail to notice the different textures. His hair is silky, so silky that it feels wet. Before Mickey, I had never run another person's hair through my fingers. Now, whenever we are apart, this is the memory of him that I carry with me, at my fingertips.

He releases me, switches his attention happily to his shoes. 'So she's off buying a stack of presents for you, is she?'

'We're not big present buyers,' I say to myself in the mirror. 'Which suits me fine. Because I can get away with buying bath salts.'

In the corner of the mirror there is a flick of his floppy hair. '*Oh darling, you shouldn't've.*'

I glance at his reflection. He is bent over a shoe, grinning. 'Not for you,' I protest. 'In fact, the time I save by buying bath salts for Mum, I shall spend worrying about your present.'

'Worrying about how to raise the massive funds, you mean?' He switches jollily to the other shoe.

I sigh. 'What am I going to buy for you?'

Growing around me in the mirror, adding his own soft shakes to the purring floorboards, he is suddenly behind me. He places one hand on each side of my head and massages vaguely, messing my hair again. 'I have everything,' he says smoothly into the mirror, 'I have you.'

'Mickey!'

'What?'

'My hair!'

'What?' A more urgent, impatient *What?*

'Oh' – I take his hands, lift them away, pause irritably with them, and then drop them gently together in mine onto my chest – 'nothing. Nothing.'

He drops his black head down onto mine, kisses my black crown. 'You look perfect,' he insists quietly.

I squeeze his hands. 'To you, perhaps. But Mum is less charitable.' And I do not want her to start prying into my life.

He takes my comb, and I feel the tiny teeth nibbling the tangle at the back of my head. In the mirror he is frowning, eyes down-turned, lips hard. '*Less charitable*,' he repeats, derisively, before protesting in refutation, 'She's your mother.'

'So? Biological accident, as far as she's concerned.' I am watching his face, which is creased with concentration, and anticipating the regular twitch of his wrist behind my head. 'Maybe I should have my hair cut short.' Strange that I have always assumed that if I had my hair cut for convenience, then the reason would be arduous foreign travels or regular swimming or something, not afternoons on my bed with my boy-friend.

'No,' he says sternly. And now, thinking, 'Your Mum is more charitable to you than to me.'

'Don't be melodramatic, Mickey. She likes you well enough.'

He smiles down over my head at my reflection. 'But perhaps she wouldn't if she knew the fine detail.'

'*Fine?*'

I sense the comb sweeping down a length of my hair. I explain to him, 'It's just that she is not very good with strangers.' And now I shrug, between comb-strokes, to disown this sentiment.

'I'm not a stranger,' he protests.

'No, yes, I know that.' I shrug again: Don't-ask-me. The tiny teeth twang on a new tangle. 'All I know is that she is not too good with people in the house.'

He melts away behind me, sits back on the bed, but his eyes remain in the mirror in front of my face. 'Wouldn't Christmas be different if we had our own children?' he muses.

'Expensive.'

His face buckles into a smile. 'Girls are so romantic,' he says sarcastically.

'But it *would* be expensive,' I counter jauntily.

'Well, yes, but I was thinking of the excitement . . .'

I swivel on my stool to face him. 'Do I detect,' I tease kindly, 'that someone here is mourning his own childhood?'

He reaches into my lap for my hands, holds them inside his own, then opens them, and searches my palms. 'It'll be nice to have a place of our own,' he says eventually, conclusively.

But this reminds me of Mum. 'She'll be here in a moment.' I snap away from him and shut the dressing table drawer.

'What have you bought for Danny?' he is asking me.

'Oh, Danny's easy,' I say, gathering everything that I want to take downstairs with me: 'A record. The latest Peters and Lee.'

He laughs and drops back down onto my bed.

'Okay, okay, I admit it: they were sold out of Peters and Lee, so I had to settle for The Specials.'

'Do you suppose that there *is* a latest Peters and Lee?' He is shimmering with wonder.

'I suppose there's a latest everything; but some more latest than others.'

Suddenly, looking down at him looking up at me, I feel the heaviness, the thickness, of all those years behind me when I looked at him but he did not look at me, when I looked alone. What changed, for him, and how, to leave him looking at me like this? For me, there was never a time when I was not in love with him. I saw him when I was eleven and new at school, and I have been in love with him ever since, I have been waiting for him ever since.

So what did he think of me during those hundreds, no, thousands, of days? I have asked him, of course, but he will not give me an answer. He implies that the past, before me, Before Us, is unworthy of consideration. I suspect that he did not think of me, or perhaps very little. I was a friend. If he did think of me,

I suspect that he felt that I was *Nice Enough*. But for me, of course, the past four years were full of dreams and plans and passion, full of *him*: calm and certain amid his twitchy friends in classrooms; and perfectly proportioned among the ragbag of squints and quiffs in the cloakroom. Most importantly, the past four years have been full of his blue smile.

Now he is asking me, 'What should I get for my sister?'

'You're hopeless,' I soothe. And the past four years have been full of suffering: there were arguments with him; and there were his other girlfriends, Tanya Thin-eyes Duncan, Hayley Palely Prentiss, Jackie Moore. There was a Christmas – two years ago? –when, for some long-forgotten reason, we were not talking to each other. Which did not matter, in a sense, because if he was not talking to me, then he was stopping himself, and if he was stopping himself, then he was monitoring every moment, conscious of every occasion when he would have spoken to me. And of course it does not matter now because I have him.

I take one of his hands and look at the flat fingers, the soft square ends and short neat nails; so different from mine, my frail fingers with tough bolts of bone, my tiny plump pads and long white tips. Holding his hand, squeezing an impression of it into my own, I look again into his face and I can see him as he will be in ten years' time when he is twenty-six, and then, after a careful blink, as he was ten years ago when he was six. This is easy because his eyes, blue rocks, are landmarks in the shifting skin. By contrast, my own eyes are flat, sunken. But I do not envy him his eyes because I have them to see, to watch. And I will have them for my children. Sometime in the future we will make his eyes again, and then again. I look down over his body, so flat inside the soft shirt. I sit down on him, astride him, for a moment. 'Do you think I should buy a present for your sister?' It occurs to me that I should sit very still, very carefully.

'No,' he protests. 'Why?' He rubs my thighs with his flat hands.

How long until we are alone together again? Christmas will be worse than usual, because everyone is home.

'I like her. I'd like to buy her something.'

'I wish girls wouldn't wear trousers,' he says, his fingertips following the creases in my jeans.

'Mickey!' I admonish lazily, and dismount, drop down beside him. I nestle my nose onto his head to breath the scent of the wet black hay. 'What should I buy her?'

'I don't know,' he replies, irritated not by me but by the stubborn button on my jeans.

'Well, is there anything that she wants?'

'Yes. She wants an engagement ring from Stuart. Do you reckon that you could fix that?' His head scrapes back across the pillow, so that he can smile at me.

I pull him on top of me, to feel the weight of him all over me; every cell of his body hauled down onto every upwardly straining cell of mine. 'We must go downstairs in a minute,' I wheeze, beneath him.

'Mmmm,' he says.

'What will your parents think if Sarah and Stuart get engaged?'

I think that he shrugs but it is difficult to be sure because he is lying down.

'What would they think if *we* got engaged?'

'Too young,' he manages ruefully through a mouthful of my hair.

I shoot one hand through his hair, from front to back, switching the roots. 'How old do you think we'll be when we have our children?'

'Don't know, twenty-two, twenty-three; that's supposed to be the best time, isn't it?' He raises his head again but lowers his face onto mine, his lips onto mine, and nibbles bitelessly.

'Twenty-two *and* twenty-three?' I protest between the little kisses. 'If I have a baby when I'm twenty-two *and* when I'm twenty-three, I'll end up in nappies myself.'

'Not *and*. *Or*.'

We snuffle our laughter in a longer kiss, and loosen more clothes.

After a moment I ask him, 'How old was your Mum when she had Sarah?'

'Don't know,' he murmurs. 'Normal age.'

'I think mine was twenty-two or twenty-three,' I muse, 'when she had Danny. Or something like that.'

'When she had something like Danny?' He raises himself so that he can inflict a smirk down on me.

'Ha ha,' I allow. We shift together so that he can drop back down onto me and lay comfortably between my legs, but suddenly, simultaneously, it is obvious to both of us that we are in a position, *the* position, so that he is poised to push inside me. He nudges, once. We look at each other.

'We shouldn't do this,' I think aloud, slowly.

'No,' he confirms.

We do not move. I dare not move in case I take him inside me. We are still looking at each other, and now, gently, he coaxes my lower lip from beneath my tooth, runs his fingertip over the stinging bite mark. I lift my head from the pillow to kiss him, and take him back down with me.

'What about your Mum?' he whispers.

'Don't worry about her, she doesn't like threesomes.'

He despairs of me with a laugh which warms my face. And nestles into my band of muscle. This is Decision Time.

'Well?' He is watching my face very closely for clues.

I try to continue to think, principally of Mum coming through my door in a moment or two, but now there is nothing in my world except this smarting and the certainty of its soothing. 'Coward,' I tease Mickey gently. We will have to be very quick.

'Wait,' he says. He pulls away from me, and reaches around to the back pocket of his jeans. I watch him tear open the packet very precisely, and put on the condom, *apply* the condom. His downturned face is dense with concentration, his fingertips beat a certain rhythm on the unfolding rubber. I shut my eyes and listen to the wail of Danny's music buried beneath my floorboards. I try to identify the track, then its location on the

LP, until Mickey shifts between my legs with a deep denim rustle of our loose jeans. I open my eyes into his.

I am sure that I can hear the crackle of rucking rubber as he pushes inside me. I pull him even closer to me, pull him quickly through the confusion of pain and numbness until he is lying much deeper in me, in the soft free space that has been waiting for him. It occurs to me now, too late, that our effort to stay as dressed as possible will not fool Mum, if she finds us here. And I realise that I have pulled Mickey so close to me that there is virtually no room for movement. But every tiny movement is magnified. I am listening into the depths for any sudden sound, for the click of the front door, but Danny's music rocks smoothly beneath us. And Mickey squeezes me, inside me, onto me, and I know that there is nothing else as good as this, that there will never be anything better than this, and I am right to risk everything for this; or, no, not *right*, because there is no choice, this is simply how it is. He is beginning to pull further away from me, each time, promising so much more with his return that I rush to meet him. How would we look to Mum, struggling like this in our wrinkly jeans? *Guilty*.

I listen harder, for sounds on the path, sounds beneath and beyond the low whistle of denim on denim and the slap of thin clean rubber onto, into, my stickiness. Suddenly, and suddenly breathlessly, Mickey says, 'I'm sorry,' like a warning, and then pushes harder, several times, and I realise that these are the pushes for which I have been waiting, for which I have been lying here in wait: *Don't be, Sweetie*, and I follow every milli-metre of these last few pushes inside me and then my body replies, my muscles squeeze of their own accord around him, my burning bloodstream strikes up into my heart and pulses away down my legs. And now, afterwards, there is nothing but a deep blanket of warmth with the refreshing rinse of his sweat on my skin. But now the thought of Mum, which drags me from swirling sleepiness. 'I hate to do this to you,' I tell one of Mickey's fiery ears, 'but we have to hurry.'

He stirs with a hot sigh and a bleary kiss for me. 'I love you,' he manages, and pulls carefully from me. He is gone, but my insides echo his presence. I slither from beneath him, and off the bed; dress myself again, cover myself, feeling sticky and sore and suspect.

I tackle my hair in front of the mirror, hearing behind me the peeling of rubber from skin and then a reluctant zip. I study his reflection. The smooth skin below each cheekbone is burning with blood flow, and his normally sleek hair is rumpled. He seems to sense that I am looking at him because suddenly he returns a smile to my reflection, a reflex smile, dizzy, eager to please, whilst ineffectually tidying his hair with a few pats of his hands. I swell with the familiar ache, but this time prickled with panic: how will I manage to live for even a moment without him? 'I love you,' I tell him.

He laughs lightly. 'I know. You've just shown me, remember?'

'What is it like for boys?' I ask him.

He sits attentively on the edge of the bed, his hands together in his lap. 'What . . . ?'

'You know, the *actual* . . .' My comb is very loud in my hair.

For a moment there is no movement at all on his face, and then he shrugs hugely: 'A tingle, sort of.'

A tingle? How sad. No heart, no legs.

'Do you want the comb?' I ask him. I am being ruthless with my hair.

He shrugs again. 'When you've finished.' Then he smiles the same frizzled smile. 'I didn't even stop to remove my shoes,' he says, incredulous, glancing down.

I was not wearing any shoes, because this is my home. I look beneath the dressing table for my slippers.

'Who's Mrs Dutton?' he asks, behind me, in the same happy tone.

A twitch of my heart, and I turn to him. 'What?'

'No, *who*?' Still smiling, he waves a piece of paper.

What do I tell him about Mrs Dutton? And I had been so sure that he knew everything about me. But perhaps he knows everything that matters. I have not thought about Mrs Dutton for years: how I know her, why I visit her.

'That's my Christmas card list,' I say, vaguely.

'Well, yes, it's hardly your Christmas present list; not unless you've suddenly come into a lot of money.' He brightens the grin, cheekily. 'So who's Mrs . . .' he glances again at the list, 'Dutton?' He shrugs sweetly and replaces the list on my bedside table. 'That's all.'

Yanking my soft slippers over my toes and slapping my heels down onto the backs of them, which Mum is forever telling me not to do, I start, 'She's an old lady. I visit her, sometimes.' Mickey's shoes are twitching to Danny's rhythm. 'You know,' I try to explain, 'she's old, she has no one else. Or not many. Not nearby.' This is true. And this is all he needs to know. More cheerfully, I add, 'I don't go there very often. Just . . .' I shrug, to imply that I choose when I go but in accordance with my own criteria, too complex to explain: instinct, perhaps, mixed with history.

'Birthday and Christmas cards,' he concludes for me: 'That sort of thing?'

'Yes,' I agree. That-sort-of-thing: I realise that I do not know the date of Mrs Dutton's birthday. She has a birthday card for me, every year, apparently bought from a local newsagent; on the front, a pastel pink cutesy cartoon of a lady with a basket of flowers, or, worse, a photograph of a girl with no hairstyle on a horse or in a dinghy at sunset, and then, wispy inside the card, one of those brain-damaged rhymes. Often, in the local shops, I wonder who buys these cards, conclude that they are convenient for people who are in a hurry, and then I remember Mrs Dutton, who is never in a hurry. Usually my card waits for weeks on her mantelpiece for me to visit.

'Saint Zoe,' Mickey teases, apparently delighted.

'Well, it's not for ever, is it,' I confide. 'I've been visiting for years, so I might as well go along, continue to go along, whilst I'm around.'

But now I want to tell him a little more, or to try to tell him.

'She talks about the old times.'

He is looking very carefully into my face but I sense that he is not listening to me. He is not interested. And this stops me; I stop myself, I will keep this to myself.

'Like old people do. You know.'

I snatch the list. 'I must write some of these tonight, I must do them all by the end of the week.'

Perhaps it is not so very odd that, when I was young, I felt that Mrs Dutton's old times were my own old times. I was drawn to old times. They came brightly to me in television programmes, *Upstairs, Downstairs*. And more sedately in lessons at school, soulful sepia eyes on the smooth ink-scented pages of our History Workbooks, and the coconut-shell clamour of horses' hooves inside our classroom radio. And perhaps from Mum, too, who was so often tearing off her memories in my presence: the lodgers, their gems of phlegm rattling the prominent bones of their little chests; and her little liberty bodice, which was anything but. I have always liked stories; that is my trouble. 'Come on,' I tell Mickey, 'let's go downstairs and start looking innocent.'

Turning from the bottom stair into the hallway, I see Mum through the kitchen doorway, and my heart bristles. 'She's here,' I hiss, incredulous, to Mickey. I make a mental note to slap Danny, who should have warned us. Mum is still wearing her coat, but scattering a work surface with the paraphernalia of tea-making: pot, caddy, cup, strainer. She turns towards me as I bound through the doorway trying to look — what? — healthy? optimistic? sporty, even? Trying to look like the type of girl who has everything on her mind except boys and bed. The type of girl who I might have been if I had not met Mickey. I am not confident of my success. Even if I look normal, is it possible that I smell different?

'Where have you come from?' Mum asks, ripping into a packet of Ginger Crinkles.

'I've been doing my Christmas card list,' I reply, sprightly, flapping it.

She glances beyond me. 'Hello Mickey.' There was no lift in her voice.

'Hello Mrs Fox,' he replies mildly. He stands beside me and looks with interest at the tea pot.

Mum turns back to me. 'So,' she drawls wearily, 'do you have enough?'

I think fast, but to no avail. 'Enough what?'

'Cards.'

'Oh. Yes. Thanks. Where's Danny?'

She inclines her head towards the noisy, buzzing living room. 'Keeping those punk rockers company, presumably.'

I let *Punk Rockers* pass without correction, despite Mickey's grin. I ask her, 'Does he know that you're home?'

Her face sparks with irritation. 'How do I know?' Then she grumbles, 'Has your father rung?'

'Don't know.' Suddenly I think better of this. 'No.' I take a packet of pretzels from the top of a shopping bag and pull apart a seam.

'Zoe, don't do that! They're for Christmas!'

For Christmas? Christmas what? Christmas lunch?

'Put them in a tin.'

Suddenly she is asking Mickey, politely, 'Do you have family over for Christmas?'

'Not really.'

I skim the tin across the shelf inside the cupboard.

She asks me, 'Are you having tea here?'

Tea, telly, bath, bed. Dad will work late, and Danny will be out with Claire. Me and Mum, and tea, telly, bath, bed. 'I'm going over to Mickey's house,' I say, although this is news to all of us. I check with a quick glance at Mickey, and encounter no resistance. 'Now,' I add.

Mickey stretches.

'You'll have something to eat at Mickey's house?' She looks at Mickey.

He nods.

'What is it?' I check, as an afterthought.

Inside her huge stiff coat, she floats back around to me. 'What is what?' she asks faintly, eyes bloated with tiredness.

'What's for tea?'

'Oh. I haven't decided.'

'Macaroni cheese?' We often have macaroni cheese when Mum is late, when there are no plans for anything else; because there is always macaroni and a packet of cheese sauce mix in the cupboard.

'If you like.'

If I like? 'I'm not having any,' I remind her. It was a helpful suggestion, not a request.

'Not even if it's macaroni?'

'No, I'm going out.'

'But do you want me to keep some, if it's macaroni?' She is stirring her cup of tea, although I do not know why because she does not add sugar.

'No. Thank you.' *Yes* would cause complications.

Danny crashes through the door from the living room, but I intercept him with an expression of cold fury.

'What?' he asks me, offended.

A clever strategy, if only he realised, because how can I complain, in front of Mum, about his failure to tell me that she was home?

'Nothing,' I reply, pointedly, before being unable to resist adding, '*thicko*.'

'Zoe!' Mum leaps to his defence as briskly as usual.

Danny is whining, 'What have I done?'

But Mickey says, 'Hi, Dan.' His eyebrows twitch, to say, *Women, eh?!*

And Danny glances happily at him; mumbles, 'How ya doin', mate?'

Mickey's eyebrows twitch again, this time to say, *Fine*. And how different from a girl, who would say, *Well, ACTUALLY*, and then go on to give details.

I am staring at him, thinking how he would not feel so fine if Mum had caught us together in my bedroom. But if I tried to point this out to him, if I could possibly point this out to him now, I suspect that he would say *But she didn't, did she?* This is always the case with him, and with Danny too, with Dad, with men: everything is always over, always in the past, and I or Mum or Gran are Making-a-fuss. Men hate fuss. Mickey is still smiling knowingly at Danny.

Mum is asking Danny, 'Are you in or out tonight?'

'Out.' His face brims with a smile. 'Mumski.' He pokes at the shopping bags. 'Happy shopping?'

'Will you have something to eat before you go?' she asks.

'How long?' He glances from the bags, the contents, the contents of the contents, Russian-dolls of wrapping, to the clock on the wall.

She blows across the surface of her tea. 'Well, not yet. I'm not in, yet.' She sips, wincing. 'Three-quarters of an hour?'

He pulls apart a packet of peanuts. 'Oh no,' he explains: 'The love of my life awaits.'

'Yes,' mutters Mum sceptically.

'Claire waits for no man.'

'No.'

Danny lunges and sprinkles peanuts into our open palms.

'Steady on, with those, please,' Mum protests. 'I've only just bought them.'

'I'm off in twenty minutes or so.'

'*I'm off now*,' I tell him, pointedly.

Politely, he expresses interest and surprise, widening his eyes. 'Oh. Where're you going?'

'Mickey's house.'

Beside me, Mickey shrugs.

Mum continues, 'Danny, do you want any food saving for you?'

He turns vaguely towards her. 'Er. Yes. No. Yes.'

As I turn to go, I hear her telling him, 'Well, I'll save some for you anyway.'

Dinah

·············

I listen to Zoe and Mickey passing down the hallway and swilling momentarily in the porch: Zoe shuffling into her shoes on
the doormat, then both the coats brushing the walls, the steel nib
of a zip ringing on a radiator. The front door opens, filling the
hallway with the low boom of night-time air, and then it slams
shut, shaking the whole house, and leaving us alone.

'Did your Dad call?' I ask Danny, starting on the bags of
shopping.

'Home by eight,' he reports, through a layer of peanut grit.

'How long had Zoe been upstairs with Mickey?'

'Don't know.' He picks up and frowns furiously at a packet of
cashews. 'What are these?'

I take them from him. 'Well, you're *supposed* to know,' I
remind him, gently. *I* am supposed to know. I am supposed to
watch over her, warn her. But do I have any influence over her?
Have I ever made any difference to her? She has unfurled into the
world regardless of me.

Sod the shopping: I sit down at the table with my cup of tea.

Danny draws a box of breakfast cereal from a carrier bag and
stretches with it to the top shelf of the cupboard. 'I'm not Zoe's
keeper.'

'I don't want her to get pregnant,' I tell him. Because pregnancy seems perfectly possible, to me: Zoe will continue to
unfurl, into pregnancy. I force a little smile, to encourage Danny
to talk to me.

He is pausing, absently squeezing a bag of crimson pot-pourri
which I have bought as a spare Christmas present. 'Never ever?'
he twinkles eventually.

117

'Very funny, Danny,' I counter dryly, but with some relief.

He crashes the packet of pot-pourri back into the big bag and says, 'Teach her about contraception, then.'

My fingers are melted around my cup. It is strange to think that people who use saucers have chosen to go without this warmth. Why am I having this conversation with Danny? Surely this type of conversation is for mothers and daughters, if at all? But, of course, I have always known that I would never have any such conversation with *my* daughter. I never have *any* conversation with Zoe. She is always somewhere else. She is a secret-keeper. I glance at the clock to check how long until Derek returns home. 'Do you think that she needs teaching?' I try gently.

He laughs, but rather humourlessly. 'Well, *you* seem to think so.'

He is leaning back against the draining board, arms folded loosely, one foot slung across the other. His hair has stayed stuck in tufts, showing the route of his fingers. His pale blue eyes illuminate me. I know that he is smiling hugely inside although there is only the merest trace on his mouth. He is so like his dad. My mother used to say about Derek, *You know where you are, with him.* Certainly I know where I am with Danny. The back of my nose stings with sadness when I realise that if his dad had been born into this later generation he would have been like Danny and I could have talked to him, no, he would have talked to me.

'No,' I tell Danny, 'I have no idea about Zoe.' And this is true: it is possible that she is very prudish. 'And, anyway, it's not *just* Zoe; because there's *Mickey*. And there's peer pressure.' I find *Peer Pressure* in the magazines in the waiting room of the doctor's surgery, in the pages of advice for mothers, in articles on mothers' advice to their teenage daughters. Eagerly, I explain: 'It's not that I think badly *of Zoe*.'

'Perhaps you shouldn't be having this conversation with me,' he sighs.

I soothe my own forehead with my warm fingers. 'There's no one else.'

'Perhaps if you're worried about Zoe, you should *talk* to her.'

'She's not here.'

He deflates in exasperation. 'Well, no, not at the moment . . .'

'Do you sleep with Claire?' Danny's girlfriend, Claire: seems nice. Nice parents, certainly, whom I have known for years, from Saturday Swimming Club. In those days Claire was a gorgeous little girl, her green eyes tilted, lifting her cheekbones with them. Her lips were made in a smile. Nowadays she covers everything in make-up. And I bet she hates the colour of her hair, the rare colour of her hair, for which there is no name because orange is wrong and none of the others, gold or strawberry, are quite right.

Danny uncrosses his ankles, shifts taller in front of the draining board. '*Oh no*,' he starts in sing-song sarcasm, 'we go down to the Baptist Hall every evening and play table-tennis.' Now he sighs and says, 'Of course,' both emphatically and dismissively.

Of course. Of course. I am trying to persuade myself, *Of course*. And I am trying to remember why I asked him. And suddenly I worry that he will ask me in return: do I sleep with his dad? What would I say? Yes, sort of, sometimes?

He shrugs nonchalantly, but confidently, self-righteously: 'We love each other.'

I want to know *where*. Here? And *when*? But where else? And *how*, I want to know *how*, because he is so little, no, so *young*, so how did he get himself into such a position, how did he know, no, how did he find the confidence? He has been locking me out of the bathroom for years. He is even reluctant to sunbathe. So little, so young? He is old enough to be married. Does he want to get married? No, please.

'We want – you know – to be together,' he says, more enthusiastically.

What is the rhyme? 2gether, 4ever? 'You want to get married?'

He smiles pityingly at me. 'Well, not this side of the next ten years, no. For a start, Claire's training will take years.'

I remember that Claire wants to be a dentist. Is it possible to *want* – really, truly – to be a dentist? And not simply to want the salary or the hours or something?

He is peering at me. 'Why? You want us to get married?'

'No. No.'

'We do love each other,' he reiterates. 'We can get married any old time.'

I wonder what would have happened to me if I had gone to bed with everyone with whom I was in love when I was eighteen? Nothing, presumably; not if I had managed to avoid pregnancy and disease. Except that Derek might not have married me. But perhaps *I* would not have married *Derek*: because what would have happened if I could have married at *any old time*? Of course, there were girls who did sleep with boys: we knew of them, Patricia Hallett who lived in our street with her deaf brother and their massive immobile mother, and Sally Gibson who was an usherette at the local Roxy. A lost virginity was like a dreadful disease: they had *had sex*. (Why is sex still something that we have, rather than something that we do?) It was the very worst that could happen to a girl. But now I cannot remember why. Yes, I can: it was worse than slavery, somehow; it was a boy using a girl and leaving her in ruins. But were there no boys in love, in those days, no Dannys?

My mother never told me anything about sex. I remember her response when, after several years of marriage, I told her that I was pregnant: 'Isn't that nice!' As if it was happening somewhere else, to someone else.

Slowly I tell Danny, 'I can't stop you doing whatever you want to do.' I imagine that Derek would say something similar, so I feel that I have done my motherly duty.

He relishes this, laughs at me. 'I know that.' Then he asks, more seriously, 'Would you want to?'

I had never thought of it this way. After a moment, I say, 'I suppose that it's pregnancy that matters. Avoiding pregnancy, I mean.'

He stretches, turns to take a cup from the draining board. 'Taken care of.'

I want very much to ask how, but I resist. This is not a chat with a friend. Asking my own eighteen-year-old son for these messy details would be as bad as checking that he is going regularly to the toilet. 'So, I have only Zoe to worry about,' I say, lightly.

Drinking from his cup of water, he raises his eyebrows, saying nothing.

'Sixteen isn't eighteen. She's very young.'

Glancing at the clock, he rinses the cup in a steaming silvery stream of tap water. 'People marry at sixteen,' he says briskly, replacing the cup precariously on the draining board, 'and once upon a time, they married at thirteen . . . nine . . .'

'Yes, and nowadays we're civilised. Can't you have a word with her?'

'Which word did you have in mind?' He grins at me before turning his attention to his reflection on the black window panes: more specifically, the reflection of his hair.

'Please, Danny?'

He glances briefly at me 'She's sixteen,' he says helplessly, as if this places Zoe beyond help. He seems undecided about whether to flatten or fluff his hair. 'We're only young once,' he says, before leaving me alone.

Caddy

·············

No doubt the chair is here because this is the porch of a church hall and churches rely upon old people for custom, and old people rely upon chairs. It is the first seat that I have found today which is not the sill of an indoor fountain. So I am no longer Christmas shopping, but waiting here on this chair in this porch whilst Ruthie and the children grapple with the Craft Fayre. There are plenty of people passing through the porch, so I am not lonely. There is a small stone plaque high on the opposite wall, which I can read if I peer and improvise. The inscription tells me that it commemorates Stephen Poultney, who was a member of the congregation of this church and died aged thirty-three in 1865 in the Something province of China, where he had been working for two years as a medical missionary. The porch gusts with people stamping dampness from their boots into the doormat. When Stephen Poultney died, he was a year younger than my daughter Ruth is now.

He must have been a very brave young man: I cannot imagine going to China nowadays, let alone in the 1860s. It must have been even further away, in those days. What a desolate place to die, especially when he had gone to cure. How did he die? How did the news of his death ever reach home? And what news? Did they ever know exactly how he died, or exactly when? Different continents, different calendars. And who arranged for the plaque? And who, how many, paid? Although there is no date of death, the inscription is otherwise unusually lengthy: the whole story, *medical missionary* and a specific location, a string of strange italicised words instead of a mere *China*. And so it caught my eye, and my sympathies. What will happen to it when this building is pulled down? He died so long ago now that there will be no one left alive who knew him.

I remember the small plaque on the wall of the old railway station (which was rebuilt a few years ago with a huge floodlit concrete lake of a car park). It listed the local lads who died in the Boer War. There were seven or eight names, I suppose. And I knew some of them, some of the surnames, local surnames, *Fitzpatrick* and *Darling*. When I was young, I used to gaze at the plaque because the Boer War was being fought when I was born. Nowadays most people in this country do not know that there was a Boer War, and even fewer know the reason. And *of course* they do not know, because what does it matter, what difference did it make? Nowadays it is as if the Boer War never happened. Few people know the cause of the First World War. The Second World War? Yes, easy: Hitler. And the Second World War was recent. My daughter Ruthie was born during the Second World War. Evie was born during the First.

Ruthie was my late baby, my mistake baby, although not my mistake alone. Now, through the flapping doors, I can see her, and not see her (Now-I-see-her-Now-I-don't). With each snap open of the huge lens she is bigger, closer to me, and I notice that she never seems to look any older. She is not so far from forty, yet her dark hair remains free from grey veins. Perhaps she uses – what is it? – *Grecian?* She *looks* Grecian. Her hair is thick and dry, not shiny. (Matt?) It is the curly type of hair but without the curls. It has not quite bothered to curl. Her eyes come towards the doorway now and I can see that their black stones hold more light than the shiny pale eyes of the people around her, in which light simply swills. She looks like her father's sister, Lettie. No, Lettie is dead, so she looks like Lettie *looked*. When she was a little girl, she looked like Evie had looked. If there is such a striking similarity, why did I never feel that Evie had come back as Ruthie? I never did, not even for a moment.

Now I concentrate on her as she comes close to the champing doors. She appears to be talking to herself, but of course she is talking to the children (as if there is any difference). I know that she has no memories of Evie's life. In fact, it occurs to me now that she probably knows nothing about Evie, who was born a whole generation earlier. Except, of course, that she was born and then she died. But it is more, or less, than Ruthie's lack of memories: it is that Ruthie is no one but Ruth. She is different. From everyone. She is more herself than anyone else I have ever known. Ruth, black and white. No grey matter. All spirit.

Now the doors are frantic in the frame: she is here, behind the doors with the pushchair. I rise to help but I am slow and someone else is there before me. Ruthie jabs the pushchair through the narrow doorway. In the pushchair, Polly seems unconcerned. Her brother Joe jostles Ruthie's knees, in a clingy sulk. I notice, for the first time, the red piping down the long seams of Ruthie's jeans, disappearing into the tiny turn-ups. And I think of Ruthie's *genes*: strong, because both my grandchildren are dark, not fair like their father. A long time ago, Ruthie had a black boyfriend for a year or so, and I wondered whether, eventually, I would have half-cast grandchildren. Why half-cast? Why not twice-cast, black *and* white?

I do not often see Joe and Polly, but I rarely saw my other grandchild, Graeme, who is Peter's boy, who is now no longer a child but twenty-six. Peter and Valerie moved to Falkirk before Graeme was born. Falkirk is in Scotland; Graeme, on the phone, has always had a Scottish accent. He calls me *Grainy*. I suppose that Joe and Polly call me *Grammar*. They live in London, although it never seems like London to me, whenever I visit. There are no red double-deckers in their road. There is no smog. My sister Connie, who started in service in London, used to tell me about smog, which so often filled her half-day off each week, sometimes so thickly that she could not see her own shoes. From Ruthie's road, there are no views of St Paul's or the Post Office Tower. Once we went from Ruthie's house to Hyde Park for an afternoon by the Serpentine, but the journey – more than an hour of bus and train and bus again – took longer than my own journey on the train from here into London.

When Ruthie left home, left me, more than twenty years ago, it was for teacher training college. There was only me to leave, because her father had been dead for several years. I remember watching Clem the first time he saw Ruthie: reluctantly, frowningly, he bent over the crib; reluctant to be a father so late in his life, reluctant to acknowledge his mistake-baby; and as he bent slowly into the crib, his frown was knocked from his face by a furious little foot. Ruthie was the last of my babies, and the biggest, the strongest. When she chose to go to teacher training college, it was because her best friend was going. But the friend, in the end, failed an exam. Ruthie went alone; still went, because, she said, she quite liked children, and there was nothing else that she wanted to do. In fact, she wanted to be an actress. And even if it was true that she quite-liked-children, she hated classrooms. So, after college, she went to London to become an actress. She worked on the stage, on-and-off, for years, and had a day-job waiting in the dining room of a firm of City solicitors. Then she married Simon, who was the chef – is still a chef, which means that he never cooks at home.

They have a lodger, a young student. 'More cooking for you,' I complained to Ruthie, when she told me.

'I don't cook for him!' she laughed. 'He leads his own life. He's never home.'

Their home is a basement flat. They call it a *garden* flat, which, I suppose, is accurate, because it has a garden, a long, old garden, not the type that I expect to find in London. It is edged with foxgloves, tall, unsteady, mottled, and the central feature is a picturesque ruin of a birdbath. Whenever I went to stay in their flat, I stayed on the fold-down sofa, which I am now too old to do. If I fold-down, these days, I stay down. The flat is different from how I imagine the homes of other modern young mums. There are no sparkling work surfaces in the kitchen; no surfaces at all, solely the small draining board and the huge wooden table.

Ruthie covered everything in the flat with paint; or, if it was already painted, she stripped it bare. There is an old fireplace (for me, gas is a godsend) which has a thick swishy red surround and mantelpiece. But all the doors are bare. The kitchen table is the exception, always having been bare. I suspect that the splinters are a trap for dirt, but scrutiny is impossible because Ruthie likes candlelight. The candles, stuck inside the necks of old wine bottles, die their messy deaths but remain in view, fossilising. And more bottles appear, with fresh candles. I wish that Ruthie could remember the thrill when our house in Kenwell was given electric lights, when she was very small. As well as furnishing her kitchen with splinters and candles, Ruthie chose old-fashioned plain names for her children. *Joe*, I do not dislike the name, but I knew so many old Joes; and *Polly*, two-a-penny Pollies. People say that everything comes around again, back into fashion, but is this true? Because what about Gladys? What is so very wrong with Glad? And Doris was once a pretty name. And Mabel, May-belle. And my little brother's name, Stanley: how can Stanley be so very different from today's Ashley, or Stan from Dan? And will today's plain, popular names become fashionable in the future? The names that I heard so often from Zoe: Jason, Jackie, Tracy, Gary.

Coming towards me, across the porch, Ruthie is rattling at Joe: 'You can't just snatch things from Polly, for no sodding reason.' People are looking around, towards her, but she remains oblivious to them. And even if she was aware of them, she would alter nothing. Other people do not exist, for Ruthie. Is this a bad recipe for an actress, or a good one? 'For Christ's sake, Joe,' she concludes loudly. She is so very different from me, in so many ways. Different from Iris, and Peter, who as children were more like me, quiet like me. Not so different from Evie, I suspect. Evie could have been a grandmother, too, like me, by now, (and *me*, a *great*-grandmother!); she would have been old enough, by now. But who knows? Because her world was different from mine, so she could have been anything, anywhere. And who cares? Not me, because she could have, would have, done whatever she wanted, and I would have, could have, been happy. I wonder what she would have shown me. But I will never know, not even from Zoe because nowadays the world, Zoe's world, is different again.

Joe's little face is sealed with a pout. Sometimes I wish that he would answer back to his mother. But, then, I am hardly a good example. And this time, as usual, I say nothing to Ruthie; instead, I ask Joe, 'Do you want a mint?'

He nods miserably, and takes one.

'Polly?'

'Mmmmm.' She sparkles wickedly, and I hand one down to her. Then I point the tube at Ruthie, but she frowns ferociously and flaps it away. 'Let's get out of here,' she says, although she is already doing so. Joe clings to her, visibly awed by the mint inside his mouth. I follow. When Ruthie reaches the street, she blows through loose lips, like a horse. She always makes a fuss about fresh air, despite having chosen to live in London.

As we step out, I can see that not far down the road from us, plodding unseeing towards us, is Mrs Fox. My heart clenches. I have not come across Mrs Fox for years. I see Zoe, occasionally, whenever she visits me, sitting briefly on the arm of an armchair, and smiling dutifully. But I never see Mrs Fox. She is deep inside a dowdy coat, like everyone else in the street. In the old days she had a distinctive cap of dark blonde hair but now she has streaky flicks, stiff silvery feathers. Coming across the sign for the Craft Fayre – a blackboard chained to a lamp post – she hesitates and glances towards the church hall, her eyes on silvery wings of skin.

'Hello Mrs Fox.'

The glance switches to me. 'Goodness,' she breathes frostily. 'Caddy Dutton!'

'Christmas shopping?' I nod cheerfully towards the church hall.

'Oh. No.' She sighs heavily down her nose.

But I am already asking, 'How are you?'

Her eyes are watery inside thin lines of black pencil. 'Fine-thanks-and-you?'

I nod and murmur enthusiastically in reply. But I am aware that Ruthie has begun to shuffle; somehow she manages to shuffle with the pushchair. 'This is my youngest daughter, Ruth, and my grandchildren, Joe and Polly.' In turn, I indicate Mrs Fox to them: 'Mrs Fox.'

Ruthie says, 'Hiya.'

Mrs Fox replies, 'Yes. Hi.' But, frozen, she is staring down at Polly as if she sees a ghost. No, not a ghost. Because suddenly I realise that Polly has done the trick. Real, live Polly: a younger version of Ruthie; but also, as Mrs Fox can see, a younger version of Zoe. She has shown Mrs Fox the truth.

Mrs Fox's eyes skate from Polly over Ruthie to me. And she manages, to me, 'She's not very like you.' This was said from the corner of her mouth, as her eyes returned to Ruthie. She blinks, breaks the spell, says quickly, more politely, to Ruthie: 'You're not very like her.'

'You can say that again,' smirks Ruthie in reply. 'I'm the image of my dad. Was.'

Looking onto Ruthie's smooth smirk, I can think of nothing momentarily but the dry webbing of my own old face, the millions of crackless cracks like old bone china.

Ruthie shuffles the pushchair.

I take a deep breath. 'And Zoe's fine, you're all fine?' Somehow we are already moving apart from each other.

'Oh yes.' Then she hesitates, shrugs, adds: 'You know, hectic.'

I smile my sympathy. 'Happy shopping, then,' I call to her, 'and give my love to Zoe.'

And she almost replies, but not quite, because she is intently watching Polly as we leave.

Starting off with several strong pushes, Ruthie is whirling easily ahead of me through the stiff cold air. Her dark hair is rising and falling rhythmically on her head; reassuringly rhythmically, puffed up with air for a second, and then drifting downwards with the next. I smile to myself because I know that if I said to her, now, 'That woman whom we just saw...' she would reply, 'What woman?' She is eager to go to my house, to prepare the children for the seven o'clock train back to London.

When she rang me to tell me of her plans for this visit, I asked, 'Is Simon off work, then?' Because he works evenings, now, in a restaurant. 'Can he fetch you from the station?'

And she replied, 'No, but my much-maligned lodger,' and this was said heavily, of course, 'has offered to fetch us in his mate's old banger.' Hearing my silent disapproval, she added cheerfully, 'Keeps me young, Mum.'

'And turns me grey,' I muttered.

She shot a derisive laugh down the line. 'You've always been grey, ever since I've known you.'

Zoe
....

Turning to shut the front door behind me, I sense her in the darkness, now see her, and snap the two together into one single instant. My breath leaps so loudly back into me that I am sure she hears. So I bolster this whisper of fear with a blast of protest, '*Mum*.'

'Where have you been?' This could have been a whisper, careful not to ruffle the quietness; but I know that this soft hiss rises from a fierce threat. Her arms are folded, her shoulders hunched, her silhouette is an avenging angel.

'Out,' I yelp, angrily. 'What are you doing, standing there in the dark?'

'I know *out*, I asked *where*?' The words burn the cool air, fizz towards me.

I have done something; or something has happened while I was out and I should have been here. By not being here I have failed her and she is livid. My stomach turns and burrows. 'What is it? What's happened?'

'Nothing's *happened*,' she sneers, full of her secret. 'I asked you where you've been.'

'*Out*,' I insist, to make the point that this answer usually suffices. '*Mickey's*. Where do you *think* I've been?' My skin flashes with the memory of the warmth of Mickey's house; and an echo of his mum's laughter curls deep inside my ears. And now nothing. No one. Where are Dad and Danny? They have been put to bed; and she has been waiting for me.

She must have found something. Durex? No, surely not, I am sure that there are none here. Letters? What letters? There are no letters. No, she has *found out* something. Someone has told her something. The reflection of the lone lamp in the living room is a red ulcer in each eye as she leans towards me to warn, 'You have been getting away with too much for too long.' And suddenly she is gone, slipped through the open doorway into the living room, taking her secret – my secret? – with her. I lean back on the wall, knowing that she has been trying to frighten me but trying to remind myself that the fear was coming from her.

Today, in contrast to last night, Mum has barely looked at me. This morning she was cradling a headache in splayed fingers, her eyelids flickering low over a diffuse, pain-dizzy gaze. And now, this evening, as she moves so fast around the kitchen to clear away the dishes that she could be trying to pack up and run, her eyes are sending me short but definite flashes, dot-dot-dash. Flashes which I refuse to decipher. I am making myself a cup of coffee, a small cup, for a few swigs before I leave for the evening. My own movements are restricted by my coat: I reach up with difficulty into the cupboard for the jar.

'Zoe.' Her tone is pointedly weary, apparently reluctantly dutiful, implying that I am simply another part of the scenery in here, to be similarly organised. 'I want you back earlier, to-night.'

Drawing the jar from the shelf, I prickle inside my impossible coat, and shrug my arm back into the stiff extended sleeve. Earlier than when? Earlier than last night? Until last night, she did not pay any attention to what she terms my *Comings and goings*. I decide to say nothing, to decline acknowledgement, in the hope that this order will become background noise, along with all the others, *Tidy-your-room* and *Fold-your-clothes* and *Clear-your-plate*.

But I fail, I cannot resist: 'What time have you scheduled for Danny's return?'

She stops emphatically by the sink and stares blindly into the plug hole: a pose, to illustrate that her anger is barely under control. 'I'm not talking about Danny, I'm talking about you.'

'Because I'm a girl,' I finish for her, and strike the rim of my cup with the stem of my spoon, unnecessarily, loudly, twice.

She swivels around, snatches me into her wide eyes. 'No,' she says, 'you're wrong.'

'Danny never gets any of this crap.'

'Don't say that word!'

'He comes and goes as he pleases.' I chuck white-hot water from the kettle into my cup; the coffee flares, like blood splashed with hydrogen peroxide.

Her eyes narrow. 'He comes and goes as *I* please, and so do *you*, and I want you home earlier from now on.'

'Why?'

Groping unsteadily backwards for the sink, her reply is as loud and hard as my question: 'Because I do.' Rolling her palms over the rim, she thinks better of this, and tries to elaborate: 'Because I've let you get out of hand.'

'But not Danny.' I dip to my coffee.

'But not Danny,' she repeats emptily.

'*Because* he's a boy,' so I spin into a wail, 'you're *much* worse than Dad.'

She shouts back, 'Maybe your father has never cared enough to make a fuss about anything.' Hastily composing herself, straightening, she hisses, 'If your father can't see what's going on in front of his own eyes, then that's *his* problem. But *this* is something that I won't let happen.'

This? This *what*? Why am I suddenly such a problem, a threat, so out of control? I hiss back, 'Sometimes Danny doesn't even come home at night: do you know that? Do you know that he creeps in at six o'clock in the morning?'

Her face stiffens, whitens: plaster of Paris to hold firm her response. 'He's older,' she says, flatly.

'Oh, *loads* older,' I whoop with sarcasm.

'You're more vulnerable.'

'I'm *a girl*, you mean,' I taunt, stepping around her to slosh my coffee into the sink. Because I am going out now. And I will stay

132

out for as long as I want.

Beside me, she does not move, nor even turn her head towards me. 'I *mean*, you're *different*,' she says to the space in front of her.

'The difference is that I'm a girl,' I add decidedly, but dismissively; calm now that I am on my way.

'What's different,' she counters slowly, 'is that I can't trust you.'

I have been sauntering away but now my attention snags. I turn, and she is watching me. Simply watching me, her eyes saying nothing. No clues. Why, suddenly, this need for trust? She is my mother, I am her daughter: where does trust come – or not come – into this?

Dinah

....

Zoe leaves through one door and Derek ambles in through the
other. Rolling from slipper to slipper. As soon as he is through
the doorway, he halts and begins to swat the nearest Formica
surface with his freshly, messily rolled newspaper. Absently,
gently, regularly. The surface is one which I have recently wiped.

'Don't do that.'

His eyes track mine to the newspaper. He shrugs, and drops
his arm to his side. Too late, he tries a limited smile. 'Is there a
problem?' he enquires, before adding airily, 'Apart from the
newspaper.'

I want to say, *Why don't you go back to your paper, your
beloved paper?* An absurd but favourite phrase from childhood
comes to mind: *Why don't you marry it?*

'Dinah?' he prompts, 'A problem?'

I manage, 'Nothing that I can't handle.'

A shallow, slapdash smile. 'Sounds like it.'

Incredibly, there was a time when I liked his inoffensive,
inconsequential sarcasm. I suppose it felt comfortable.

'Is it Zoe?' he is asking.

Unwittingly, I nod. Anger rattles silently in my throat.

'So, what's the problem?'

What's your sudden interest? I warn him off: 'It's between me
and her.'

'But we're a family,' he protests, his words rolling high with
dismay.

Don't make me laugh. But unfortunately I do laugh, and brittly.

He starts swatting his thigh. 'Come on, Dinah,' he whines,
'what's up?'

Unfortunately, he does not mean *lately* and *in general*. He wants to know what has happened now, here, between Zoe and me; what has happened to disturb, momentarily, his peace. And he wants to know so that he can make it all right again. Which, in this case, is impossible. I used to think that Derek could make everything all right. But all he ever has to offer is a quip or two. Which is Danny's habit, too, but differently: Danny's aim is to hold the moment, to lighten it and turn it around, to see something new. Derek's aim is to brush it away.

He shuffles and leans back perilously close to my clean surface.

'You shouldn't give her a hard time,' he reasons softly. 'She's a good kid.'

'Oh, you think so, do you?' *Well, I could tell you a thing or two.* But could I? Even if I wanted, *could I?* No. Because he would have to see for himself. How strange, that I have never listened, have always relied upon my own eyes, and now I have been tricked by them. Or tricked by the light. Because tricks of the light can and do happen. But not reincarnation. But for Derek to understand, he would have to see. To see what I saw. I saw what Caddy and Zoe told me about when Zoe was a little girl. I saw how convincing, saw how much Zoe had kept from me, saw how she must have taken apart our world – the world of Zoe and me – behind my back. Yes, what I saw was betrayal: hers, of me.

When I saw Mrs Dutton's granddaughter, I saw how strong I will have to be to put my world together again. Until now, I suppose that I have lived my life thinking that everything would be fine if I made my own little world, had my own little family: *at least I would have this.* This was what I was led to believe. By whom? By Derek? I was certain that if life was bad, then at least I knew how bad. Well, I was wrong, I did not know how bad: my own – my only – daughter spent her childhood under the impression that someone else was her mother. *Was?* Who knows what she believes now? *Believes?* Remembers, feels, suspects, hopes. This is complicated. This is not how my life is supposed to be: I have been let down. And now I will have to pull this family up, together, bring this family into line. Family? I have no hold, have never had a hold over Derek; and I do not doubt Danny, I *know Danny*, I know him better than I know his father. He is my son. He is so obviously Derek's son; and if he is Derek's, then he is mine. But, I will have to bring *Zoe* into line.

'She's no trouble,' Derek is continuing, 'not really.'

'That's because she's never here,' I tell him.

He reflects on this with an inward smile, not much more than a wince. 'Good, because Danny – in there – ' he cocks his head towards the noisy living room, 'has been driving me m–'

'*DEREK*!' This conveys my seriousness, and my exasperation; but what is it that I want to say to him? Nothing. I want him to shut up. I want to think, and he is a distraction.

He pauses for a moment before straightening slowly, stiffly, and saying sadly. 'You haven't been easy to live with, yourself, lately, you know.'

So I end up saying, 'Why don't you leave me alone?'

To which, of course, there is no answer.

Zoe

....

Nowadays her eyes never leave me. Eyes? Her whole face never leaves me, turns after me; and with the face comes the gaze, sweeping, passing over me, licking me with warning. Nowadays her whole body crooks towards me, forever ready to pounce. And if she loses track of me, she finds another way. Yesterday afternoon, when I came home from school, she was looking through old photographs. Without turning to me, without lifting her eyes to me, she simply said, 'I should never have let you have your hair cut.' My own gaze skipped over the knuckles of her shoulder and down into her lap. On the photograph in her hand was a little girl. Five years old? Seven? I did not know, I could not guess, I can never guess. But of course I knew that she was me. Me and not me. She had been me, I had been her. I looked closer, longer. In the photo her bony legs dangled from a parachute of a dress. Even so long ago, Mum would never have had such a shapeless dress for herself. 'Shame about the dress,' I remarked.

Her eyes rose like bruises. 'I bought that dress for you for your sixth birthday,' she complained, as if this were justification enough.

This morning Mum's silvery stare is flexing all over the kitchen to stay with me. It is she who is moving, not me. I am sitting with my elbows on the table and my head in my hands over a bowl of cereal. The cereal had seemed like a good idea at the time. Two minutes ago. Mum is clearing away, washing up, wiping down. She is never late to finish breakfast, not even on a Saturday. She asks me, 'What are you going to do today?'

'Go out.'

'Again?'

This needs no answer. Instead, I raise my eyes to Danny's. He is jabbing a knife into the toaster, ringing its thin steel ribs, trying to recover his piece of toast. I inform him: 'You'll electrocute yourself.'

'It's off at the plug,' he mutters.

Mum has whirled from me to him but now she comes back again. 'Where are you going?'

I remind myself that I do not have to answer this. But I want to say his name, to rattle her with his name. 'To see Mickey.'

Slapping her cloth around the draining board, she pretends to muse: '*We* never see Mickey, these days.'

I concentrate on finishing my mouthful of cereal before reminding her, 'That's hardly surprising, since you decided that he couldn't come here any more.'

She stops the slapping, stops the games. 'I didn't say that he couldn't come here, I said that I was sick of you two skulking off to your room. If he wants to come here – if you want him to come here – then he should stay down here and talk to us, he should behave like a proper member of the family.'

I switch full beam onto Danny: *Proper member of the family? Talk?*

She continues muttering, but to herself, poring over her own peculiar wounds with satisfaction: 'All that whispering behind closed doors . . .'

I stop listening; I tilt my bowl to pool the dregs of milk.

Suddenly her voice is direct again: 'You could try doing some homework, for a change.'

Is this about homework?

'You could try making something of yourself, unless you want to spend the rest of your life stuck around here.'

No, this is not about homework.

'You could try showing some consideration for the rest of us. You could try, *just try*, not to treat us as a disposable family.'

What is all this *us*? I try to enlist Danny's support but his focus is on the toaster. The piece of toast is on the point of his knife. The point of one tooth is on his lower lip. He and the piece of toast are balanced.

Mum is leaning over the table towards me, driving all her weight down onto her fists on the tabletop.

Quickly I protest, yelp, 'I'm not treating anyone like anything.'

She begins, very low, 'You think you're special, don't you, Zoe? But you're not, not really. You thought this would be easy, didn't you? But you can think again. Because if I have my way, you won't turn your back on your family.'

I do not know what she means. 'I will,' I shout back into her puffed up face, 'if you carry on like this.'

'No *ifs*,' she threatens, 'but for better, for worse.'

Danny is turning in the haze in the corner of my eye, and saying, 'Leave her, Zoe.' Or perhaps, *Leave it*.

But I have already snapped to Mum, 'Well, you'd know all about that, wouldn't you?' Her eyes click with realisation: wider, or narrow? I do not know; but I do know that there is no going back. 'You and Uncle Gerry,' I rasp, to finish.

I cannot believe that I have done this. Not when I have spent my life trying to avoid referring to him. Trying not to notice him. And how do I *know*? *What* do I know? Nothing. No specific memories. Simply a sense, as certain as a smell. A feeling from my childhood. The feeling of my childhood. Mum and Uncle Gerry. No stories to dispute. Now, in front of me, around me, nothing is moving. Danny's eyes are still on me: they do not move to her, they stay on me.

'Don't look at me like that, *I* haven't done anything wrong.'

His eyes are saying, still saying, *Shut up*.

'No, because someone has to say it.' Shout it? 'And, anyway, what's the matter with you, lately? Don't you care about what's happening?' About what is happening to me, about what Mum is doing to me. *You don't care about me, any more, do you, Danny? You of everyone. You and everyone.*

Mum uncoils smoothly from her crouch over the table. Her face swells and darkens with an uncomfortable smile. She takes one step back from the table but seems to look down on me from much further away. 'Well, well,' she sighs, sticky-sweet, 'you've certainly shown your true colours.' And she turns momentarily to Danny to check, casually, 'See how she turns on me?' To me, she says, slowly and emotionlessly, 'You think you know everything. But you don't know me.' A twitch of the tight smile. 'I know you,' she says, her voice hollow, 'But you don't know me.' And she turns and walks slowly from the room.

Danny chucks one hand into his hair and sighs hugely, preparing to say something.

But I say, incredulously, accusingly, 'You *knew*. You *knew*, too.' *About Mum and Uncle Gerry. And you said nothing, for all these years*. And now, as far as I am concerned, there is nothing more to say. So I stand and leave, too.

Dinah

....

Every evening, the main room, the living room, bubbles with Derek's television. Bulletins and adverts, no difference, *Buy this*. Whenever I have to go into the room, the telly roars like rapids, far too frenzied, and I cross carefully, afraid to look down. The voices carry on, hectoring me, regardless: government ministers, car salesmen, comedians, film critics, police inspectors. What do they know about anything? When I go to bed, the voices sink below me, busy but inconsequential, to become a comforting feature of darkness, like the chatter of crickets in summer. I wake from my doze when the noise stops and the silence starts. The silence clicks into place below me with the flick of Derek's finger on the light switch in the hallway. Hearing the squeeze of the bottom stair, the groans of the subsequent steps, the sigh of the bathroom door, I turn thoroughly into sleep. When Danny and Zoe are home for the evening, they have their own sounds: Danny's sound is the revving record player; Zoe's sound is the boom of water into the thin shell of the bath, followed by the squeaks of her body on its plastic floor. None of them seem to speak to me. But they seem to watch me, so I am forever waiting for them to say something, feeling that they have something to tell me. With Zoe, in particular, I am waiting. I am playing this by ear.

This evening, so far, everyone is home. Through the kitchen doorway I can see that Zoe is sitting on the stairs, flicking through a booklet. I do not know if she was on her way up or down when she stopped and sat down; I do not know if she is absorbed or simply pausing, scanning. I did not realise that she was there, I am trying not to follow her around the house. But a moment ago Danny called up to her, 'What's that?' He is below her, by the front door, searching his coats and jackets.

She has not raised her eyes from the pages. 'Nottingham,' she replies eventually. 'University.'

I call through the doorway: 'University already? Nottingham? That's a long way away.' This is the first time that I have spoken directly to her since she was so rude to me three days ago. I have resolved not to snap or shout, to go gently. Stealthily.

Still she does not lift her eyes. 'Everywhere's a long way away,' she mutters.

Apparently Danny has found whatever he was looking for, because he turns away from her and comes towards the kitchen, flapping a small slip of paper, probably a ticket. 'Sis,' he calls jauntily over his shoulder, 'Don't do it. Don't go. Choose life.'

Her eyes slide low in his wake. 'Oh, yes,' she spits her sarcasm after him, towards me, 'I have a lot of that around here. And, anyway,' she drawls derisively, returning to her booklet, 'Choose *money*, you mean.'

He halts in the doorway, turns around, swings towards her, hooking himself to the frame with one hand. 'Money *means* life,' he laughs, and flaps the ticket in his free hand.

She frowns him away.

Passing me, he calls cheerfully to her, 'Just you wait and see: too much History will leave you with a nasty overdraft and no job.'

I step through the doorway into the hallway, and peer up through the banisters. 'You're going to do *History*?'

She turns a page, reads, turns again. For this long moment there was no reply, but now, bent over this new page, she mutters, 'What did you think I was going to do? Astrophysics?'

From the kitchen, Danny is happily yelling a warning: 'I don't want a hippy for a sister.'

In response she sends a glance of thorough disgust over my head, and shouts back along the hallway, 'You don't know *anything*, do you?'

I must go carefully if I want her to talk to me. I prompt, 'Zoe?'

Her eyes drop blindly to me, and focus with anger. 'What?'

'I didn't know that you were planning to do History.'

She turns pointedly to the booklet. 'Perhaps you didn't ask.'

I swoop and catch my patience. And try again, try to try again. 'I mean, I thought you were going to be a teacher.'

A *tut* rips her sullen silence. I have no idea what this means. She does not elaborate.

'Why *History*?'

She pokes her face between two white wooden bones and stresses, 'Because I'm *good* at *History*, okay?'

'You're good at *French*,' I protest.

She returns to the booklet and her reply comes over the whisper of slippery pages: '*And* I'm good at *History*.'

From here I can see nothing but the bright colours of the pages turning behind the white bars. 'But what *use* is History?'

She slaps together the covers of the booklet. 'What use is *French*, if you're not in France?'

Behind me, in the kitchen, Danny hoots an appreciative laugh through a mouthful of something.

I retreat as she thumps down the stairs, and return hurriedly to my initial point: 'Nottingham's a long way away.' From me? From Caddy Dutton? From here, from all of us? Why so far away?

From the foot of the stairs she skims the booklet across the hallway onto the telephone table. 'A long way away from what?' She tackles her coat, which is hanging by the door.

It is my turn to hold a hard, dense silence. To wait for her to come around. I do not know if she has an answer.

When she has retrieved her purse from her coat, she continues resentfully, 'Anyway, the cost of living is cheaper, up North, so you should be pleased.'

Is this really what she thinks? I try to catch her eyes for clues but she is fussing down into her open purse. So I tell her, fairly kindly, 'Don't be melodramatic, Zoe. Money isn't good but it isn't *that* bad. You can go wherever you want. If that's what you want.'

She is huffing over the purse, threading up coins one by one with her thumb-and-forefinger into the folded palm of her hand. Counting, and not quite under her breath.

'And anyway,' I laugh quickly, painfully, fraudulently, to signal a joke, 'all I meant was that it's a long way for you to haul your washing home.' I am fast-swallowing my frustration, becoming faintly dizzy on this anger which is brewing for myself and for her. Because surely this mention of washing is supposed to be part of the routine for mother and teenager, part of the double-act, well-rehearsed, well-meaning, a firm family favourite. But, predictably, we are a flop, horribly, embarrassingly.

Bang on cue, she misfires, 'I'm quite capable of doing my own washing.'

Oh, I do not doubt it, I do not doubt that you, Zoe, are capable of everything and anything.

She is asking me, 'Can you advance me a couple of pounds so that I can go to the pictures?' And somehow this is all the more threatening for the lack of any wheedling, pleading, or hint of blackmail. It is stunning, in fact, for the lack of everything, including interest. For her unspoken *Take it or leave it* when surely this should have been my line. I would love to go to the cinema. Tomorrow I am meeting Maxey in town: her suggestion, shopping. Should I suggest that we go on to the cinema? But I know Maxey's answer: *too tired.* Perhaps I could go, tomorrow, with Zoe; I could meet up with her, on her way home from school, and make my suggestion. And then she would be my captive audience. But how can we meet? I do not drive, so there is no excuse, no lure of a lift home. Whenever we are both in town, we make our own ways home. We have never been companions.

Already Zoe has grown weary of her new cool tone and is complaining, 'We're not going to spend the evening here, watching *Panorama*.'

We: Zoe and Mickey. 'There's Mickey's house.' I am wobbling inside but I will not relent my new rule: no bedroom. No doubt this is the rule in Mickey's household. In every household. Belatedly, I am playing the part of the proper mother, and Zoe will have to learn to live with it. Eventually, this will help us.

She mutters, 'I've been there all week.'

I nod behind me. 'There's the kitchen.'

'*You're* in the kitchen.'

I refuse to rise to the bait, to give her an excuse to flounce away. Instead, I turn and search briskly for my purse in the drawer of the telephone table. 'What's the film?' I enquire, brightly.

'Is the money conditional on the type of film?' Muttered behind me, but audible. After a pause she decides to reply, but reluctantly: '*Life of Brian*.'

I turn, interested. 'Brian who?'

She tuts to the ceiling before calling, disgusted, to the kitchen, 'Did you hear that?'

The reply, blared through another, bigger mouthful, is mercifully indistinct. So I remain ignorant of what I have said wrong. Although nowadays, anything – *everything* – that I say is wrong.

She holds out her hand to me, palm upwards. Shows me the thin pink scar, the flick-knife skid of her lifeline. Blueprint; hand-print. What is the saying, God gives us one and we are born with the other? Or, are we born with one and we grow the other? Inflicted with one. Whatever the saying, I know the theory: we are one half intractable, and one half malleable. With Zoe, which hand has the upper hand?

I lay the notes in her palm.

Her 'Thanks,' is surprisingly light, short but sweet, as she skips for the stairs.

As I approach the kitchen, Danny displays a considerable effort to clear away the remnants of a snack-making extravaganza in which a jar of gherkins seems to have been involved. Since when have we had gherkins in the house? Since forever, by the look of the jar. Cheekily, Danny is reassuring me,

'I'm clearing up, I'm clearing up!' Endearingly, he is oblivious to the brushing of crumbs by the underside of his sleeve to the floor. Presumably he noticed my look of horror when I saw the gherkins, because now, lifting the jar, he says cheerfully, 'Yes, I thought so, too,' before wrinkling his nose to add, 'I suppose there's a sense in which it's nice to have been right.'

I have shut the door behind me, I am leaning on the warm boiler, lazily, dreamily. I have been despairing for several days, but now, suddenly, I feel optimistic.

He flings a dishcloth down in front of him onto the table, and announces, mock-seriously, 'I'll clean behind the cooker, this weekend, if you're good.'

'Danny?' My voice surprises me.

He glances wide-eyed from his first wet stroke of the tabletop. 'I mean it,' he says. Turning down over the table he smirks to add, '*If* you're good,' before rounding on the second stroke.

Do I go backwards or forwards? There is no going backwards, there is never any going backwards, there is merely swerving. So, I can swerve: I can talk to him without telling him what I have seen. He would not understand; the only people who would understand are Zoe and Caddy. And they are the very people who must not know what I have seen. Because they must never think that I believe. But I do not want understanding, I want information. I ask Danny, 'Does Zoe ever say anything to you about Mrs Dutton?'

He stops, blank. Stops my heart. 'Mrs Dutton?' he muses, emptily. Slowly his eyes sink beneath a frown. 'New teacher?'

My heart has begun to beat again, but tentatively. 'No,' I try the grown-up name, 'Caddy Dutton.'

The frown continues downwards and oozes into a low shaking of his head.

'An old lady,' I prompt. 'When Zoe was little, she used to go to her house a lot.'

His head is still swinging, slowly, but perhaps this is momentum, perhaps he is busy thinking.

'Come on, Danny,' I coax, 'You remember.' *You must remember.*

'Is she still alive?' He carries the cloth in both hands to the sink, to shake free the crumbs.

'Yes.'

'No,' he decides, 'She doesn't ever mention her.'

'Did she ever?'

'Mention her?'

I nod, nervously.

'No.' He rinses the cloth. 'Not that I remember.'

Please remember.

He pauses, cloth dripping. 'Why? Is something wrong with her?'

My heart squirts a plume of scalding blood. 'With Zoe?'

He twinkles his eyes and rolls them gently to the ceiling. *'With this old lady.'* Below, the cloth twists, stiffens, dries in his grip.

'Oh. No.'

As he passes me, leaves the room, he is humming a tune. To which he adds the beat of his feet on the stairs. And only now, hearing this rising scale, do I realise: if he is going to clean behind the cooker, then he is not going to stay with Claire. He always stays with Claire at the weekend. But not this one. I did not listen for what he did not say. I did not ask. Now I turn after him, through the doorway, look through the white pipes of the banisters to see his feet disappear upwards into the ceiling. His footsteps continue along the landing, rising over me and dying away.

Zoe

....

I can see Mum, and she can see me. She is coming up the stairs.

The voice of the telephone continues to squeak into my ear. 'And, Zoe, he said that he stayed in, last night, and listened to various albums. Can you believe that he said that? *Various albums!* Who would ever, ever say *Various albums?* He really is so awful. I can't let this go on.'

Across the landing, the banister creaks as Mum leaves the top stair, projects herself inside her long untidily tied bathrobe. Her frown, focused on me, is heavy too.

The voice in my ear is momentarily not a voice but a sigh. 'I suppose that I used to think that he was quite sweet, that he was quite interesting; and I suppose that I thought all this would get to Jamie, because he's Jamie's friend. But he's *not* really Jamie's friend, is he; not *really*. And, anyway, what do I care about Jamie any more? Jamie can fuck off.' Another sigh into the crackling static.

Mum reaches the doorway, stops, looks down at me. I am sitting on her bed.

The voice hisses, 'I must do something about this because nowadays, whenever I am upstairs with him, all I can do is lie there and wish that he would hurry up and finish. And that's awful, isn't it?'

'Yes . . .'

'And he's so superior. Well, superior to everyone else, not to me; to *me*, he's *soppy*. In fact, I wish that he would do his superior act on me, because it might make him a bit more interesting.' Suddenly the voice squeals, shoots out from the phone: 'And he has long nails, Zoe! No *thank* you. Creepy!'

148

I dare not look again at Mum but concentrate on my fingertip which is running gently over the dial.

The voice is concluding, 'Do you know, every day I look at him and then I look at Davey Draper, and I know that Davey Draper is the one for me.' There is momentary silence; then, 'What's the matter?'

'Yes,' I say firmly.

'What? Is there someone there?'

'Yes.'

'Oh. Right.'

'Better go now, but thanks for calling.'

'Yes. Right.'

'See you soon, then. Bye for now.'

'Yes, bye. Call me later.'

Mum says, 'Who was that?'

I release the twin black nibs from beneath my fingertips and replace the receiver before answering truthfully, 'Jane.'

'But you saw each other last thing last night!' Mum wails. 'What can possibly have happened during the night so that you need to talk to each other this morning on my phone?' The frown forms a dart in the slack skin of her forehead. 'Thanks-for-calling, *nothing*. I wasn't born *yesterday*. *You* made that call.'

I snap back, 'Danny's always on the phone, he has just rung Claire.'

Her eyes bulge with anger. 'It was a two-second call, to check times for this afternoon. *And* he *asked*.'

'*She* called *me*,' I rage, hoping to convince by indignation.

But Mum retreats, muttering, despairing, 'You're *worse* and *worse*, *week* by *week*.'

I hurl some sarcasm after her: 'Oh, I *wonder why*?'

She calls, coldly, 'One day you'll have your own phone bill;' then, flatly, as she waddles away, 'Mickey is here, his car has drawn up outside.'

'Here?' I protest. Suddenly the morning – full of reading, radio, and, later, a shower – is nothing but a fading flavour in my mouth.

She flicks a sarcastic glance over her shoulder, 'Well, yes, here, unless he has come to see Selina-next-door.'

She thumps onwards across the landing and I skim across the bed to the window. I look down on Selina's head, in the garden next door: woolly yellow hair cleaved and travelling in a long plait to vanishing point. She is squatting and soothing her cat Tomkin. He is a glinting black crescent of fur on the sunny stones of their pathway. I know that she often talks to Tomkin for hours. She is twelve. I can remember when there was solely Selina next door, but then came Jake, Jess, and Anna-Maria. Selina's whispers to Tomkin pass like wind or water through all the other noises of their house, the chattering of pots and pans, the babble of a couple of recorders and the harping of a violin. I look beyond our twin gardens to the road. Mickey's car is lifeless in front of our house. Our doorbell screams.

'Answer it!' screams Mum.

I crash from the bed onto the landing and down the stairs, sensing Mum peering out from the bathroom above me. 'I forgot,' she calls, quieter: 'post for you, on the end of the banister.'

I snatch the small white envelope and grab at the door.

'Surprise,' says Mickey.

'Yes,' I say, standing back to let him pass, and prising open the envelope. 'It is. I thought we were going over to Martin's to watch *Lassie* this afternoon.' Superfluously I add, 'For a laugh.' But this is the official version, because I still cry at Lassie films.

In passing, Mickey kisses me on the cheek, then flings up his hands in a shrug: 'I'm not arguing. But I thought that it would be nice to see you now, too.' He looks unsmiling and steadily into my eyes and says, 'I don't feel that we have seen very much of each other, lately, alone.'

I think I know what this means, although I do not know if he knows that I know. I tell him, 'I was supposed to be doing some reading this morning; when am I going to read all that stuff for History?'

'Zoe, it's Saturday,' he insists, following me into the living room. He sighs, sweeps around me and sits on the arm of the settee. 'What's that?'

It is a card from Mrs Dutton. A photograph, a silhouette, of someone who looks like Selina, sitting beneath a tree. I slip it back into the envelope. 'Nothing. A birthday card.'

'A bit late, isn't it?' he laughs.

Mum leans through the doorway and nods at Mickey. 'Hello Mickey.' Now she nods at the envelope. 'What was it?'

I protest, 'Is there no privacy in this house?'

She shifts her weight from one foot to the other, rustling the bathrobe. 'Doesn't look like it.'

'Birthday card from Mrs Dutton. Satisfied?'

She straightens, bathrobe rising; eyebrows rising, too. 'But it's not your birthday.'

'No, but it *was* my birthday,' I announce to them both.

'Early for next year,' sniggers Mickey.

'Does she usually send you birthday cards?' Mum's words are strung with loops of curiosity

'No.' Which is truthful: she does not usually *send*. Usually I call on her, but I do not seem to have been there for a while.

I glance at Mickey. I could have gone to see Mrs Dutton this morning. I realise, now, that a visit is very overdue.

'You two off out?' Mum asks sourly.

I return to her. 'Of course.'

Her face shrugs and she flounces from the doorway.

'Come on,' says Mickey, snatching my hand and pulling me from the room.

'Where to?' I flop along behind him.

'A drive?' He halts at the coat rack. 'Jacket?'

I shake my head. 'Not if we're in the car.'

He presses me down onto the bottom stair. 'Shoes, though.' He reaches for my pair with one hand, lifts them together between fingers and thumb.

I complain, 'I'll do it.'

He places them on the carpet in front of me, and I slide my feet into them.

Outside, as we approach the car, I wonder if I should ask him to drive to Mrs Dutton's house. I could tell him that it is essential that I go now: now that I have been reminded, now that I should thank her for the card. I have never been driven there before, and I would love to slip so quickly to the end of the Causeway and then through the estate: Roads, Streets, Lanes, Avenues, Crescents, Walks, Drives, all similar, all with the same name, Westerbury. How long to drive there? I do not drive, I cannot translate walking into driving. Five minutes? Ten? Or two or three? And then I could slip as quickly away, when I have done my duty. But what will I say to Mrs Dutton? I could say that I have been busy with homework. My excuse of homework, aimed at grown-ups, is similar to the excuse of period pains which I reserve for boys or male teachers or Dad: mysterious, dreadful, placing me instantly beyond their suspicion or reproach. In fact I have been busy with Mickey and Mum; busy, with Mickey, trying to avoid Mum. So busy that I am becoming tired of both of them. On the path, the spillage from the steep track of the sun is scalding my eyes. It strikes me that I cannot ask Mickey to spend this beautiful morning with me in a dim room stiff with three-piece suite; in a room with a collection of ornaments which has gathered, drip-drip-drip, like a muddle of stalagmites.

'Drive to where?' I ask him inside the car, pitching my question above the initial efforts of the engine.

He concentrates briefly on the rear mirror. 'Somewhere scenic?' *Scenic* is not said seriously.

Mrs Dutton's estate is definitely not scenic, despite the colours of the houses. On a visit last year I found that the Council had decided to paint the grey pebble-dashed houses pale pink, or blue, or green, or yellow. Mrs Dutton's house was yellow – she said *primrose* – and her next-door neighbour was *rose*. I do not know about primroses, but it seemed to me that the house was the colour of the pansies in Mum's window boxes. But I suppose *primrose* sounds better than *pansy*.

'The fields near the railway?' he suggests.

I close my eyes and think: as we come along the road we will see little splashes made in the deep dry yellow fields by straying walkers and the occasional vehicle. And closer, I will sense the soil, hard, loose, fragrant, like biscuit. 'Yes,' I tell him, 'that'll be nice.'

I am surprised at how soon we reach the edge of town. We are approaching the very last shop before the countryside. Its front is lined with small black plastic buckets holding thin bunches of flowers. But if it is the last shop in town, then it is also the first, and no doubt these flowers will drift back into town in the cars of visitors. Now we are passing, and rocking, the ice-cream sign on the roadside. It swings inside a metal frame which is weighted to the kerb with an elephant's foot of concrete. Why ice-cream? Why does ice-cream warrant such a sign, why not milk or chocolate or fruit or magazines? We have passed the last shop, or first shop, and suddenly we are nowhere. But it is a familiar nowhere, full of the grey road newly marked with careful sweeps of clean white paint, and frilled with an untidy hedgerow. We swing past the huge tree with a hollow trunk, a hole which is presumably home for something? Birds? Squirrels? Now we pass the terrace of cottages. Perhaps they belong to one of the farms, because this is farmland. But there are no farmhouses, no farm-yards or barns. Perhaps they are hidden from the road.

We turn off the road and the car stumbles reluctantly across the tough brittle tracks. We often come here, but not usually during the daytime. I gaze out at the gaggle of stalks disturbed by us, goggling at our windows. Mickey stops the car, and the stalks become calm, then aloof. He switches off the engine, which settles eagerly, competently, much more so than whenever it is required to start. Behind us, the sun-licked road is a thread of grey mercury stretching across distant fields. Mickey turns to me. The raw sunshine is scouring his eyes, rinsing away the colour, so that they sparkle like clean cut glass. 'Don't worry about that History,' he says softly. 'No one ever does any background reading.' He shrugs happily. 'It muddles. All you need are the facts.'

'I know the facts,' I reply with a smile.

He laughs. 'I'm so glad that you decided to come here with me. I feel that I haven't seen you properly for ages.'

I do not know what to say to him, I do not want to say anything, so I lean across and kiss him.

I savour this huge silence stitched with little noises, our own little noises, the yawns of our warm old leather seats beneath us and the ticking of our tongues in each other's mouths. Occasionally I hear the swish of a car on the road behind us. After a few moments, Mickey pulls gently away from me. He looks across at me with an expression, *the* expression, which is both hard and soft, full of his intensely focused eyes. 'Shall we get into the back?' he whispers.

Nonsensically, I glance into the back seat, as if this will help me to make a decision. 'No,' I confide, 'not here.'

He shifts on his seat and suddenly there is more distance between us. 'Why not?' His voice flutters slightly with surprise.

'Not here.'

His face stiffens. 'What's wrong with here, all of a sudden?'

I did not expect this to be difficult. 'Not in daylight.'

'What's wrong with daylight, all of a sudden?' He makes an attempt to laugh, but unsuccessfully, humourlessly, impatiently. 'You're so paranoid, lately.'

I glance around: in front of us, the embankment waiting for one of the slow local trains; behind us, the road, suspiciously empty. Most of this car is made from glass, and it is buzzing inside with sunlight.

'It has been nearly two weeks,' he whines, incredulous. His pale irises are suddenly small in the paler, airy, whites.

I know what he is referring to, and I feel slightly sick at the realisation that he has been counting the days. I had assumed that whatever we did when we were alone in my room was something which simply happened; that whenever it happened, it was a bonus. But now that we are rarely alone, he seems to think of nothing else. So, Mum's effort to turn us respectable has backfired. Which I would find funny if I were not so fed up. Now it seems to me that there is nothing more to our relationship than the back seat of his car. There is nothing more, in his eyes, *to me*. Until recently, left alone, we were fine, there was nothing wrong between us. On the contrary, we were in love and everything was right. I realise that I am breathing very carefully. I raise my eyes to look at him. His face is drawn into a pout, I am sure that it is a pout, and I am sure that boys are not supposed to pout. I cannot guess what he will say next: I do not know whether his complaint is merely a whine or a deeply held grudge. And is he complaining, or blaming?

And do I care? He is waiting for me to speak, but I have nothing to say. I did not bring the subject up, and I would not have chosen to do so. Now I want to close the subject with as little effort as possible, and go. 'It's not my fault,' I start, 'it's my mum's fault that we're never alone.'

'We're alone now.'

I ignore him, so he counters, 'It *is* your fault. You're always too busy to spend time alone with me.' This is said sceptically, spitefully. 'Last night it was Jane and Sandra and Simon and Lee. Every night it's Jane, or Simon, or Robin, or Louisa . . .'

I want to see them because they want nothing from me.

'I have to see them sometime. And, anyway, they're your friends too!' Immediately, I regret raising my voice.

'All I know is that we're never alone.'

I examine my bitten nails. The sudden chill in my stomach surprises me, telling me that I can imagine nothing worse than an evening alone with Mickey, without my friends. Ludicrously, I wish they were in the car with me now.

I do not speak, so eventually he starts again, but much more quietly: 'And I suppose we're off to see Jane again tonight?'

I had never realised that he was so jealous. 'She just *happens* to be *there*.'

He blows this away in a huge rasping sigh.

'She *is* my best friend, Mickey.'

He turns towards me. 'Well, why don't you sleep with her, then?'

'Maybe I *should*.'

He starts the engine with a savage tweak of the ignition key. I am pleased with *Maybe-I-should*. I must remember to tell Jane. I manage not to smile, and, instead, close my eyes and anticipate the movement of the car. But nothing happens. I open my eyes again and see that Mickey is staring through the windscreen and tapping the steering wheel with both hands, lightly, soundlessly, but insistently.

He turns to meet my gaze. 'Why are we continuing with this?' he asks blankly.

'Well, you started it,' I whoop indignantly.

'No, not *this*. I meant, why are we continuing to see each other?'

My heart refuses me; drowns momentarily in blood and leaves the rest of me bloodless, cold and weak. 'Because we're in love?' I manage, but so caustically that this is immediately in doubt.

'But what's the point?' he despairs, his forehead folding. 'Because if it's like this now, what will it be like when we both move away?'

It occurs to me that there was a time when I would have been impressed by this – this anguish at our impending separation – but now the only expression which springs to mind is an old one: lily-livered. No other expression will suffice. Looking into his stern hot face, I say silently, *Lily-livered*. No other expression contains enough ridicule. Because *I* could have made the effort to keep us together. Because what are a few miles, between lovers? In the olden days, romances survived wars. Our own separation could have been romantic: new places, new homes, our own homes, whole weekends alone together.

I shift the emphasis slightly: 'I didn't realise that you were so up-set by all this,' meaning, *You SHOULDN'T be so upset by all this.*

'And you're not?' he goads savagely.

And I'm not. So, is he right? Is he right that I am wrong, that something is wrong? Am I less in love? And if so, what do I do? This is all too sudden. And too drastic. Must I do anything at all? If we were married, we would continue; this would be a down in the legendary lifelong sequence of ups and downs. There would be no decisions to make. But we are not married: we have always said that in our own eyes we are married, but now I see that we are not. And never were. He starts to shift the car, turning the wheels too sharply, grating the tyres against the brown hairy shell of the earth. The bottom of my door jangles with small stones. He is glaring through the windscreen. The air in the car burns with his fury. I sit very still amid the lurches, and barely breathe. I suspect that we are going back home. I breathe with the gear changes. The car is turning back the landscape: the terrace of cottages, the hollow tree. Within a few moments the dry bright icing of morning sunlight on the fields crumbles away into the tracks of habitation: hedges, fences, roadsigns, buildings, cross-roads.

To cap it all, Mum starts on me as soon as I come through the door.

'Do you see much of Caddy Dutton?' she asks, apparently conversationally. She is standing on the bottom stair. I want to go up the stairs. So, do I have to stop here, now, on the worst day of my life, and think about *Mrs Dutton*? And what does Mum mean by *much*? Is she going to try to force me to go around there? Some mad new plan, rule, of hers? I must answer carefully. I decide upon a surly, 'Sometimes.' Realising that she is not going to budge and that I cannot easily pass her, I divert to the living room.

She follows me. 'Recently?'

No, not recently. *Think. Lie.* 'A couple of months ago.' I have no idea how many months ago. At the moment, I do not care. Lately, life has been full of duties, dragged low by duties.

'And how was she?' The tone remains polite, a tinkly variation on a theme.

How was she? I drop down onto the settee, and drag the newspaper from the coffee table. *She was old.* What more can Mum want to know? Mrs Dutton was, is, was, an old lady. End of story. Unless Mum knows something that I do not know. 'Okay,' I reply, with an upward tilt, a hint of a question, *Why-do-you-ask?*

But Mum is not listening to my questions, she is pressing on with her own: 'Does she still say things about her daughter?'

This strikes a different chord, a strange chord, but faintly. The answer is *no*, but, 'What things?' I scan the front page of the paper, but the stories are all economic.

Above me, Mum's reply is delayed; she misses a beat, seems to settle reluctantly for, 'Things about the daughter who died.'

I shrug, Mrs Dutton has not talked about Evie for years and years.

'No.'

Although I do not look up, I can see that Mum remains standing over me. The shrug had been to send her off, to shrug her off, to signal that I am not interested, that I do not want to talk. All I can think of is Mickey, in the car: his hand, its hard, whitened grip on the gear-stick.

'She *did* talk about her, though, didn't she, when you were a little girl?'

Years and years ago? 'How do *I* know?' Briefly my irritation squeezes into an upward frown.

Which was a mistake because she is drawn down to perch next to me. Suddenly she is all knees. 'Of course you *know*, Zoe,' she reasons, not particularly patiently.

'You were *there*,' she says, a whistle of exasperation in her words.

I do not reply, so she starts again, swivelling to focus more firmly on me, turning-the-screws: 'Have you ever met her youngest daughter?'

If I leave, she will follow me, she will follow me to my room. But if I sit this out, she will go, soon, and leave me in peace. So, resentfully, I tell her, 'Her daughter died.'

'No, the *other* daughter.'

I slap together the smudgy wings of the newspaper. 'They both died.'

'*No*, there's *another* daughter.'

This is wrong. The story was, *two little girls*. There was a boy, Mrs Dutton had a boy, but for some reason he was unimportant, he was not in the story. I slap the newspaper into my lap, and turn to Mum: 'How do *you* know?'

'I've seen her.'

'What do you mean, *seen her*?'

'*Seen* her. In the street. Recently.' Her face is expressionless in mine.

And no doubt mine is expressionless in hers. Because I cannot follow this conversation. How can all this have been brought on by the birthday card from Mrs Dutton? Sharply, I question her: 'How did you know that this girl was Mrs Dutton's daughter?'

'Woman,' she corrects.

'Woman,' I concede. Stupidly, I had pictured her as a little girl.

Mum adds, 'She has a little girl of her own, and a little boy,' before returning to her reply: 'I *knew*, because Caddy Dutton *said so*.'

I lift and rattle the newspaper. 'So?'

On the other side of my mottled wing, Mum is muttering, musing, 'Her name is Ruth.'

'Oh, *yes*,' I tingle with relief, suddenly remembering something. Something? *Someone. Ruthie.*

Turning towards me, Mum's eyes spring huge, round and white, to match her knees. 'Have you ever seen her, them, the children?'

'No.'

'Mrs Dutton has never shown you any photos of this woman and her children?'

159

'*No*.' I crash the newspaper into my lap. '*Look*, I *will* go and thank her for the card. I *will* go, I *promise*.'

But Mum seems not to have heard; she seems to be thinking, and says simply, 'I never asked about what she used to say to you.'

Pointedly resurrecting my paper, I complain, 'When?'

'When she used to say that you reminded her of her own little girl.' The reply comes faultlessly, smoothly, bravely. Without looking directly, I can see the shine of her eyes, I see how they are wide and clear and tough.

'I don't know,' I grumble into the newspaper. Because is this necessary? What answer will suffice, will ensure that she leaves me alone? And in what tone? Does she want fond reminiscence, cruel dismissal, or clinical detachment? The page in front of me frowns headlines about car production quotas and firemen's wages. I look for the Diary, which usually shows a photo of a filmstar hurrying through an airport corridor with a small child flung around the neck like a fox fur. 'She used to say that I looked like her.'

'Yes,' confirms Mum lightly, meaning *obviously*.

What else? 'And that I did the same thing with my hand,' *the same as her little girl*. A nervous habit: I demonstrate the alternate taps of my little finger and ring finger onto the tip of my thumb. I have to concentrate because I have not done this for a long time, not since I was little.

Calmly, Mum says, 'I do that.'

'Do you?'

'Yes.' She demonstrates for me: similar, but with simultaneous taps of the two fingertips.

'And I licked keys.'

'You *what*?'

'*Licked keys*.' The photo in the Diary is Lady Di. No airport, no children. No hurrying. No shoulder bag, no jeans. Hands held together. Ankles pressed together. A smile, no sunglasses.

Mum whoops, outraged, 'You never *had* keys.'

I give up on the paper, toss it back onto the coffee table. '*She* had keys. And I used to lick them.'

Over the flurry of paper, Mum is continuing to flare, 'But that's *disgusting*. I *told* you about germs.'

I push myself up from the settee. 'I know,' I complain, explain, 'I didn't do it *all the time*. I didn't *mean* to do it. It was a *habit*. I must have liked the taste.' Momentarily I have forgotten how we came onto the subject of these keys. Certainly I have forgotten the taste of them. 'The taste of the metal, presumably.' Just as I love the smell of coins; the rusty, raw smell of coins.

Below me, craning up, she wails her protest: 'Now you're going to say that I didn't give you enough iron or something.'

This is so ridiculous that I am stopped in my tracks. Emphatically weary, I patronise her with, '*No*, but I *will* if you *want*.'

She starts to scrabble from the settee, but she is so much slower than me. Stoked up on indignation, she yells after me, 'I bet *Mrs Dutton* said so.' To stop me in the doorway, she warns, 'Mrs Dutton is a confused old lady, you shouldn't have let her upset you with a load of old rubbish about her daughter.'

My hand freezes to the door handle, but not because she is right. But because she is wrong. And she could not be more wrong. Mrs Dutton is never confused. She is slow and clear: she thinks, slowly and clearly, before she speaks, slowly and clearly. And she has never upset me. Unlike Mum, with her ribbons of thought: tattered, loopy, knotted. Which tie me in knots. And, anyway, no one makes up my mind for me. Ever, on any subject. But there is something else which, even before I speak, is seeping from me to rattle the door handle. I turn, briefly, to send her coldest smile that I can kindle, and to suggest, 'Isn't this concern about my childhood a little overdue?'

Dinah

....

I can do nothing right. I try to be nice, and what is her response? A slam of the door. Leaving silence eddying in its wake. And my heart. Because I have been jumpy, lately. Now she starts on the stairs: so, she has decided not to leave the house but to go to her room, and I will not see her again until she wants something from me, food or money. Each step on the stairs is a thump.

She is a harsh judge of me: *overdue concern?* What does *she* know about concern? When has she ever had to think of anyone but herself? I did not take to motherhood; but when it happened to me, I did my best. No, I did not giddy her with hugs and kisses; I do not have the genes for bubbly, cuddly love. But *concern?* Her whole life, I have been here for her; I have had to watch over her since she was nothing but a swelling of my stomach. She took over my life, but not until she had taken over my body. When she was a button of cells she was sunk so hard into me that, all day every day from the moment that I woke, my body strained to throw her up.

As soon as she was born, she knew her own mind. But I did not, I never knew her mind. She never let me in on her secrets. Of which there seemed to be so many. And I still know so little about her; she still tells me nothing. I did not know that she kept in contact with Mrs Dutton, if only via the odd birthday card. I have always respected Zoe's privacy, I have never pried. And for her whole life we have rubbed along, if uneasily. But sometimes you need to know what someone thinks. And for us, this time has come: I need to know what she has going on in her mind before I can start to think straight again. I need to know what she thinks of Caddy Dutton. And what she thought, when she was a child. I need to know if she believes Caddy Dutton; I need to know if my own daughter refuses to believe that I am her mother.

The slam of her door shoots through the feeble frame of this house and into my bones. There is more of me in her than she realises: like me, she is brittle, she has to spend all her energy holding herself together.

Zoe

....

Mrs Dutton is tiny, peering around the door; the door, in comparison, is huge and heavy. The yolks of her eyes run up me, and I watch her recognising me: something which I have never seen before, something she has never needed to do. Is this because she is so old, now? Or have I changed? Her little face fattens into a smile, and the doorway grows wide. She answers my unspoken question for me: 'My Goodness, you've grown!' But is this the truth, the *whole* truth? Has she not shrunk? And now she is shrinking further, stepping back to allow me into the house. Her face, her hand on the door, every bit of her that I can see, is cracked by thousands of lines. *How old is she?* I realise that I have no idea. She was always old, I never thought of her in terms of a specific age. But now I want to know. 'You've had your hair cut,' she says, 'and it's very nice.'

Following her into the dim front room, so different from my own home, Mum's home, Mum's huge windows and curtains of huge orange leaves, I say, 'I've come to thank you for my card, my lovely birthday card . . .' There is a smell, I recognise as the smell of this house. A strange, sleepy sense of recognition, like the pull of a dream which has crept into the next day; the pull to complete the dream when the moment has gone and there is nothing but the slow-motion real world. 'I'm so sorry,' I hurry, 'that I haven't come around until now.' My visit defined: explanation, thanks, apology.

'Oh, don't be silly,' says Mrs Dutton, closing the door behind me.

I turn abruptly towards her, peer wide-eyed through the shadows. To find her baggy smile.

'What matters,' she coos, 'is that you're here now. It's so nice to see you. Sit yourself down.'

I turn back to negotiate more shadows, to try to locate somewhere to sit. 'I can't stay long,' I start again, before I can stop myself, 'because I have to meet my boyfriend in town.' This is a lie, surprising me much more than Mrs Dutton.

'Oh, well,' she is purring, 'never mind, just stay for a cup of tea.' She shuffles past me towards the kitchen.

'Do you have coffee?' Lately I have begun to hate tea.

'I think so,' she calls cheerfully. 'I keep a jar for visitors.'

Glancing around this stiff shiny room, I wonder who visits.

She laughs. 'Gives *me* palpitations.'

Palpitations? A phenomenon which Mum has begun to claim for herself, in recent years, along with other strange ailments: cramp, ringing-in-the-ears, tight chest, puffy ankles, dry eyes. Old people's ailments?

'I've had exams,' I call, compelled for some reason, no reason, into another lie.

'I can see,' she calls back happily, over the boom of ignited gas beneath the kettle. 'You look exhausted.'

Do I?

'Did you pass?'

Pass? 'Yes.' Of course. *Passing* is not the problem.

She wanders towards me but stops in the doorway, fidgets with her apron. Torn between me and the kettle. 'Still clever at school, then?'

Does she want an answer? Surely it is not for me to say. And clever in whose book? I smile briefly, pained: *I suppose so, fairly.*

'Boyfriend, now, though,' she encourages, approvingly.

Why, oh why, did I mention Mickey?

'Must be difficult to find the time, now, to settle to those books.'

I have to stop this. With another lie. 'He helps me.' I explain. 'He's older.'

'Older?'

'A year older, he's in the year above me.' Talking about him like this, as though he is still my boyfriend, almost convinces me. And it *was* true, *has been* true, not so very long ago, hardly any time ago at all. I am fairly sure, now, that this is not what I want, that I do not want him; but what *do* I want? For the moment, for Mrs Dutton, this half-lie, white lie, is easier.

'What's his name?'

'Mickey.'

'And he's at school with you. Isn't that nice?'

No, not at the moment, not at all. We have not spoken since our row in the car, although we see each other every day. Glare at each other every day, and turn away. And I have seen him looking at Sarah Goodwin. And it is a look that I know very well.

'And how long has this romance been going on?' Behind her, the kettle is rattling on the stove. Soon I will have my coffee. Soon.

'About six months.'

He looks like me, we have the same black hair, and until recently I thought that he was the same as me, that we had the same thoughts, the same feelings, the same plans.

'Goodness, you'll be getting married before I know.' She chuckles and turns to attend to the kettle. 'Milk and sugar?' she calls. And now, 'Zoe?'

Hearing her stumbling towards me, I release my face from my hands and straighten briskly, telling her, 'I'm okay, I'm okay, I'm sorry.' *Don't touch me.*

'What is it?' she is saying, but slowing down, slightly wary.

Her words are weals of pain, which I do not want to hear. I do not want sympathy, it hurts. I busy myself with a hunt up my sleeve for a tissue. 'It's nothing,' I sniff, desperately.

She stops in front of me. I see the hard hands turning in the soft white apron.

'Everything's going wrong,' I tell her.

I sense that she sits slowly, painfully, in the opposite armchair. 'How can everything be going wrong, Zoe?' A whisper, warm with amazement.

'It's Mum,' I start, not having known where to start, still not knowing what to say. 'She never lets me see him.' I swallow a sob.

'Never?' She is leaning forward, straining forward. 'But you're seeing him today, now, after me, aren't you?'

This was said so kindly, so soothingly, that I smart. 'I never see him *properly*, now,' I explain. 'Mum's on at me all the time.'

'My mother was the same with me,' her voice is very close, and I hear the brush of a laugh through the words. 'With me and Clem, I mean.' The laugh rustles. 'You know, *Clem*,' she stresses, but lightly, awkwardly, shyly.

I do not know, but I listen quietly. Quietly is the only way to listen because she is whispering.

'But she came around in the end,' she says calmly. 'They always do. They have to. Because you know who's right for you. And if he's right, he'll wait for you.'

I blurt, 'But she has gone mad.' There is no other explanation. 'And she's driving *me* mad.' I begin to cry steadily now; not for Mrs Dutton, but for myself. I am talking to myself, listening to myself. But I can see that Mrs Dutton is flapping a hand, perhaps to stop me, to catch my attention, or perhaps to try to unravel this mess.

'Zoe,' she pleads, gently, 'tell me what's going on.'

'Nothing in my life has been right since she started.' *Started to turn on me.* 'Everything I do is wrong, all of a sudden.'

'All of a sudden?'

And it is only now that I realise that, until this moment, Mrs Dutton has been sounding as if she doubts me, however slightly, kindly, sympathetically. And now, oddly, by choosing this moment to change her mind, she is wrong again, because I am wrong, because surely Mum has always treated me like this. Treated me as a dead loss. Everyone knows how Mum treats me. But Mrs Dutton is also right, I am right: it *is* all of a sudden.

'Since when?'

I look up at her. 'A couple of months, now.'

'Does she know that you're here?' She is eerily calm: *Emergency, under control.*

'Yes, no,' *She knew that I would come here sometime to thank you for the card,* 'I don't know,' and I don't care. Because why should it matter? How can this simple visit be wrong?

'Don't tell her.' Said very definitely, implying a specific plan.

But what plan? Is she going to suggest that I come here, to her, for help, for refuge? What help can this old lady be to me?

'Has she said anything about me?'

Another lie, 'No,' but unfortunately over-zealous, with a tell-tale squeak of indignation, a ring of untruth.

She does not let my lie pass until she has held a heavy pause. 'Well, *if she does,* I want you to tell me.'

More conditions, more threats. Currently my world is full of them. I am becoming used to them. I nod, careful not to commit myself in words. Playing along.

Satisfied, she says brightly, 'Tell-you-what: you bring your young man around here.'

Is this the plan? Much worse than I had anticipated. More complicated.

'And you can have time alone to talk together in peace.' Now she laughs, painfully self-conscious, 'Well, apart from me, but you don't have to worry about me, I'll keep out of your way.' Shyly, she adds, 'I'd very much like to meet him.'

Yes, but he does not want to meet you. Because he does not want anything to do with me, he does not want to *meet me.* I tell her, 'I'll see what he says.' And perhaps I would, if we were on speaking terms. 'Mrs Dutton,' I say, suddenly, 'I'm very sorry, but I have to go.' To get out of here. To be by myself.

She withdraws into her chair, slightly shocked: 'Already?'

'I've remembered something,' I lie, desperately, 'something that I have to do in town before I meet . . .' I cannot say his name, I let his name fall into the flurry of my standing and shrugging of apologies.

Sitting below me, she is tiny, deflated by dismay. 'You don't want your coffee?' Only her hands are hard and brilliant, on the arms of her chair.

Looking down, I focus on not telling her that I have begun to feel faint. Wrenching myself around, I manage to murmur over my shoulder a final, heartfelt, 'Sorry.'

Caddy

What could I have done? Could I have stood between her and the door, stood my ground, barred her way? No, of course not. So I am still here in my chair, holding the arms of my chair, still hearing the click of the door behind her, the punch of the brass nib into its socket. When Zoe began coming here, when she was a little girl, she could not reach, could not open the door for herself. Not for years. She stayed here until I let her go. Not that it ever felt like that, of course. No, not that it ever *was* like that. So, how was it, then? A joint decision, I suppose: I do not remember, because how can I, why should I remember who opened the door? They were all joint decisions, when to come and go, what to do. Or, surely, not decisions at all, but natural, foregone conclusions: we had a shared sense of what to do and when, how. Now, suddenly, I have seen, heard, that everything is different. That *we* are different. And naturally: because she is a teenager, now; she has a life of her own, boyfriend trouble, homework, exams, mother trouble. But this is new ground for us.

Dinah Fox would have stopped her, just now, would have rushed in front of the door. And hence the problems between them. What is she hoping to achieve, by her tightening her hold on Zoe. *Achieve?* She will *lose*. She will lose Zoe, unless she is careful. We both will. If I do not want to lose Zoe, I must tread carefully. Or tread not at all. Stay here. Wait. And she will come back. In time. Of her own accord. She will come around. And this is all I want: not to lose her.

Is Mrs Fox's behaviour worse because of what she has *seen*? Seen Polly, seen Zoe in Polly. I caught sight of Mrs Fox before she had noticed me, us – when she was alone, left to her thoughts, and what I saw was an unhappy woman. Withered mouth, thinned shoulders. Dissolved eyes. Did her glimpse of the truth make much difference to her? At the time, I felt not. I felt that, if anything, she would give up a little more. And now, hearing of the trouble between them, their skirmishes over the boyfriend, I am more certain. Mrs Fox has her hands full with the usual problems. And, anyway, what could she do, could she even *hope* to do, now that Zoe is grown up? Why should Mrs Fox matter to me? All I want is for Zoe to come to see me, occasionally. Preferably warmly. I do not wish for much. I shall not want much from Zoe because I learned from Evie: the greater the want, the greater the loss.

Dinah

There was nothing different or difficult about Mickey. He meant no harm. I could handle Mickey. And he could have been useful to me, I should have worked harder on him. But now, suddenly, he is gone, and there is someone new. *Dominic*. Not that we have been introduced. I only ever see Dominic on my doorstep. In the dark. He only ever seems to come here after dark; his eyelids quivering, pained, in the light which I switch on to snare him. Usually I can catch him: I watch him leave his car and slink up our path to our doorstep, where he tries to sidestep my sudden beam, to slouch in shadow and wait for Zoe.

He never has to wait for long. Because Zoe watches for him. Waits for him. Suddenly, overhead, her sounds cease: no more shuffling between bedroom and bathroom, no more hairdryer, no phone conversations, no words with Danny. She cuts herself off from us, from her world, veils herself in net curtain. Before I hear his car, I hear her feet on the stairs. She runs to him, to follow him wordlessly into the darkness, into his car. But there is a moment when she is trapped between the two of us: at the foot of the stairs, whirling into her coat, into stiff sleeves, under the bright hallway light. And it is then that I watch her eyes buzzing his face, trying to read him.

She told me his name, when I asked. Then I wanted to know: is he from her school? She said yes. Said rudely, to warn me: *no more questions*. But one more question: I asked her where he lives. She said, 'St Andrew's Lane, satisfied?' and flounced from the room. Every evening, from my place in the hallway, I can see that this doorstep Dominic thinks too much of himself. But that he knows the enemy: Mickey was wary of me, but this boy is scared in a different way. Scared in a real way, nothing to do with schoolboy deference: I detect that he has plenty to hide.

For someone so intent on shadow, he is oddly keen to draw attention to himself: since when have boys been dying their hair? When he runs his fingers through his hair, I see that the tips, the nails, are stained a matching shade of yellow. Mickey was shiny and solid. This new boy is too thin. Mickey was wide-eyed but this boy's eyes are small and too bright. Mickey was the-boy-next-door, but I have never seen a boy like this new one: the messy hair and clothes, the contempt in his eyes. I wonder what Zoe tells him, has told him.

Danny is no help. Whenever I ask him about Dominic, his eyes reel: he seems reluctant to even think about him. At the very most, he sighs, 'I've *told* you, he's not worth worrying about.' But I *have to* worry about him.

Zoe

....

Behind Dominic, his mother peers from the warm shadows of the hall into the high-pitched brightness of the cloakroom, and calls to me, 'Hello Zoe.' My return smile is swiped from her view by the coat which swings in his wake from one of the hooks on the wall. Undeterred, I call back, blindly, 'Hello.'

'Come on,' Dominic says into my ear, stepping swiftly past me, down from the doorstep. I take the doorknob and turn back to the darkness of the driveway. But suddenly the door is heavy in my hand and I turn to find his mother reclaiming it from me. 'Dominic,' she calls over me from the doorstep, 'we're popping over to visit Grandma and Grandpa very briefly at about nine.'

Ahead of me, he barely turns, but raises a hand. I have no idea whether she is requesting his presence or merely informing him; I have no idea whether his raised hand is agreement or dismissal. And I wonder, do *they* know?

When I glance again, his mother's place has been taken by his sister. She is wearing a very long shirt and nothing else. 'Dom,' she calls, 'are you passing a post box?'

'No,' he barks.

'Hello!' I add hopefully.

In reply, she grins and rises onto her bare toes to send me a frilly wave. Their little sister wriggles into the space beneath her armpit to shriek after us, 'Domino! Maltesers! Please!' Her glasses are flashing into the darkness, too big for her tiny face.

With a sharp click of his tongue Dominic swirls around, swelling rapidly with indrawn breath. I cringe in anticipation but he continues treading backwards until he turns ahead of me behind the hedge. Without further requests, the door shuts, and everywhere is dark. I turn past the hedge to find his face in the brief grip of match light. It polishes the mother-of-pearl tone of his skin. And stokes the red hair which remains, despite the bleached spikes and the new Crazy-Colour green forelock. Mum refers to him as Lawrence of Arabia but I do not know why because he does not look Arabian to me. He concentrates with breathtaking intensity on the end of the cigarette, then relaxes instantly with the first drag. He whips the damp air once with the match before dropping it from his bony fingers.

'Emily wants Maltesers,' I smile.

'Sod Emily,' he says mildly, and strides off.

I laugh and hurry behind him. 'Where are we going?' I link my arm with his, having selected the non-smoking side.

'I don't know. Does it matter?'

'Why do you think Francesca wanted a post box, at this time of evening? She has missed last post.'

He glances down at me. 'As I recall, Francesca didn't want a *post box*; she wanted us *to go for her* to a post box.'

'Charmer,' I tease.

'Not so much of a charmer that I'm prepared to spend my life running errands for people. Least of all my sodding sister.'

'You're so mean to your sisters, and they're so *nice*.'

He marches on, wincing at the cigarette. I can see the firm dark track of pencil along his lower eyelids. His eyelashes, lacking pigment, are nothing but a flurry of tiny spiders' webs when his face is close to mine.

'Is she going out with anyone at the moment?' I enquire politely.

'*Going out*,' he sneers. Then, 'I don't know. No doubt she's knocking off some of my friends behind my back. And why are you so obsessed with my family?'

'Do you have to go with them to see your grandparents?'

'No.'

So I decide to try: 'Oh good,' I enthuse bravely, 'because Mrs Robinson's on.'

He halts, scrutinises me, seems to swallow a large proportion of the cigarette. 'What?'

'Mrs Robinson.' I have to sing, 'And-here's-to-you, Mrs Robinson . . .'

He laughs; tilting his head back, laughing over mine. '*The Graduate*. What time?'

'Half nine.'

He nods slowly in approval.

'Can we watch it?'

He twinkles at me. 'Of course we can watch it.'

'Can you run me home afterwards?' I try to twinkle back, although we have already agreed, on the phone, that if I came over here on the bus, then he would run me back. The problem is not the lack of a car but that he has very little money for petrol.

'I said I would, didn't I?' he replies happily, flinging the stub of the cigarette into the gutter. Then he sighs and says, 'Poverty is so *soul-destroying*.'

From here I can still see the house. It is grey, stone, massive. It is called The Rectory. I have never been entirely sure about rectories: I am fairly sure that they are – or were – religious, but how do they differ from vicarages?

With both hands deep in his pockets, he resumes his march. 'At least we can enjoy a few hours without the presence of my darling family.' But it *is* a darling family.

As I reach him, he flings both hands into the air. 'I have to get away from here,' he hisses loudly. Turning to me, continuing to step, but backwards, he is suddenly cheerful: 'Guess where I was when I first saw *The Graduate*?'

I shrug eagerly.

'California,' he announces.

I am impressed. 'How?'

He has turned away, flapping his hand. 'My uncle Robert. Lives there.'

'Oh.'

'I wish my parents knew a Mrs Robinson,' he snaps, utterly

disgusted with them. Then, more interested, 'Well, they do, actually. Know a Mrs Robinson, I mean; a real, live Mrs Robinson.' He rolls his eyes: 'But she's no Anne Bancroft and she's more into the local Tory Council than hotel rooms.'

I am not sure whether to sympathise. 'Do you really?' I ask conversationally.

'What? Do I *what*, really?' We are on a main road now and the street lamps wash their distinctive tone into his hair.

'Wish that your parents knew a Mrs Robinson?'

He laughs uneasily at me. 'Of course I do. Just as you go for those older men.'

'But I don't.'

'Of course you do.'

'I *don't*.' I wish he would not tease me.

'You're just saying that.'

'No, *you* are.' I try to lessen my impatience with a laugh. '*I* don't *just say* anything.'

He shrugs.

'And where are we going?' As far as the horizon, the road is lined with semis. They are unlike the semis where I live: they are fat and white; why do they bother to be semis if they are so big? Each one is topped by a sparse web of black timbers, and bulges at the bottom with a bay window.

'As far as the war memorial?' He shrugs again. 'Then we can go home, because They'll be gone.' He blurts a sigh of relief. 'I have got to get away from here. If I've managed a C this time for Maths, I'm off, I'm not hanging around here all year for one more try. I think I'll go to Paris.'

Paris? The Eiffel Tower. Notre-Dame. Suddenly Paris seems further away than usual. How can I stop him from leaving me here? 'What will you do there?'

'As little as possible.' He stares gloomily ahead, and shakes the packet of cigarettes inside his pocket.

'But where will you live?'

The packet appears in his shaking hand, and he dishes a

cigarette into his mouth. It is startlingly long and white, held very lightly between his lips. I remember the tiny pink-tipped sweet cigarettes which Danny and I used to buy from the local shop. It is a shame that the real ones do not taste or smell as nice.

'I have a friend.' The cigarette wags. 'I'll sleep on his floor.'

'You have a friend in Paris?'

How does anyone from here have a friend in Paris? Perhaps it is a pen-friend. I had a pen-friend, but she lived in Nancy and she was not a friend. The friendship was a delusion of my French teacher, who suffered the characteristic jolly delusions of all French teachers: that France is nice, that walls stuck with maps of the wine-growing regions are nice, that fourth formers want to learn to speak French. I do not know most of Dominic's friends because they did not go to our school. I do not know where they have come from. They work in theatres and play in bands. Dominic was at school with me, but he was two years ahead of me, which was a big gap, which *is* a big gap. I knew him by sight; I knew the sight of him. Everyone knew the sight of him, shivering miserably, interestingly, in the corridors: the red roots of his yellow hair, and the matching yellow fingertips; the eyeliner, two thin dribbles of dark chocolate. He was notorious for saying to the Headmaster, when in trouble yet again over the colour of his hair, 'I think that you are projecting your own anxieties about going so grey.' I never thought that I would be here, now, with him. I got to know him when I began to go to his local with Jane. During the days, the evenings, after Mickey.

'A friend of a friend. Does it matter?' A dense wad of smoke buds from his mouth, and then a smile slides slowly across his face. 'You can come too,' he teases, 'and you can work the streets to earn us some cash.'

'Thanks, Poppet.'

'*Poppet*,' he repeats derisively, then adds, 'You don't have the face for a life of vice.'

'But you do,' I answer immediately.

He winks at me. 'Yes, I do.'

'Wasted, I meant.'

But he preens mockingly. 'Yes, I am, aren't I.'

'Do you speak French?' I ask him, to shift the subject.

He peers sharply at me. 'Don't you?'

'Well, *school* French, yes . . .' *Je m'appelle Zoe, je vais bien merci.* Not enough to survive, surely.

'Anyway,' he shoots pale smoke into the air, 'I might go to Berlin, I've loads of friends in Berlin.'

Berlin? 'Do you speak *German?*'

His eyes slot sideways. 'German isn't *difficult.*'

I listen to the steady warm thuds of his shoes. How does he know everything? How is he afraid of nothing?

He says, 'Do you want to come to a party on Saturday?'

'Where?' I mean, whose?

'Out at Adlington.'

Who could possibly live in Adlington? There is a signpost to Adlington – Milcham 3, Adlington 6 – on the road out of town. It is on Dad's short-cut route to the motorway, so we have driven through it occasionally on the way to the airport, on the way to a holiday.

'We can probably have a lift,' he says doubtfully. Then he explains: 'Toby.'

I nod thankfully, although I have met Toby once or twice and I do not like him. I do not like the prospect of being stuck in Adlington, waiting for Toby to sober up and calm down before he drives me home. Or worse: *not* waiting for him to sober up and calm down before he drives me home. 'What about getting back?'

Dominic says, 'Oh, don't worry about that.'

Carefully, I tell him, 'I'm not sure that I can.' Why am I such a coward? Why am I so nervous of his friends? 'I promised Jane that I'd help her baby-sit the Richardson twins.' Almost the truth. And it can become the truth, if I do go over and sit with Jane. Jane-to-the-rescue.

He says nothing.

'I could come along later.' But I know that I cannot, that I am safe, because there will be no Toby to bring me.

He turns suddenly to me. 'Do you want to come along to a gig next Thursday? In the room above The Anchor?'

I try to sparkle with enthusiasm, although I am contemplating the prospect of smoke and red light bulbs and noise and drunk boys, versus *Yes Minister* and a hot bath. 'Who?' And I would have to catch the bus, the number forty-one, which is notoriously, painfully irregular.

He reflects my apparent enthusiasm: 'A few of my mates, they've been together in this band for a couple of months now and they're brilliant.'

Briefly, I am interested: 'Will Danny know them?'

He flings the remains of his cigarette into the hedge and sneers, 'No. It's not your brother's type of music.'

As ever, he is too quick to judge: I know that he has even less idea of Danny's ever-changing taste in music than I do. Nevertheless I do not say this but try again: 'Danny has lots of friends in bands.'

He laughs triumphantly. 'Won't be your brother's *friends'* type of music.' He twinkles at me.

'So why will it be *my* type?' I enquire reasonably.

He whirls around and grabs both my hands. 'Because it's brilliant,' he enthuses, pleads.

It is difficult for me to refuse him anything when he pleads so enthusiastically. I play for time: 'Thursday night?'

'I *think* it's Thursday night.' He has lost interest; or, more likely, has no interest in the details. He is not keen on details.

I wince my apologies. 'I might have to go late-night shopping on Thursday because Mum wants me to help choose an eighteenth birthday present for Aunty Maxine's David.' A lie. A very unlikely lie.

No immediate response: his gaze drifts with a passing car before he murmurs, 'You need to get out more often.'

Do I? Ahead of us the road runs down a hill: a runway, endless, the seams sewn with lights.

'What are you going to do for *your* eighteenth?' I ask him.

He laughs and hooks his arm around me. 'What do you think I should do?' He squeezes me, smiles down at me.

I shrug, curious.

'Because my parents' – and *parents* is hot with exasperation – 'want to take me out for a meal.' He rolls his eyes. 'I'll only ever have one eighteenth birthday, and I have no intention of spending the evening across the table from my parents and my sisters in some restaurant, slurping prawn cocktail.'

I wonder where a family like Dominic's goes for birthday meals. Dad takes Mum to the local Chinese sometimes for birthdays. He took us all to the Carvery once for a treat when we came back late from holiday, tired and hungry, and there was no food at home and the shops were shut. On holiday we eat sometimes in restaurants, at square tables with gingham tablecloths. Always chips, and always ice-cream. On the tables there are little brown glass bottles with cocked spouts, and baskets filled with pieces of crusty bread. If possible we take a table on a terrace under vines. Back home, we go for pizza sometimes when we are shopping on Saturday in town. I have had prawn cocktail at weddings.

He is leaning into me. 'Eat-your-heart-out, Buñuel,' he sings into the street. Then he shifts against me, peers down onto me. 'Have you seen that film? The one where they sit around on toilets and have to excuse themselves to go off alone into a tiny room to eat?'

I widen my eyes. '*The Sound Of Music*, isn't it?'

He laughs. 'You *haven't* seen it.'

'Exciting plot?' I tease further.

'It's satire, my dear,' he pronounces archly, before briefly squeezing me again. 'And where would we be without satire?'

'Same place as we are now?'

He sighs. 'You have no faith, Zoe Fox. And no sense of humour, either.'

I decide to smile angelically and say, *Oh-but-I'm-kind-to-animals*, but he says, 'They'll ask you, so say no.'

He explains, louder, 'They'll ask you to come to the meal. But say no. I don't want a meal. It's my birthday and I want to go out and get blitzed.'

They'll ask *me*? They'll ask *me* to come to their family meal, to the coming-of-age of their first-born, their son-and-heir? They'll ask me to sit down with them, with his mum in a fawn cashmere cardy with buttons of pearl, and his dad with the warm voice and silver hair; they'll ask me to sit alongside Francesca's pout, sit in Emily's polished gaze? Did Dominic tell them to ask me? I sneak a sideways glance for clues: as ever I see nothing but the hard ripple of cheekbone in the smooth surface of his face, and a small round silver eye. Or is this his mother's own decision, perhaps after consultation with Francesca? Or did Francesca initiate, insist, *Ask Zoe to come*, whilst she was flapping around the kitchen in her long shirt? Because Francesca seems to like me.

And her opinion is vital to me because she saw the others: each one, it seems, a friend of a friend of a friend, Lucys and Sophies and Penelopes; each one, it seems, a whole world older than me. And Francesca is honest; unlike Dominic, who is forever running scared and keen to cover his tracks. Dominic is not a natural, but I have staying power. Enough for us both. Everyone-needs-someone, and we need each other. No one else will do. We are so very different from everyone else, there is no place for us in everyone else's everyday world. I will have to try hard, to be hard on him, but eventually he will see that we are made for each other. Quietly, gently, I take a deep breath, to fill myself with him: the smell of his coat, which is the rich smell of The Rectory; the smell of his hair, which is the smell of supermarket shampoo, friendly family-sized bubbly amber gel; the smell of his cigarettes, which is the secret smell of the inside of his mouth.

'How much cash do you have on you?' he asks me.

Sleepily, I draw myself away from him, reach inside my warm

pocket for my purse. 'Seventy pence,' I tell him, after a brief investigation.

'Great,' he says in disgust. 'We won't be nipping into the pub, then.'

'No.' And I do not care. I would rather stay here, alone with him.

We have reached the war memorial. He leans back on the stone ledge and pulls me towards him, to face him, to stand between his knees. He looks very closely at me, and his thin lips hook a smile.

'What?' I demand. 'What?'

'How did you get this wonky face?' He lifts a hand in front of me and then I detect the peel of a fingertip landing on my own lower lip.

'Oh, that. I've always had it. I fell over, I suppose.'

'Careless,' he teases breathily. Suddenly the fingertip dissolves and his lips are there, but barely, moving slowly and dryly over mine. It hurts me physically to be so close, pulls me apart and burns me. His breath stings me. He straightens slowly away from me, briefly switching the flow of blood in my veins so that it stretches after him. I concentrate hard on the cold air, to cool myself. I am held so close to him that I cannot fail to notice that this passion is mutual. I close my eyes and switch my concentration towards an effort to stay perfectly still.

'There'll be no war memorial for us.'

I open my eyes.

'I mean, there'll be no one left to build war memorials. No one to read them. Not next time.' I shift so that I can look at him. He directs his frowns into my face. 'No more chances,' he muses quietly. 'Countdown to meltdown.'

'We'll-all-go-together-when-we-go,' I whisper to him.

Frowning harder, he grumbles, 'Not funny;' insists, 'I'm serious.'

Did I say that it was funny?

'I wish I knew how much longer we have left. We've yet to

scrape into the eighties, I don't suppose we'll reach the nineties.'

'Dominic . . .' I protest gently, pressing both my hands from his cool forehead into his fierce springy hair.

'What do you reckon?' he continues. 'How long?'

I try to comfort him: 'Dom, it *may* never happen.'

His eyes slip away from me. 'And you'd like to believe that, wouldn't you? You and the rest of your kind; you and a billion other gullible people.'

I turn my hands to my own hair, complain, 'You're the one who says that economics is everything. Why would a government want a nuclear war? What money is there for a government in a nuclear war?' I am surprised by this, and fairly impressed. I am learning to stand up to him.

He refuses to look at me. His eyeballs move beneath the membranous lids. 'Governments aren't rational,' he manages eventually. Is the bitter tone for the irrational governments, or for me?

'But rational enough to do everything else for economic reasons?' I snap, 'You're being inconsistent, Dominic.' And in more ways than one, because usually he champions irrationality.

He glares at me. 'So, you really think that someone won't push the button someday?' he demands, incredulous, furious.

'It's not *my* fault,' I remind him indignantly. 'And, no, as a matter of fact, I *don't* think that it *won't* happen. I've seen those diagrams too, you know.'

His eyes cloud with confusion.

I sweep my hands through the air in search of the words. 'Those clocks. Midnight.'

'Zero hour,' he corrects sullenly.

I listen to the regular swing of cars on the road behind me. It is not raining but the tyres are squashing surface water. 'I mean, what can I do about it all?' And particularly *now*; at this particular moment in time.

'You could try getting angry,' he says resentfully.

'I *am* angry, *most* of the time.' But *now*? On our evening together? Pre-Mrs-Robinson?

'*All* of the time.'

I am surprised to find that I am angry *with him*.

He takes both my hands loosely into his own. 'Look,' he implores, 'if I wasn't angry, it would mean that I wasn't angry about the prospect of losing you, which would mean that I didn't *care* about you. And you wouldn't like that, would you? Think of it like that.'

I would love to try, but I doubt that I can remember back to the start of the sentence.

He sums up: 'Think of it as *for you*, because it is, partly.' He is watching my eyes very closely. Now he dimples amicably at me, and his grip tightens around my cold hands: both a squeeze and a shake. '*Someone* has to fight your corner for you. You trust too much in fate,' he says, sadly and kindly.

Trussst in me . . .

'Maybe fate has done me nothing but favours.' I surprise myself again, and bite down hurriedly onto my lip.

He reels, whistling his derision. 'If you carry on like this, in five years' time you'll be married with three kids.'

'No I won't,' I protest angrily. For someone who so often refuses to listen to anyone else, he has an unfortunate tendency to lecture.

'Yes you will.'

'No I won't.'

'Yes you will. Especially if you stay hanging around with guys like your Mickey.' He savours *Your Mickey*, and excitedly tilts his chin in defiance.

So this is about Mickey; this is jealousy. 'He's not *my* Mickey: remember?' I laugh, or half-laugh because I do not want Dom to doubt me. I made sure that Mickey was no longer *my Mickey*.

'Ah, no, he's not your Mickey at this precise moment in time,' he twinkles, 'but that's where your heart is.'

'No it isn't.'

'Yes it is.'

'Your word against mine,' I hurry, 'and I should know.'

'But I can *see*.' He grins sharply, conclusively.

'But, strangely, you don't seem to know how long it takes to make a baby: if I'm going to have three babies in the next five years, then I'll have to start very soon.' I return the grin. He says nothing for a moment, so I continue, 'And what will *you* be doing in five years' time?'

He shrugs grandly. 'Who knows? Winning huge prizes for my novels?'

But not for your modesty.

He deflates slightly, and stares over my shoulder into the road. 'But I don't know if I care. Five years is a long, long time.'

I sigh and lower my forehead very gently onto his. 'No it isn't.'

'I wonder if we'll still know each other?' he ponders.

'Well, if we make the effort, then we will.'

'Sometimes I feel that I've already known you for a long, long time.'

I have never known anyone like him: I lift my head to look at him and, unexpectedly, he reminds me of a little boy in a summer somewhere, with thin hard white limbs glittering in dull loose clothes.

'Which means that I trust you, almost.'

I stroke my lips over the pale fur of an eyebrow.

His face follows mine, nuzzles upwards. 'Do you believe in reincarnation?'

I murmur, 'Do we have any reincarnation after The Bomb?'

Between small kisses he replies, 'Of course not. There's nothing after The Bomb. Except perhaps dinosaurs, or something, eventually, I suppose.'

'Dinosaurs? We come back as dinosaurs?' I breathe a faint laugh into his mouth. 'Shucks, I won't be able to fit back into my old clothes, I'll need a whole new wardrobe.'

Holding me away from him, his hands on my shoulders, he insists, 'It's not funny,' but his seriousness slants into a smile.

'But I'll make you laugh in the end,' I tell him, knowingly.

'I don't know about the future,' he counters, jollily, 'But in the past you were probably burned for witching, you black-eyed temptress.'

I resist his grip, return to him, and start again with a tiny kiss on the tip of his nose. 'If you say so. And what were you?'

'Ah, well,' he teases, 'Leonardo da Vinci, Oliver Cromwell, Van Gogh – the list is endless, do you want me to go on?'

'No, I think I've got the picture.' I kiss him wordless. Then, pausing for breath, I wonder, 'Do you think Leo and Olly and Van ever thought they would end up as you?'

His hands are cupping my bottom, a perfect fit. '*Thought* isn't the right word,' he hums into my ear. '*Hoped*, or *wished*, perhaps.'

'And do they all have to be famous, your previous incarnations?'

'Of course they do,' he reasons cheerfully, 'because how else would I know them?'

I take another breath which I intend to turn into words, but fail. 'Well,' I sigh it back out, 'You have me foxed.'

This is his favourite joke of the moment; he ripples with delight: 'No, *you* have *me* Foxed.'

'Perhaps you're not supposed to know who they were,' I reason, suddenly interested, almost managing to ignore the flick of his laughing tongue in my ear. 'Perhaps you're not supposed to know too much about the whole process.' I dodge his tongue. His eyes are flecks in the darkness. 'Because if you did, if we all did, then it wouldn't work, would it? It would become too complicated. It would . . .' I dig an incisor into my lip, to sharpen my concentration . . . 'stop going on.' I shrug hopelessly.

He kisses me very definitely for a moment and then murmurs warmly, 'Like all the best things. Best not to think too hard. Or not to think at all.'

I stiffen inside. On the outside, I start to shake. I am thankful to be so close to him that he cannot see me. We are both acutely aware that we have not yet found a time and place when we can be truly alone with each other. But we both know that this is only a matter of time. And I know that I am, have been, waiting, ticking furiously for him.

He tips his cold blue gaze directly into my eyes and asks flatly, nonchalantly, 'What contraception do you use?'

What *do* I use? 'Nothing.' *I* use nothing. 'I mean . . .'

He is nodding confidently. 'You're not on the pill,' he concludes correctly.

I do not reply and nor do I move. I am waiting, still, but differently now. For more comment from him? for a conclusion? But he shifts me, rises with a yawn, hangs one arm across my shoulders, and says, 'We don't want to be late for Mrs Robinson.'

Caddy

....

'So, how are you?' Zoe is asking me again, lacing this enquiry with
a dash of smile. She is not sitting in the chair but on its arm. Barely
sitting, and pivoting, turning to track me. The smile signals the
tone: friendly but formal, the verbal equivalent of a handshake.

So, she wants an adult exchange of pleasantries. Which is new.
'Fine,' I thank her, making the effort to match her brightness.

She smiles again; a crack, a seep of a smile. I can see that she
does not know what else to do now that our exchange has taken
us nowhere. Since she arrived in my doorway, a minute or so
ago, there have been a lot of these smiles. And they are new too.
Certainly they mark a contrast to her other visit, last month.
Today she seems to be steeling herself. I feel that she is holding
her breath, that I can hear her holding her breath. Usually I have
to catch and keep her attention because she seems to be somewhere else, usually she will sit on the arm of the chair because
she is barely here, but today she seems to feel she is too much
here, and is flinching.

I sit down opposite her. She smiles again, briefly, and loops
some of her new shorter hair onto the hook of her ear, settles it
around the small curled body of her ear. 'I've come to apologise
for last time,' she says.

'Oh, Zoe,' *Don't-be-silly* . . .

'Look,' she interrupts, reluctantly, lightly, quite sharply, 'I was
awful. I'm sorry.'

'Zoe, really.'

'I was in a bit of a state.' Her fingertips flit to her ear, trace the
cupped hair. 'It was a bad time.' She shrugs stiffly.

'You were upset,' I soothe.

189

She shrugs this off. 'Everything was on top of me, a bit.' Another shrug. 'That's all.' These shrugs seem to have taken the place of the smiles.

I smile for her, but broadly, and gently. 'And now?'

I expect another brittle shrug but she is stilled. She looks to the window, fixes on nothing but net curtain. Her lips part but no words come.

'How is the romance going now?' I prompt.

The frosted gaze returns, twisted and wrung empty by her surprise; and she echoes me, 'Romance?'

'Mickey,' I urge, gently.

Nothing changes on her face but her voice falls flat: 'Oh. It isn't. He isn't.' She tries to finish with one of her smiles for a flourish, but it is too brief, unsure. It is apologetic.

'Oh.' Having so badly lost track and bumped so hard into her again, I try to adjust to this new Zoe, to this month's version: *no Mickey*. I knew that this could happen. I should have been more careful. It is me who should apologise.

But her eyes narrow to attention and she says briskly, 'Don't worry; *I* don't.' Swiftly her fingernails rake the hair which brackets her ear.

'So, what happened?'

'Nothing.' She looks down onto the linked hands which rest so easily on her steeply sloping lap, one thumb lying across the other like a pair of tiny dozy white mice. 'I don't know what I ever saw in him. He was boring.'

When she looks up again and I can see that her eyes are dry and resolved, I offer, 'Would you like a coffee?' Another pleasantry, but noisy in the back of my mind are the memories of her tears on the previous visit. If they were quiet tears, how have they made such noisy memories? Why am I – why have I been – so worried by those tears? Why so worried, if they were simple tears over Mickey?

Apparently glad for the change of subject, she is shaking her head vigorously and reassuring me, 'No, thanks.'

Coffee was easier to mention than the jacket. She has not removed her jacket: is this because she is not intending to stay for long, or is she waiting for instructions, for an invitation, from me? And if she is not eager to stay, will an invitation hurry her away? Coffee was an offer, but removal of the jacket would be a request. Fidgeting on the arm of the chair, she does not invite requests. Her eyes are dry but I cannot see through the tears of her previous visit. Her tears. She came here and cried her desperation for a few moments before drying her eyes and going away. And then I saw nothing of her, until now. She left behind her tears and I faced them every day. I waited because I knew that she would come back for them, come to take them back and tidy them away: Mickey or no Mickey, there would be some solution for those tears. Every day I told myself to wait one more day before going to find her. And, in the end, how was I wrong? Because here she is.

No, I waited because I did not know what else to do. And now I realise that I need to do more. But what? Until now I have been happy to watch, to watch over, to watch out for her; but now she is old enough to start making mistakes, or bigger mistakes, and faster, and to hurt for longer. And I want her to be happy. How nice if someone can come happy from this mess, and perhaps there is no chance now for me or Mrs Fox. Suddenly I doubt that my watching, over, out, will suffice; I will have to *guide* Zoe. Remembering the angry accusations of her previous visit, I remind her: 'But don't you think that your mother caused the problems?' *The problems between you and Mickey*.

She sighs heavily down her nose to convey weariness. 'Mum caused problems, but they brought out what was already there between us. Or not there.' These final three words come low and bitter, her mouth hardly moving around them. She strikes the hair behind her ear and says, sharply, 'Anyway, I don't want to talk about him.' But she *is* talking about him: 'He didn't care about me. What he wanted was a wife, or something. *Someone*. He wanted *someone*.' She stops herself, checks herself, with a hard shrug. 'He wanted a cosy set-up . . .' The words stop and she shrugs again, differently: not too many words, suddenly, but too few.

'And you didn't?' Who can resist a cosy set-up?

'No.' She turns her hard, black, shiny eyes onto me. And her mouth shuts firmly: her final word.

In the end. 'Ever?'

The eyes reel away with impatience and her mouth opens for a fierce sigh. 'Ever is a long time off.'

Is it? How old was I, how much older than her, when I met and married Clem? Perhaps time is different nowadays. Longer. Lives are longer. Decisions can take longer.

'There's someone else,' she says, suddenly. Confides. Is this a secret? As close to a secret as possible, from her? The words slipped quick and surly from her but I sense that she wants, no, *needs* them to be here between us. *Pass the parcel.* She needs my response before she can continue. Her breath is held in somewhere beyond the slightly open mouth, the mouth which is open in readiness, and her eyes burn on this held air. Entrusting me, and mistrusting me. Her sole defence is to watch me, hard.

But what do I say? *Someone else?* Already? Life is *faster* nowadays. 'That's nice,' I manage. 'What's his name?'

'Dominic,' she says. The name sparks from her heartful of breath.

So that it is me, now, who flinches. But why? I try to laugh off my unease. 'And *Dominic does* care about you,' I confirm, jollily. But I am not thinking of Dominic, I am missing Mickey. I never met Mickey and already he is gone. Already he belongs to her past. She has a past which I cannot know.

I notice that she is thinking about my throw-away question; frowning down her thoughts onto one tooth, into her lower lip. 'He cares about everything,' she says carefully, downwardly, perhaps inwardly, before hauling her gaze decisively upwards to emphasise this conclusion with a flat dark dare of a look into my eyes.

I manage, 'Does your mother like him any better?'

She coughs a laugh. 'She hates him.' This comes confidently, and breezily. Now slightly softer, more relaxed, she reflects, happily, 'He's not her type.'

'Who *is* her type?'

'True,' she chirps, failing to realise that my question was genuine. 'So . . .' she shrugs hugely, and carefree, 'in for a penny, in for a pound.'

'No, who *is* her type?'

After pausing to consider, she decides, admits, 'Not Dad,' the words airy with surprise. 'Or not at the moment, anyway,' she qualifies, more surely. 'Maybe Danny, she seems to think he's wonderful.' And now her own silent comment on her brother: a savage wrinkle of her nose.

'But you like Danny, don't you?'

'He's okay,' she replies, the words rolling high on more surprise, 'but I suppose we don't have much in common any more.'

'Anyway,' I hurry, 'that's not what I meant. *I meant*, who is her type *for you*?'

'Oh, *me*.' Throwing her fingertips behind her ear, flexing her hair, she flashes me a sheepish grin: not much more than another flinch, and this time blurred by weariness. '*No one's* her type, when it comes to *me*.' And she adds, 'Definitely not Dominic.'

She wants to talk about Dominic. Which is fine by me, because if she talks to me about Dominic, then she will talk about herself-and-him, she will talk about herself. '*So*,' I start, with as much of a sense of mischief as I can muster, 'what is Dominic *really* like?'

But as I lean forward in my chair, she leans back, away, and now her gaze is drifting over my head and around me, around the room. The sole focus is in her eye-tooth which ventures, briefly, tentatively, onto her lower lip. As if she is testing that the lip is still there, still feels pain. 'He's different,' she says, finally, flatly. Apparently she is already bored.

She has not given me the whole story; she has given me a version. The-edited-version. Highlights? Far from high. *Edited?* She has given me nothing. 'How?' I try to enthuse, 'How is he different?'

Her gaze snaps onto me, but lightly. Her face is washed smooth by surprise. Is she surprised by my interest, or more specifically by my question? Or by her own forthcoming reply, the thoughts of Dominic which are hidden from me, honey-combing beneath, inside, the smooth surface of her face? Eventually, without any obvious enthusiasm, she replies, 'He doesn't care what people think.'

I smile, although I do not know why; a reflex, perhaps, mere politeness. 'But presumably he cares what *you* think?' I check, hopefully.

She frowns, a faceful of irritation. 'We think the same,' she says, hurriedly but definitely.

My questions, her answers, are leading me nowhere. Apart from the fact of his existence, Dominic remains unknowable to me. Because she is determined to keep him to herself. And I am not at all sure that I want to dwell on him, I am not at all sure that I like the sound of him. But I have no choice: I have to know about him, because I have to look out for her, and go further, go *with* her. 'Is he from your school?' I hope that this sounds simply conversational.

'Was.'

'He's older than you?' How much older?

'Two years.'

Like Mickey. Like Mickey was.

She coughs, stifles this sudden bark with a soft fist; and moves slightly on the arm of the chair. Is she going to leave? 'And how is your mum, with you, in general, these days?'

Her eyes and eyebrows flutter. 'Worse, she seems worse,' she says, oddly chatty all of a sudden. 'She seems to want me to have no life at all.'

'Zoe . . .' I protest, uneasily. *A bit strong, surely?*

'It's true,' she says, almost cheerfully. Belligerently cheerfully.

Perky with incredulity. 'She wants to know where I am, every minute of every day. Not Danny, though. She never says a word to Danny. Which is because he's a boy. Although, of course, she insists that's not the reason.'

It is cold in here. Which is why Zoe has not taken off her jacket. Heaving myself from my chair, I head for the unlit fire. 'Does she give you a reason?'

'No. Or no reason that makes sense. Says she can't trust me, says she won't let me turn my back on her.'

I pause in mid-bend by the fire, drawn by the little shrug, the flip of her shoulders. Suddenly warm from my exertion, I check, 'Do you want this on?'

She looks down onto me. 'No,' she mutters, continuing the puzzled tone, 'I'm fine.'

I crank myself upright. Zoe is staring through me. There is no movement on, in, her face. But beside her face, a black wing of hair flies high on her fingers and then slowly downwards, backwards, to settle with the rest of her bob. 'She's possessed, obsessed, whatever,' she guesses. 'I think it's her menopause.'

I think not. Sitting back down, on the edge of my chair, I am heavy with dread. Blindly, I lift the new wide-eyed tone from Zoe, turn it around and slide it back to her: 'Would she not want you to come here?' The tone, from me, rings untrue: because, yes, I want Zoe's confidences, and I want them uncomplicated, I want us to talk as equals, to search for a solution together; but no, unlike her, I am not clueless. I think that I know, now, the reason for Dinah's behaviour. I remember the look on her face when she saw my little granddaughter. This clue of mine is hard to hide, it feels huge and hard in my throat, my eyes, my hot face. Is Dinah doing what I thought she would never do? Is she fighting for Zoe? But fighting who? Not me. I have heard nothing from her. No, she is fighting *Zoe* for Zoe.

Zoe is saying, 'She doesn't know I'm here.' With a helpless, faintly dismal shrug she explains, 'Nowadays I make a point of not telling her where I'm going.'

'But if she *did* know?' *I have to know, I have to know the worst, I have to be prepared:* Would she try to stop Zoe coming here?

Something twitches Zoe's face: puzzlement? irritation? 'But she *doesn't* know.'

'Would she try to stop you coming here?' I feel that these spectacular heartbeats of mine are visible in my eyes, that I am laid wide open.

'How *could* she stop me coming here?' Squeaks and blares of frustration.

My heart thumps out, 'I don't know. You tell me. Could she?'

Oblivious, she continues, 'How can *anyone stop* me from doing *anything*?'

'Has she said anything about me?' Slapped into the air between us, this sticks like an accusation.

She is guarded, behind her frown of irritation. 'What do you mean, *said anything about you*?'

Now it is me who is irritated; I shrug, try to shrug off my irritation. '*Said* anything; *mentioned* me.'

'No,' she sulks.

'Zoe.' *Please. Answer me.*

'I've told you,' she lifts her head high, 'she has some odd ideas. I've told you, she's mad.'

'What ideas?' *Precisely?*

Her gaze slides resentfully around the room, but she relents to grumble, 'Suddenly, she wants to know everything about me. So, she has begun to go over my childhood. And, of course, you came up.' She shrugs to convey nonchalance, but stiffly, unconvincingly.

She is so brittle. She is angry with Mrs Fox, not with me. But I cannot risk switching her anger onto me. So I resist the urge to delve; I decide to stick to what is important: 'Why don't you tell her that she can't stop you coming here?' Because this, surely, is all that I want, from her; all that I have ever wanted.

She snaps, 'I'm not telling her anything.' And stamps this with a furious frown.

She is still having her argument with Mrs Fox, but now I need her to have *my* argument with Mrs Fox. Because Dinah could ruin our lives. What I have left of my life. I must help Zoe to understand. We must both be prepared. 'But,' I start to reason, to plead, and suddenly I feel as if I am pleading for my life, 'she has had this her own way for too long.' *For the whole of your life.* 'She has never considered anyone else's point of view.'

'I don't need to tell her anything,' she continues, scathingly. 'Because whatever I want to do, I'll do:' and this, very angrily; and because there is no one else here, this anger is for me.

I have to turn her back to Dinah, to the problem, our problem. 'Zoe, listen, this is not some squabble about bedtimes or something, this is *important*. She *believes*, now.'

Expressionless, clueless, Zoe utters, 'Believes what?'

'Believes in you and Evie.'

Still nothing, only those wide eyes scanning mine for clues. '*What* about me and Evie?'

Which is tricky, because I have never had words for this; not proper words, solely this feeling. I have never had to use words for this with Zoe. She always seemed to have the same feeling. 'That you're back,' I try, eventually. 'That you're Evie, and you've come back.'

Suddenly Zoe's blank face breaks into a laugh. 'She wouldn't believe that,' she laughs, surprisingly kindly.

For whom is this sudden, surprising kindness? I smile automatically in response, but anxiously, because I have to tell her, 'She *does* believe it.'

'She *does not*,' she snorts, apparently very amused, flicking her gaze to the ceiling. 'My mother would never believe something like that. I'm not even sure that she ever let me believe in Father Christmas.'

I have to tell her, 'She saw Polly. Polly: my granddaughter, Ruthie's little girl. Did she tell you that she'd seen Polly with me in the street?'

Zoe says nothing. She is focused firmly on me.

So I continue, 'Polly and you . . .' But I stop. All I have to say is, 'It was so obvious, Zoe.' I am surprised by the low hum of my tone, the gentle thud of defeat in my words. 'I could see from her face that she knew.'

'Knew?' Zoe seems to have said, echoed this word without moving a muscle on her face; this word, this echo, seems to have come from somewhere else.

'She knows who you are,' I confirm, gently.

'You're mad,' she says, quite thoughtfully, rising from the chair.

'Zoe . . .' An exclamation? A plea? A reprimand? *Sit down . . . ?*

She yelps, 'So, this *isn't* madness?' Furious-eyed; flapping, throwing, one hand aimlessly into the room, perhaps towards me.

'It's the explanation,' I interrupt, fairly forcefully, 'for her behaviour.' *Try arguing with that.*

'Look,' she threatens, retreating behind the chair, leaning onto the back of it, 'I don't know what my mother has said to you, nor why, but let me tell you that she believes *nothing*. Truth is irrelevant to her. All that matters to her is to make sure that *I* don't believe. Because she wants me to have nothing of my own, no life of my own, she wants me under her control.'

I start to explain, ' But that's *because* . . .' then find that I have stopped, switched instead to urging, 'Tell her, then; tell her that you *do* believe.' Suddenly I know that it is not true that Zoe is all that I want, the mere presence of Zoe. There is more: I have wanted to *be believed.*

Zoe is focusing on me as if she is surfacing from sleep to find me at the foot of her bed. As if she does not yet know me, nor herself. Momentarily she is no one. In a matching tone of voice she manages, 'But I *don't* believe.' She is sleep-talking, her eyes wide to compensate.

'Yes you do,' I remind her.

'No I don't.' She is starting to believe herself; listening too closely to herself, leaning too heavily onto the words, tipping the tone from puzzlement to justification.

'You've always known,' I counter.

Suddenly she blazes, '*What* have I always known?'

Under her black-burning gaze, in the glare of her challenge, I shrink, fumbling for words. 'That you and Evie . . .' She *knows* that I have no words for this. Or *should* know. Crossly, I leave her with, 'You remember.'

But she simply repeats, '*What* have I always known?' And now answers for herself: 'A load of old stories.'

'Zoe . . .' *Come on* . . .

She flails back from the chair and throws her arms to her sides, mutters, 'I don't believe this.'

Bizarrely, I find myself pleading for her to, 'Ask your mother.'

'You're both mad,' she says quickly but resignedly, more to herself than to me. And immediately, before I can appeal, she says, informs me, 'I came here to apologise.' The following pause is so brief that it never happened, that it has slipped between one moment and the next and now she is finishing: 'Which I've done.' *End of story.*

She reaches the door, and I want to call to her. To tell her that I want her to come back, regardless of whatever she believes. I *want to* want her here, regardless; but, sadly, shockingly, I do not.

Zoe

·········

It is mid-afternoon but smells like late night. I decide that I cannot clear up the mess on the table until later. Francesca called us to the kitchen an hour or so ago, having made a grill-pan full of cheese on toast, stilton sprinkled with walnuts.

'This is very nice of you,' I cooed appreciatively in the doorway.

'I wouldn't do it for *him*,' she laughed, glancing behind me to Dominic. Sisterly love? I turned to see him digging his fingers crossly into his hair. Francesca finished, 'But it's nice to see *you* properly for once.'

When I had arrived, this morning, she was in the living room, kneeling in her pyjamas on the floor amid cardboard boxes of old records. 'You should *hear* some of these!' she enthused. And I did. All morning her discoveries followed us at full volume through walls and the ceiling. Often she sang along, almost as loudly, in snippets: *I can see clearly now the rain has gone*, and then a moment later, *It's gonna be a bright (bright) bright (bright) sunshiny day.* Or, *Heaven must be missing an angel.* I was particularly impressed by *I'm gonna make you love me* complete with *Oooh yes I will, yes I will.* Above the noise, in Dominic's bedroom, I asked him, 'Where do these records come from? They're too old to have been bought by Francesca or you. And I can't imagine that they belong to your parents.'

He sighed wearily and said, 'A cousin dumped them on us, years ago. They're mixed in with some old stuff of my parents'. It's all crap.'

The old stuff was classical, orchestral and some piano: when it was sweeping through the walls and ceilings it sounded to me like film music, although I did not know which films.

We came downstairs to lunch to 'My sweet Lord'. Dominic interrupted Francesca's happy humming with, 'You're too young to remember this.'

'No I'm not,' she wailed, and then sang louder as if to prove her point, although was not difficult because the singing consisted mainly of My-sweet-Lords and Hallelujahs.

'No one's too young to remember this,' I explained to Dominic. Then I told Francesca that when I was at primary school I spent playtimes on the edge of the football pitch with my best friend Jackie Moore, watching the objects of our desires (mine, for a long time, was Adam MacKenzie), singing, *Here I am, Take me in your arms, And love me*. I told her, 'We both sang *Here-I-am*, then Jackie sang *Take-me-in-your-arms*, and I sang *And-luuurve-me*.'

Francesca and I squealed with laughter, and Dominic said, 'You're kidding.'

I turned on him. 'Adam MacKenzie was *very cute*. He was a big favourite with the girls.' Sadly, he did not age well and was nothing special by the time he was thirteen.

'No,' Dominic said blankly, 'you're kidding that you used to go after the boys like that.'

'Why not? Didn't you fancy any of the girls at your school?'

Francesca hooted a laugh: 'There weren't any girls at his prep school. The choice was between the Games master and the class hamster.'

'Fuck off, Francesca,' he said calmly. 'Don't be so crude.' Then he returned to me. 'The only girls in my school were in porn mags.'

Francesca and I tutted in unison. 'Hardly the same,' she muttered, in disgust.

'No?' he sneered.

I announced loftily to Francesca, 'It's not his fault; he needs re-educating.'

'He needs re-*something*,' she managed.

Now, after lunch, Francesca is folded over the window sill,

dangling a cigarette into the garden, and gripping the phone between a hunched shoulder and dropped chin. She is still not dressed. Low grunts alternate with sudden screams of delight. The cigarette was begged from Dominic: 'Post-prandial,' she said, 'and since I did the prandial, I think it's the least you can do.' And it was she who had insisted that we have something to drink with our lunch. She had stood in the middle of the kitchen murmuring thoughtfully, 'What can we have, what can we have?' And then she had ushered me into the dining room, to the drinks' cabinet. We peered together into the dense dark glittering stalagmites until suddenly she swooped. 'I'll tell you what they never, ever drink,' she said triumphantly: 'This!'

It was cherry brandy.

'Have you ever tasted this?' I asked Dominic, enthusiastically, after my first sip.

'Disgusting,' he said. He had not taken a glass.

'It's wonderful, isn't it?' Francesca agreed. 'Like cough mixture.' She was digging spoonfuls of chocolate ripple ice-cream directly from the container. Both Dominic and I had decided against ice-cream. I did not regret the decision, but I envied her abandon.

Resentfully, Dominic asked her, 'What are you doing today?'

She slurped outrageously from the spoon, and then replied, 'Hanging around, this afternoon; having a bath. Jodie and Laura and Clara are coming over at six-ish and we'll cook up something to eat. And then Petey and some of the boys are coming this evening.'

'No,' he said.

'I'll do whatever I like,' she said breezily.

'No you won't. I've been left in charge and I say no parties.'

'It's not a party!' she managed, indignantly, through a mouthful.

He shrugged dismissively. 'I don't care what it is; I don't want it.'

'Well, screw you.'

I grinned at her.

He glowered at her. 'Look at you,' he snarled, 'you huge pig.'

She snapped the lid back onto the container, and snapped a false smile onto her face. 'Driving lesson,' she said icily, 'you can give me a driving lesson this afternoon, darling brother.'

'No,' he said.

'Yes,' she replied with the unfaltering smile. 'You're a wonderful, wonderful driver, and you can give little-ol'-me the benefit of your abundant wisdom; can't he, Zoe?'

Surprised to have to join in, I made a sound, an acquiescent sound.

'And how pleased Mumsy and Dadsy will be with their wonderful darling son!' She swept from the table to the freezer. 'So, *shift*.'

Dominic said, 'No. I'm *not* giving you a driving lesson.'

Involuntarily I made a disappointed sound, probably because I was warming to the prospect of having something to do during the afternoon. I cringed, but luckily my surprise contribution had been buried beneath Francesca's slam of the lid of the freezer.

'Why not?' she hollered.

Dominic replied, 'Because you can't drive.'

I failed to stifle a laugh.

She leaned heavily onto the table. 'So, teach me,' she said fiercely into his face.

'Not now,' he replied crossly.

'*Why not?*' she threatened slowly.

'Leave me alone. I'm not up to it.'

I tapped the bottle of cherry brandy. 'But you haven't drunk a drop of this.'

'Jesus!' Francesca said suddenly to him. 'I thought so! You've been pill-popping again, you bastard!'

I turned, horrified, to examine him. 'No,' I wailed softly to Francesca. 'He looks normal, to me.'

She switched her stare to me. 'And just maybe this *is* normal, for him, huh?'

'Proof, Fran,' he goaded. 'Don't forget proof: we all know how you hate to bother backing up your silly little opinions and suspicions. And, anyway, today I'll-do-whatever-I-please.' He was imitating her. 'Eh?' he goaded further, with an impression of her cold smile. 'In fact, I'll do whatever I please for the rest of my life now, because I'm eighteen.'

'Oh!' flared Francesca, scathingly. 'Very good! You're going to tell that to the Drugs Squad, are you?' She leaned again across the table. 'See?' she hissed at him. 'Your brain's already rotting. You are *stupid*.'

'And you're a sanctimonious bitch,' he spat back.

Sighing grandly, flamboyantly giving up on him, turning away to the phone, she said flatly, 'I don't care what you do to yourself, Dominic, but just make sure that you don't muck up *her* life.'

I nearly choked on my sip of cherry brandy. Because how could Dominic muck up my life? It was mucked up before I met him. On the contrary, he is supposed to be the *answer*.

She has left us sitting at the table, looking at the leftovers and listening to one half of her phone conversation. I have been feeling sick for a few minutes. Dominic has been reluctant to shift his attention from his cup of coffee; but now his cold white-and-gold hand creeps over mine. His gaze dips beneath mine, lifts mine to his face. 'All right?' he asks faintly.

'I feel sick,' I tell him. 'Perhaps it's all the cheese.'

'Perhaps,' he laughs.

I cannot believe that I have drunk enough to make myself feel sick. But I do not merely feel sick: I feel very light, not simply light-headed – not at all light-headed – but light-bodied. 'I might need to lie down.' I *do* need to lie down. And here, preferably.

He rises from his chair, comes around to stand behind me. 'Come on,' he whispers. And I stand, unsteadily. 'Come on,' he hushes, and I take his hand and follow him upstairs.

I wake. Dominic is asleep beside me, his breathing fuzzy on my neck. I cannot have been asleep for long, perhaps only for a few moments, because the sunshine has not moved. It is concentrated in the far corner of the room, burning the shiny flank of the huge wardrobe. I can hear, in the room below, a tinny old film, the voices as rapid and jerky as the silent images of even older films. I wonder if it is a film that I know. I listen harder, but to no avail. Which film would I want it to be? Which old films are my favourites? My brain is empty, washed through with sunlight. I have no wants. Lately I have been worryingly low on wants. A different strategy, then: which films did I see when I was little? I think that I saw *Chitty Chitty Bang Bang*, and I think that I did not like it, or not all of it: there was something scary, witches, a witch, something. The child-snatcher, perhaps: was there a child-snatcher, or was that in *Mary Poppins*? But not in *Bambi*: Bambi's mother was shot dead. No amount of happy ending would help Bambi. I was outraged that someone — Mum, presumably — took me, cheerfully, knowingly, to witness that dreadful event. At the time I felt that my life had been ruined, that there was no turning back. I also remember a film with a car called Genevieve. Was this *Chitty Chitty Bang Bang*, or something else?

Dominic stirs, beside me. I try to shift, but my limbs are startlingly heavy. I become still again and the nausea settles.

'Hello Zo-bo,' he snuffles. He is awake.

'Hello,' I reply as brightly as possible, without moving.

'You okay?' he grumbles, propping himself up, frowning sleepily down at me. He is aflame with drowsiness: the patches of his face that are usually softest and colourless — his cheeks, his eyelids — are even redder than the roots of his hair.

'Yes, okay,' I report hopefully.

'Good,' he says vaguely. 'Good, good, good.' He dips to kiss me, very lightly.

Dreamily I follow the movements of his lips on mine and the nudging tip of his tongue. Then he runs a hand around and down my body, rustling my jumper and jeans.

'I feel sick,' I tell him, without urgency, as a reminder.

'Aaaah,' he soothes sympathetically, and the hand comes to my forehead, strokes back my hair. Now holding my face with both hands, he kisses me softly and wetly. My eyes are closed and I am wonderfully warm, held very still by the weight of his body. It is strange that his frail body is so heavy. He shifts, and the mattress ripples. I hold firmly onto him. He lifts me, scoops me with one hand whilst with the other he starts to tug my jumper up my back.

'Dominic,' I grumble in protest.

He continues, methodically, patiently. I am aware that I am a dead weight. 'Dom,' I say again.

'Ssssh,' he soothes.

I manage to pull slightly and unsteadily away from him. His pink sleepiness has become burning exertion.

'Leave it,' I tell him.

'You'll feel much better,' he reasons.

Exasperated, I submit. He tugs the jumper over my head. 'Beddy-byes,' he puffs, and unclips my bra. Released, I settle gratefully back onto the bed, close my eyes and savour the tingle of cool air. The mattress rises suddenly beneath me. Briefly I open my eyes, and Dominic has left the bed, is standing at the bedside, swooping purposefully to the waistband of my jeans. He grazes his fingertips on the stiff button, muttering irritably, and then tugs and finally tips me free. Naked, I roll immediately under the duvet, hugging it as I settle on my side. I love the smell of pillowcases. Behind me, he is stripping himself of his clothes: I can hear zips and static crackle. Then the mattress throws me off balance again and chilly Dominic is stuck to my back. I snuggle further into the warm dark duvet.

'Lovely warm back,' he murmurs into the back of my neck.

'*Was*,' I grump. I settle again to listen to the silence: the stifled telly downstairs, the slow Saturday cars outside, the clock across the room on the chest of drawers.

I am drifting but he rolls me back to consciousness with several steps of his fingertips on my hip. 'Dominic, don't.' I tighten my grip on the duvet.

'Don't what?' My ear tingles with this lively roar of fake innocence. But soon the hand is on my hip again: this time, soft circular strokes of a flat palm. 'You have beautiful skin,' he murmurs. 'Softer than anything else on earth.'

I smile to myself, smile at his cliché, and draw up my knees.

'What's the matter?' he asks mildly. The stroking continues, extends, circling wider over my bottom.

'I need to sleep this off,' I reply, into the duvet.

He rises behind me, propping himself on an elbow and breathing hotly onto my shoulder. 'What?'

'Sleep.' I do not open my eyes.

His hand slips deeper. 'Don't you love me?' he laughs quietly.

His word *love* thuds into my heart. For weeks I have been waiting for this one word from him.

'You don't love me? Eh? Mmmm?' He sweeps his hand over me as he speaks, daring, tickling.

I am very surprised to find that, possibly, at this precise moment, the answer is no. 'All I feel is sick,' I remind him kindly. In fact, lying here very still, I do not feel sick, but my body is lifeless. I am toppling into sleep.

He whispers into my ear, 'Don't shut me out, Zo-bo, Zoby.'

'I'm not shutting-you-out.' Although I would if I could, for the next hour or so.

'Yes, yes, you are.' His tone is eager but even; suspiciously so.

Reluctantly I roll over onto my back, and look up at him. 'I am not shutting you out.' This was said feebly due to the effort involved in rolling over. 'What do you mean anyway, shutting-you-out?'

He replies with a kiss, blinds me with a kiss.

'Dominic?'

He ignores this, shifts heavily onto me and kisses me again. After a moment he says appreciatively, 'I am close to nobody but you, in the whole world.' His eyes fill my own.

My heart swells but unfortunately this makes me feel sick again.

'In the whole wide world, the whole, wide, world,' he is chanting softly.

I smile drowsily at him, and try to sneak back onto my side.

But his grip is stronger than I had anticipated. So I stay on my back, held more tightly. And he says, 'I mean it.' Which echoes oddly as a threat.

I am surprised to find that I am eager to reassure him: 'I know.'

'Do you?' he says emotionally. 'Do you know? Do you know that I love you?'

My eyes have been closed since the sleepy smile. Now they open to him.

'Sometimes I *really* love you,' he urges.

I am unable to breathe but perhaps this is less due to the shock of his words than to the heaviness of him on top of me.

'Let me make love to you, Zosie.'

Why do I feel so unresponsive? I wince my guilty apologies. 'Please, Dom, not now,' I manage.

But he moves on me; and the mattress moves beneath me; and I freeze. He whispers, 'Gently, just very gently.' And he dips to kiss my nipple.

'I really don't feel like it, at the moment,' I try again, trying to be stronger this time; but my voice is thinned by doubt and shame, and the words flap feebly in the air above us.

The stripped white spikes of his crown are quivering below my chin. 'Of course you do,' he cajoles warmly, murmurs to the nipple.

Of course I do. I try to feel him through my nipple, try to take the tingle of the nipple into me, and through me. But now he shifts, rises, and I hurriedly brace myself for his weight. He kisses me. I concentrate on his kiss. Dry but wet, rough and hard but sinkingly slippery. Strange. He is humming with pleasure: 'Mmmm.' This is suspicious because I cannot believe that – frozen, like this – I am giving him any pleasure at all. I concentrate harder on the kiss. Once I have a toe-hold in the kiss I slip my concentration down my body and try to feel him tingling on my skin. He is beginning to ripple on me, all over me; flecks of him all over me, so I shut my eyes. But as soon as I shut my eyes, I lose track of him and drift towards sleep. I open them again. The bits of my body which are not covered by him are cold.

'Not now,' I tell him again, surprising myself. And I am surprised, too, by my tone, taut as a plea.

'Relax,' he replies, without looking at me.

'I'm serious.' I am weary, so weary that I am swelling with tears. I want to hide inside the hot soft folds of the duvet. 'I want to sleep,' I try. 'Just sleep.'

'Afterwards,' he suggests.

My eyelids are painfully heavy. 'No, now,' I tell the room.

'Shhh,' he breathes.

'Dominic . . .' I try again, a last hope, some strange hope that saying his name will cast the spell, will compel him to listen to me.

'Shhh,' he is repeating playfully all over me.

Somehow I summon another effort. 'Don't do this.'

He looks at me. I am looking at him. Clear, clean blue eyes, and whiskery white lashes. It is impossible to be afraid of someone with such empty washy eyes and no lashes; impossible, perhaps, to feel anything. Except, perhaps – what, what is this? – a lack, a raw hole. The skin on his face is thin and colourless enough to be a substance secreted straight from the underlying bone. Now he looks away from me.

He stretches across to the bedside table, into the drawer, and takes something. I do not need to look in order to know what it is. 'Dominic . . .' I try again, hopelessly.

Lightly, he kisses my forehead. Then, ripping carefully into the little packet, he says, 'Please, Zoe,' very calmly, resignedly, slightly sorrowfully.

Please what? Please shut up? Please let me? or love me? or forgive me?

What more can I say? I attempt to move, although I do not

know why, do not know what I am going to do. But my movement makes no impression on his heavy body. I look away from
him, away from his careful preparations. The room, so familiar
to me, sinks slowly into my eyes: the dry honey peel of the pine
chest of drawers, the rusty graze in the mirror on the wardrobe
door, the ochre speckles of damp collecting in tiny waves of
wallpaper. As ever, the desktop across the room is thick with
books: always the same books, but differently sprinkled, bearing
traces of him.

Without listening, I have been hearing Francesca below me:
from time to time a twitch of the hallway, the occasional clunk
of a door closing or perhaps failing to close, bouncing back
open; earlier, some apparently tuneless humming in the kitchen,
followed a moment ago by a brusque but indistinct retort to the
voices on the television. I wish that I was watching television.
And I can do, soon. I wish that I was with Francesca. I wish that
I *was* Francesca: how is there so much life in her and so little in
me? What would she do, now, if she was in my position? She
would have plenty to say. Lately I seem to have had nothing
much to say to anyone. But it has not mattered until now. Or not
mattered so much, so urgently. I try again, one last time:
'Dominic, no.' Clear enough, surely?

He does not even look at me.

I try to move, again, but the contents of my head move more,
so much more, so I shut my eyes and freeze. And I can hear
Francesca again, sneezing. I remind myself: she is there, now,
below me, and she will be there when I go downstairs, soon. And
how difficult can this be? Dominic starts with a kiss, which is not
unpleasant, because how can a kiss be unpleasant? I think about
the kiss for a moment; and when this fails to work, I think
ahead: this should not hurt me. I have done this before, I know
what to do. Much more worrying, now, is that I hate him. How
can I so suddenly hate someone who I am supposed to love? And
how can I survive this with someone who I hate? He is moving
into position, so I close my eyes and focus fiercely inwards.

I am surprised that it does not hurt, almost pleased, surprised that I am almost pleased. Grateful, thankful. I move faintly with him because I want this to finish as quickly as possible, I do not want to be here all afternoon. Once more I look over his shoulder around the room, then shut my eyes again and wait. And wait. And now, quickly, blissfully quickly, it is over. And I can savour my first few deep still breaths. He is drifting into a doze on me. I strain beneath him and he stirs, shifts, slithers easily out of me. Briefly he lifts his bloodlit face to mine, his mouth swaying into a smile, and he kisses me softly, sloppily, saying, 'I love you.'

Caddy

....

Lying here, in bed, I keep my eyes closed, but why? If I open them, there is nothing but blackness. Nothing for them to see. So why close them, in order to sleep? Why cannot darkness, alone, suffice? Why cannot darkness, alone, bring sleep? Surely it is no effort to keep eyes open, no more than the effort required to keep a head on a pillow or an arm or leg crooked in a particular manner. And anyway, eyelids flutter, later, during deep sleep. I read in a magazine that deprivation of this fluttering sleep will lead to death. So, eyelids need to beat. Another pulse, the heart of the brain. We have to sleep. Sleep is different from rest. Rest cannot, alone, suffice. I sleep less and less, as I become older.

I could tell myself that Zoe does, or did, believe. That her behaviour is wilful denial. Yes, I think I see, in my mind's eye, her closed face: I think I can see that her face was sealed against me when she shouted and turned and left me. A face which, until then, I had always seen as plumped up with secrets. Secrets which I shared. A seal is breakable, but what use is a broken Zoe? But perhaps there is no denial, perhaps she has been careless with her memories, and forgotten who she is. Yes, perhaps she has grown away from her memories as she has grown up. So that my mistake is merely that she was moving through her life without the cloak of care and consideration, thoughtfulness and guardedness, which I thought I saw around her.

And yet I saw the look on her face. The *look*? There was no look, there was nothing on her face. All expression fled from the cold splash of disbelief. I do not know how this misunderstanding has happened, but it has. I saw that it has.

What can I do? I cannot make her see. I remember that when she was a little girl she had a book containing the well-known puzzle, the pattern which can be seen as a vase or as two faces in silhouette. For a long time she could not see the faces. And I could not help her. It was impossible to tell her how to see. But seeing the faces was not something which would simply happen to her, given time: it was something which she had to *do*. As soon as I saw the two faces in place of the vase, I knew that it was something which I had *done*. But I did not know how. I cannot tell her how to believe me. This is like love: it is impossible to tell someone to love someone else. *Like* love? This *is* love: I suppose that what I want, and have always wanted, is for her to love me. There are no steps through which I can lead her, there are no props which I can use to show her how to feel for me. There has to be a will. This has to come from her. And I have to face the possibility that it will never do so, perhaps not in my lifetime.

Zoe

....

His mother's voice chafes the stairwell: 'Dom, do you two want lunch?'

Dominic is across the room from me, standing over his swirling turntable, aiming the needle, bending lower and lower beneath the weight of his frown. Fine tuning.

Irritably, I prompt, 'Dominic . . . ?'

The needle lands, and the record screams. He relaxes, turns to me. 'But we don't, do we?' he answers, apparently reasonably, over the noise.

I glance at the door, mean to go to answer, to do the job of replying to his mother for him, but I lack the necessary energy. Instead, I stay sunk into the bed, on which I have been sitting for hours. With my eyes I take firm hold of the door and will myself, but nothing happens and it stays distant, stiff, closed. I say, 'Anyway, I'm going.' These words surprise me. They slipped out. They glisten wonderfully in the dry air between us. I am convinced by them, utterly convinced, so I am happy to brace myself for the inevitable protest. I am thrilled to be going even though I do not know *where*.

'Going?' he spits hotly, flailing a record sleeve. 'You've only just arrived.'

I had not noticed until now (*how* had I not noticed?) that he is wearing such a horrid jumper. Horrid shape, horrid material, horrid colour. Often I wear horrors for a joke; and, with jumpers, the bigger and thinner, the better. But somehow I know that Dominic is not joking. Dominic never jokes, not really. He *jokingly* jokes, but never *really* jokes. I switch my gaze to the clock: 'It's a quarter to three.'

'So?' he flashes.

'So I've been here for three hours. Or so.' Which feels like forever. How long had I intended to stay here? And why? We have been drinking coffee, several mugs; and we have been sitting here, listening to his records, and talking, barely. He has been kissing me, *wearing that jumper*. He does not seem to have washed, yet, today. Perhaps if I go, he will find time to have a bath.

'Are you coming back later?' he demands.

For what? Why should I? He sounds like Mum. I am stiff from sitting for so long in these cooling pools of cotton. The room is sunless today. I was too cold to remove my shoes. The high white shoulders of my feet are sore beneath unrelenting laces. My head hums with the thuds of doors. Downstairs the telly has been dribbling sport for hours, rattling arhythmically with the voices of commentators. 'I have some homework to do,' I mutter darkly. 'An essay on the Aswan High Dam.' I relent with a weak smile: 'Interesting, huh?'

His eyebrows spasm in response. 'Sod that,' he says.

'Yes, but if I sod it,' I explain, wearily, 'then unfortunately it is still there tomorrow.' And the next day, and the next. It seems to me that I have been looking at the title, *The Aswan High Dam*, every day for a very long time: waking to it, ignoring it throughout the day, then sleeping with it. It remains too huge to tackle. Day after day I end up examining my fingernails instead. My fingernails are more manageable. It troubles me that there is something lurking behind *The Aswan High Dam*, waiting to take its place: *Subsistence Farming In South East Asia*, perhaps. Now I turn my attention quickly to another problem: going home. No, *two* problems: travelling home, and staying home. I know that I will wait forever at the bus stop, cars dropping down the road, hot and shiny, grains of sand, quicksand. I will wait for a bus to take me back; to leave me with, leave me to, Mum. I focus on Dominic. He is leaning back on his desk, tapping his hand in time to the music, flapping one whole hand against his thigh, and nodding. 'Come out for a drink tonight,' he says.

Leave me alone. If I want a drink tonight I need go no further than the tap. Dominic means pub. And pub means small bays of black wood beneath lampshades of frilly glass. And everywhere the blank gaze of fake brass. And no escape from scummy ashtrays. And his friends, sour and sleepy. A whole evening dabbed with cold sweet liquid: small expensive amounts, tasting utterly predictable, coming sterile into endless standard glasses from those big shining bottles locked onto the wall behind the bar. The pub again. Trapped in the pub for a whole evening.

'Zoe?' he prompts.

'Actually . . .' I start, and grope for an excuse. The truth is that I do not want to have to make the effort. I will have to catch the bus, there and back, *two* buses. They-always-come-in-pairs. And *catch?* As if they are rushing towards their destinations, when in fact nothing is further from the truth. If I want to catch the bus, I will have to rush my tea. And I am sick of worrying and hurrying to fit in with other people. So I tell him, 'No.'

'But I've hardly seen you lately.'

'You saw me yesterday.' Instantly, I regret this; regret starting this.

And sure enough, he is glad of the opportunity: 'Not for very long,' he responds excitedly, indignantly. 'Remember?'

But I do not remember. I stab at the rewind button in my head but nothing happens. But why *should* I remember? Anyway, regardless of how little time I spent with him yesterday, I am not going to go to the pub tonight. I am going to do what *I* want to do, tonight. Which is not go to the pub.

'I must finish my essay,' I stress. This is the official version.

He deflates with disgust. 'You're so fucking boring.'

You're this, You're that: I hear enough of this from Mum, I do not need to hear even more from Dominic. I stand, to go.

'Don't go.' He snaps away from the desk. And his hands

216

come forward, too; but go nowhere, stay limp in front of him. 'You never want to do *anything*, these days,' he whines, pleads.

No, but especially not with you. I try to focus on his face, to ignore the horror of his jumper, the toneless turquoise V swilling around his neck. What does he ever want to do, what has he ever wanted to do? Once upon a time, pre-Dominic, I was fine, and now, post-Dominic, everything seems wrong.

'I'm tired.' There are too many people wanting too much from me. I am so weary with them. Their voices are buzzing my brain to nothing, processing my brain into soup. Which is irreversible: I cannot imagine that I will ever feel any better.

'You've been looking very drawn, lately,' he continues. This is an accusation, sharp in tone, embellished with narrow eyes.

A strange word to use, *drawn*: a grown-ups' word. For Dominic, a borrowed word. A hollow word, from him, so it fails to offend me. Rather, it intrigues me: *drawn*, in one sense not so very different from *painted*; the opposite of the true, intended, sense. But, anyway, why should I care what Dominic says? Because everything from him is an accusation. Everything from everyone, lately, is an accusation. And I do not care how I look to Dominic. This is the very least of my worries.

Jane is wearing her beret, indoors, in the late evening. She is always wearing her beret, nowadays, now-an-evenings. It came from a jumble sale. Where else could a beret come from? I have never seen or heard of anyone buying – really buying – a beret. We are sitting together on the floor, our backs propped against the seats of armchairs, listening to *Station To Station*, our recent Bowie discovery, our latest favourite. Sitting opposite, our legs outstretched; our feet meeting, almost, in the middle of the room. Also in the middle of the room is the tin of crackers, rattly with cracker-sand, next to a wooden board on which there is a wilted pat of butter and a shiny yellow block of cheese. Jane swings forward to swipe a fragment of cracker with butter. 'No Aswan High Dam, then?'

Earlier, I had told her that I should stay at home this evening to do my essay. 'No,' I confirm, 'It . . .' and I scan for the word, the precise word for precisely what the Aswan High Dam is doing to me, '. . . eludes me.' I simply cannot *think anything* of the Aswan High Dam, not even the words for its awfulness.

Jane snorts. 'They're buggers like that – dams – aren't they.'

Not that she would know, because she is not a geographer. She cannot help me with the Aswan High Dam.

I try to smile for her, but pointlessly, because she is not looking at me. She is buttering, lavishly. But I would like her to see my smile. Because I mean this smile. I appreciate her efforts to ease me into smiles. Despite the Dam. Despite everything.

Frowning over the destruction of the lump of cheese, she says, 'Everything would be fine if I could lose half a stone.'

'Really?' Which means, more precisely, *Do you REALLY want to lose half a stone?*

She looks up and mmms through a mouthful, before adding an ecstatic, 'Imagine!'

Imagine what? Imagine her, half a stone lighter? Or, imagine losing half a stone? Imagine dieting?

Beneath the beret, she darkens into a frown. 'Not that you'll ever need to diet,' she predicts scornfully, 'because you were born thin.' Her two front white teeth lower onto and snap into a cracker.

'You're not fat . . .' I start to complain.

'I'm thighsy,' she counters confidently.

'You're not thighsy.' If she is thighsy, am I? I glance down at my thighs, in their jeans, spread all over the carpet.

'And if I had a *job* . . .' She sucks the smears of butter from her fingertips.

Job? Half-stone and job? What is the connection? I am gazing at her, for clues, but her grey-painted eyelids are unfolded over her eyes, and her fingertips are slipping noisily in and out of her mouth.

'I need a *job*,' she hums beneath the slippery buttery shrieks.

Suddenly her eyes contract upwards to focus on me. 'Davey Hurrocks is going to ask about a job for me at the petrol station, did I tell you?'

'No?' At the petrol station?

'Yes. Two or three nights a week, or something.' Her gaze settles heavier on me. 'That's all right, isn't it?' She flickers doubt, waits for reassurance.

'At the petrol station?' All this is news to me. I am slow, this evening. Unease falls all over and around me. I shrug wearily, and manage, 'I'm not sure that I'd like to be stuck there all night.' In my mind's eye I see a tiny Jane – with beret – imprisoned on the roadside in glowing glass.

She is sitting very still, trying to track my thoughts. 'It's only two or three nights,' she says carefully. 'And it's a half-ten finish.'

'No – ' I dismiss the concern with her social life – 'is it *safe*?'

'You sound like a grown-up,' she says, and starts again on the cheese. 'I'm not worried about that. Surely I'll be safer locked up in there than on the streets.'

Which streets? I am unsure that the roads around here qualify as *streets*, which we can be *on*. But before I can reply, she yelps, 'Imagine the sheer joy when it's all over!'

'When what is all over?' Something, inside me, sinks. I cannot imagine anything ever being over. Everything seems to go on and on.

Gamely, she wags the cheese knife. '*The Aswan High Dam*. When *The Aswan High Dam* stops and life starts.'

'Oh. Life.' I smile feebly. I try hard to imagine, but my imagining muscle is slack. I cannot imagine Life. I cannot imagine anything any more. My head is too busy with other people's voices: Dominic's, teachers', Mum's, Dad's, Mrs Dutton's.

'Freeeedom,' she is purring, sliding the knife again into the cheese. Then she grins over her soundless nibbling and says, 'Well, it can't get any worse.'

'True.' But now the whole of me is sinking. I latch my gaze onto the floor-length red velvet curtains which replace the French windows in the evenings. And above them I see the big bright brass rings around the rail, each stuck with a fragment of the reflection of the standard lamp below, of the bulb inside the standard lamp. Each ring bearing a tiny blazing egg of the bulb. Below the rings I see the cold laval folds of material, the water-fall of red rock.

Jane says, 'What's the matter, Zo?'

I reply, 'I don't know.' And this a reflex, sheer reflex. Yet true, too: I do not know, I simply do not know. 'I can't breathe,' I marvel.

'You can't breathe?' She darts to a crouch, then freezes.

But, no, the breathing, the non-breathing, is incidental, coincidental. The non-breathing is not the matter, I do not know what the matter is. But I do know that, coincidentally, I cannot breathe. Yes, I cannot breathe.

'Christ,' says crouching frozen Jane. 'Really? You really can't breathe?'

It occurs to me that I would not like to have Jane's problem: someone, in her living room, who cannot breathe.

'You can't breathe?'

I stare at her, eyes wide open, so that she can decide. She springs, hauling me to my feet; throws one thick red curtain down the brass rail, and snaps open the door. 'Breathe,' she breathes, 'breathe,' pushing me in front of her over the doorstep into the darkness. And I do, I do as she says. And we stand, looking at each other with relief, sparkling with the black air. Inside me, the wrinkled pink sheets of my lungs are fizzing. The air inside me is bubbling, light, bright, linked, whole and broken and whole again.

'Is that better?' she is asking optimistically, urgently. 'Is that better?'

And nothing could be better. I am alive again for a moment. 'Mmmm,' I am telling her. 'Mmmm.' I am savouring the swollen night air with its high wide sprinkles of sounds. But then I look up into the black sponge of the sky.

And suddenly I am tired, tired again and even more so after all the panic. I turn limply back to the door, the warm yellow room. Jane clatters behind me, clunks shut the door. 'Do you *think* that you just *thought* that you couldn't breathe?' she asks chirpily, pleased with the distinction that she is making. She flings the curtain back over the doorway, zipping us into the room again.

'Oh Jane, I don't know.' How can I know? 'I suppose so.'

We sit gingerly on opposite armchairs.

'You've been a bit peaky lately, haven't you?' She is gaining confidence in questioning.

I nod.

Eagerly, she folds forward, forearms aligned with thighs. 'Do you think you're all right?'

'I'm just tired.' Tired of everything. I try harder: 'I feel shut in.' Utterly. By everyone.

'You're not pregnant, are you?' she asks sharply, suddenly even more forward so that she is all beret and huge loose finger-linked hands.

'No,' I answer wearily. 'Well, I don't think so.'

Her doubtful frown is sharp beneath the soft disc of black felt.

'Well, I haven't tested. But I'm not due.' I would have to wait until I am due, then wait two weeks before testing. Trying to summon the energy to reassure Jane, I can only manage another, 'I don't think so.' I am faintly surprised to realise that it is not something to which I have paid much attention, lately.

She does not relinquish me from the eye of the frown. 'You should be on the pill,' she snaps.

I shrug, lacking the energy to argue. Perhaps *Dominic* should be on the pill.

'Is everything all right with Dominic?'

She dislikes him; usually, sarcastically, calls him *Mister Mystery*. 'Yes,' I reply: everything except that I feel nothing for him. I feel nothing, I have lost my touch. I wish that Dominic would go away. But do I, really? Because if he went away, I would be on my own. Me and Them rather than Us and Them.

Jane says, vaguely, 'Boys confuse love and sex.' I glance at her, but find that she was talking to herself. Quietly she is continuing, 'If you go to bed with them, they think you're in love with them.' Thoughtfully, no, mindlessly, she is dragging the knife across the moist surface of the cheese. 'Which is the *last* mistake, *surely*, that you'd expect a *boy* to make.'

I realise that I have lost her, that she is lost in some troubles of her own. That I will lose her for good, soon, unless I am careful. I have not been a good friend to her, lately. I have not been good to anyone.

Suddenly she snaps to attention. '*Your* problem is *exams*.'

'My problem is NOT exams,' I bark before I can stop myself. Of course, I would prefer that there were no exams, but they are not the problem. By comparison, they are no more than an irritation. But what *is* the problem?

Predictably, justifiably, Jane is protesting, 'Don't shout at me, Zoe! I'm only trying to help.'

Help: the word draws tears onto the surface of my eyes. No one can help. This keen hopelessness scrabbles at the inside of my chest. The tears flop from my eyes. I manage, 'It's just that . . .' But what is the point? I have said it all a million times in my head, a million-million times, the words creaking around and around my head, old words, used words, no words of my own: *Everyone is on at me all the time, I'm fed up, shut in, closing down, I'm going nowhere, there is nowhere for me to go. Everything has gone wrong.* No, worse: nothing has ever been right.

'Oh *what* is it?' pleads Jane. 'What *is* it?' She pops a small pink rose of tissue from her sleeve, and lunges to dab at me.

'It's everything,' I wail, between the crunches of the tissue onto my skin. 'It's everything, that's all.' And Jane wipes and wordlessly oozes the sounds of denial and comfort, *No*s and *Never mind*s.

*　　　*　　　*

At my sun-licked bedroom window, with the gritty wipe of the net curtain on the back of my head, I look down on Selina. Or, more precisely, on Selina's knees: she is sitting on next door's front step and I can see her knees, raised, bony, close together like two knuckles. The knees are held tightly together by the clean elastic band of her long bare brown arms. She is so young. I must have been young once, but already this seems impossible. Opposite Selina, facing her, sitting on the lawn, there is a boy, who comes often to see her. I think that he is what Mum calls *local*, from the Crescent or one of the neighbouring roads, because I recognise him, vaguely. Mum would say that they are *courting*; adding, no doubt, that Selina is rather young for courting. Nevertheless, according to Mum, Selina would be courting. Strange, because, in a sense, all that they do, all that they ever seem to do, is sit, talking, in the garden. Why? What do they talk about? How can there be so much still to say?

I am looking down onto the top of the boy's head, I can see his warm brown hair curl around his head from the crown. The flicks of his head fail to shift the clinging sunshine, merely rearrange the yellow speckle in his hair. It is normal hair, normal boys' hair, a boys' cut from a local barber. He is young, too. He is mother-dressed, his jeans clean, his blue-and-white chequered brushed cotton shirt muzzy with washing powder. Squeaky-clean. Nothing of mine which has been clean has ever squeaked. He will be nice-looking when he is older. No, he *is* nice-looking. But young. The two of them, sitting together in the garden are so young and clean and sunny that they look like an advert.

The kitchen window is blue with evening. The kitchen is empty, cold, cleared of food, everything in cupboards, the surfaces sour with bleach solution. The cloth, fat and sloppy with chemicals, hangs over the plastic bowl in the sink, drying. Through the window I can see Selina. She is watering the garden next door. Sinking into the sunless distance she is bent like a question mark around the buzzing nozzle of the hose. I can hear the drizzle from the hose on the dry soil. It is nothing like the sound of water. But, then, I suppose that it is not the sound of water; it is the sound of the soil, dry soil, beneath the drops. I step outside through the open doorway. The deep blue air feels wet on my face, full of unfallen dew: swimming pool air, cooling, wrung through, astringent.

I wander beside the fence, trailing my hand along the top. Glancing back at the house I see Mum stuck momentarily in an unlit upstairs window, frowning down at me from the shadows like a gargoyle. No escape. But what could I possibly get up to here in the garden, her garden? There is no one else in the house: Dad is working late, and Danny left home several months ago when his job moved to Milton Keynes. I halt and tip my gaze over the fence into the darkness of next door's garden.

'Selina,' I say mildly. 'Hello.'

She turns to my voice, her long loose hair turning fractionally later and the hose merely twitching, barely faltering in its aim. She smiles, a wink of white teeth.

'Hi.'

I smile, uneasily because I am unsure that she can see. And now what do I say? Even in this rich darkness I can see that she is in love, that I have distracted her from a dream. That I have intruded. And for what? I have nothing to say.

'All right?' I ask hurriedly. Her dream-dipped face is shining without light, moony.

'Mmmm,' she replies contentedly. 'And you?'

'Mmmm,' I copy, noting that love – the appreciative gaze of someone else – has brought out her eyes and lips better than any amount of make-up could ever do.

I drift back from the fence into our garden and then onwards, backwards, into the house, slipping through the kitchen into the hallway. The hallway is half-lit from high above by the upstairs landing. Mum is upstairs, doing something, doing whatever mothers do upstairs. I look into the hallway mirror. I am shadow. Unlike Selina, I am made of darkness, not light. Will I ever fall in love again? Again? Once I thought I was, but suddenly I was not. The next time I thought I was, but I was wrong. She-loves-me-She-loves-me-not: pick away the petals until there is nothing left, or nothing which is very nice to see, nothing very much. Once, twice, I was splashed with love, lit up with love, but it dried on me, burned through me, and fell away. Something else to have gone wrong, to have left me high and dry.

From inside my bed I can hear that the morning outside is rattling with rain. Stop, start, stop, start: sometimes when I wake there is sopping silence, and sometimes, like now, the rain is back, pinging the leaves beneath my bedroom window, pitting the roof of the front porch. The seams of daylight around my curtains are the colour of putty. A rasp comes from the bottom of my bedroom door as it shaves an arc in the carpet: this, to Mum, is the equivalent of knocking. She comes through the doorway, hitching her coat onto the remaining shoulder. Actually, it is my coat, or was my coat, adopted by Mum when I moved on to another, to my current coat. It is not very nice, burgundy; it was chosen, originally, by Mum. She reaches to the back of her neck to tip her hair free from the worryingly big collar. 'I'm off,' she announces, resentfully.

Then she says, 'I gather that you're not going into school today?'

I shift feebly in the sheets. 'I don't know,' I reply weakly. I have not yet thought about this. I have been off school, claiming illness, for several days. Simply because I wanted to stay in bed. But bed is no escape. Not from Mum.

'Jane rang,' Mum presses onward.

Surprise pricks at me. 'This morning? I didn't hear.'

Mum's face flattens with scorn. 'Well, no,' she manages. Then: 'Asked how you were; I said, *Sleeping*. She said, if you do go in later today, remember to bring *King Lear*.'

No escape from Jane. From *King Lear*. From requests, orders, expectations, things to remember.

225

Mum's shallow blue eyes dribble down the bed and back again to my face.

'Going-in-today? – I told her, *Fat chance.*' Turning to the doorway, she begins to recite the itinerary of her trip into town.

'I'm taking in some dry cleaning – ' her eyelight flashes momentarily into my face, ' – I presume you've nothing for the dry cleaners? Then I'm looking in at the library, I've a book overdue, so, if you've anything to go back to the library, say now.'

I have not been to the local library since I was a child. How can Mum not know this, how can she have forgotten this?

'Then the shopping. Then swimming with Maxey, ladies' hour.'

Maxine has recently had a mastectomy and Mum is participating in efforts to restore her energy and optimism; Mum who, afterwards, at home, says, *If it happened to me, I'd die, I'd die.*

'Then a bite to eat with Maxey. Then to the travel agency, to suss out Greece. And, sometime, I must check whether those photos are ready, for Danny. And, also, there is your father's road tax.'

I nod wearily, to magic her away. My hair scratches the pillow.

'Is Dad gone?' I have no idea of the time.

She pauses, door in hand, and says, archly, 'About four hours ago.'

Then, finally, stepping backwards and drawing the door over herself, her voice becomes thin and pointed with threat: 'And I don't want anyone around here whilst I'm out.'

Nor do I, nor do I. Released into shadow, I am received back into the soft hot self-scented linen. Somewhere beyond me, the stairs boom softly with Mum's downward steps, and the hallway radiator rings with the impact of a dry umbrella. Then the front door snaps shut and the pathway cracks again and again beneath her heels until she is gone.

*　　　*　　　*

I am at the end of the Crescent: The Goldfish Bowl, as Danny used to call it — and probably still does, in deepest darkest Milton Keynes — although he knew very little about goldfish bowls, because we did not have goldfish for long. Mum said that they did not last and refused after a while to replace them. For Dad, the Crescent has always been *My Drive: I'll just park the jalopy in my drive.* Which was funny, the first million times. It is midday now, and it is no longer raining; it is nothing much at all. Drifts of cool sunshine are collecting on the pavements. I am at the end of the Crescent and I can go left or right. There was no other aim to this walk than to make me feel better, but now, at the end of the Crescent, I am stuck, because I do not know whether to go left or right. Of course, it makes no difference, in the end. There is nowhere to go, and then I will have to come back again.

Cars pass me, occasionally, rolling slowly to the cross-roads, crushing a wet glitter of tiny stones. Mrs Saunders' car was the last one, plumped up inside with a pink and blue baby-seat; the pink-and-blue baby, Timothy, gazing fatly from the window. No doubt they were going somewhere purposeful, jolly, sterilised: doctor, dentist, coffee morning. Somewhere they will go to again and again, week after week; nipping out and nipping back like the contents of a cuckoo clock. Busy but calm in their shiny red car, they are one giant road-borne smirk. Perfect, happy, with no worries. I turn back, I am going home.

Caddy

· · · · · · · · · · · · · · ·

'Caddy,' urged the telephone's voice, meaning *Listen*, 'it's Mrs Fox, Zoe's mother.'

As if the elaboration – *Zoe's mother* – was necessary. What other Mrs Fox would I know? And I knew that this was about Zoe, because why else would she ring me? So what else would I do but listen? My heart began to swell, filling my chest. I felt that whatever it was, it had already happened. Zoe had left home, or run away, or had had an accident. And now this was the news, I was a mere recipient of the news, the echo of the event. I would be left to echo with the news. It did not occur to me that it was still happening. Yet it *was* still happening. And it is still happening, now.

Mrs Fox went on irrelevantly, almost apologetically, 'I found your number in the book.'

Instinctively, I turned with the phone to the armchair where Zoe had perched on her last visit: nothing but an armchair, stubbornly an armchair, stiff upholstery, arms akimbo, empty. I blinked and when my eyes were closed, she came back to me: trim in jeans, hair short. No: short but long; short but one length. Deceptive. A bob. And very black as usual, as black as oil. I remember that she looked so like Ruthie that I spent the visit braced for Ruthie's characteristic complaint, *God, Mother*. But of course she was not Ruthie. In contrast to Ruthie, Zoe could always be relied upon to be polite. If polite is the right word, which I am beginning to doubt.

Mrs Fox continued calmly, or perhaps wearily: 'You asked me, once, to let you know if ever anything happened to Zoe, so I'm calling you from The Infirmary to tell you that she's in here.'

'In where?' I blurted dizzily. 'The Infirmary?'

'Yes . . .'

I was riding each huge shuddery contraction of my chest. 'Why? What's wrong?'

'She's fine,' she said, remotely. 'She'll be fine.'

I continued, 'What's wrong, what's happened?'

'Look,' she said, meaning *Listen* again, 'I'm on a pay phone in a corridor. 'Do you want to come here? Can you come?'

She told me to follow the signs, or ask, for ITU. So, when I arrived in the main entrance lobby, I asked at the Enquiries hatch. The lobby has been modernised. The whole hospital is, of course, bafflingly different from when Evie was a patient. A lifetime ago.

'Follow the signs,' said the woman, smiling kindly through the hatch, flapping one hand towards a stack of signs on a distant wall. 'There's a lift,' she added reassuringly.

I was scanning the signs, all long words. 'Where? Which sign?' The lettering on the signs was rather old-fashioned, very round, calm.

'There.' She leaned heavily onto the counter, craned towards the signs, repeated the wave.

But there was no *ITU*. 'Where?'

'*There*. The top one.'

The top one announced *Intensive Therapy Unit*. Intensive, Therapy, Unit. I bubbled briefly with anger for Mrs Fox, because why had she not *said*? And then I began to wonder: *Therapy?*

Leaving the lobby for a corridor, I was hit by the heat. I paused in front of a display of plaques to remove my coat: ten or so old plaques, most of the inscriptions starting *This cot was endowed in perpetuity by* . . . All of them were dated from the thirties. A decade after Evie. Some gave details of the sums which had been raised, five hundred pounds in one case, and more than a thousand in another. Some cited individuals; some, organisations. One plaque announced *The Mayoral Cot*. When I reached the Intensive Therapy Unit, at the end of the corridor, the door was shut. It was unlike the doors to other wards, it was solid, with a doorbell. On the notice under *Ring Bell* it was written in red ink that *Admission is restricted to two visitors per bed, next of kin only, no children.* What type of therapy requires such secrecy? I rang the bell and a nurse opened the door. I told her that I had come for Mrs Fox, and she asked me to sit in the waiting area round the corner.

So here I am, standing behind a screen, avoiding sitting in one of the low plastic chairs. In the middle of the semi-circle of chairs is a low table holding a couple of magazines and a box of tissues. Very thoughtful. Pinned to the screen are two pictures, paintings, of landscapes. A moment ago I heard the door open and close and then saw a woman walking away down the corridor in a surgeon's baggy disinfectant-blue trouser suit with all her hair tucked into a matching shower cap: I know from television that this is the uniform of a surgeon. Now the door opens again, and Mrs Fox peeks around the corner. She is startlingly grey – hair, skin, eyes and shadows beneath them – except for the red slash of hospital heat across her face. She looks oddly at home, rubbed clean of make-up, the cuffs of her grey-white blouse slung around her elbows. She smiles to greet me, and I leave the screens. Following her through the doorway, I glance beyond the nurses' station – their walls stuck with papers, the long counter littered with boxes stuck with notices, Don't-put-this-or-that-in-here – and I see the beds. And I re-member: *Intensive.*

There are four beds. No, *bed* is the wrong word for a complex trolley on wheels, layers of trolley and layers of little wheels parked alongside a stack of machinery of switches and dials, in front of a dull silvery panel of plugs, beneath a bright buzzing television screen. I know about these beds, I have seen these, too, on television. I know where I am, but on television it is always Intensive *Care* Unit. There is no therapy here. Nothing but green threads of life strung on the bright black screens, jumpy, jump-started. In the beds, no one is moving. The unit is shockingly airless. The huge wall of glass is dulled, tinted, the sky even more grey than in real life. In the distance the four beds, two-by-two, are very close together, with a trolley in the middle. The little square is busy with nurses, hatless, dressed in white. I follow Mrs Fox. There is no room to breathe. I see the small pool of black oil on the pillows of one of the beds: Zoe. There is a tube in her mouth, and a bag of clear liquid shining high beside her.

I hiss to Mrs Fox, 'You *said* she was *all right*.'

She is affronted, turns her tin-foil eyes on me. 'She *is* all right.' She stops in front of me on the tiles, and folds her arms.

'They're life support machines, aren't they?' I demand quietly. 'Is she on a life support machine, is she *dead*?'

'Actually,' she says calmly, superior, 'they call them ventilators. And, yes, she is on one of them, and no, she isn't dead.'

How, why, is Mrs Fox so calm? Has she been given something? Is she drugged?

I have to tell her, to warn her, to force my way through to her. My words flicker in my breath and into my throat and eyes. Mrs Fox has left Zoe's bed unanchored. How can she stand here like this, sweetly dishevelled, homely, stuck on this expanse of cold clean tiles? As if there is all the time in the world, when over there her daughter is drifting away from her.

'She's dying,' I breathe. 'Really, truly, she's dying.'

'She's not dying,' Mrs Fox is whispering in reply, arms folded, firm-mouthed.

'But without the machine?' I urge. I cannot look again. The machine is not forever. It has plugs. It has other patients waiting. I want to grab Mrs Fox's thin cotton-covered shoulders and shake some life into her and out of her through the smothered and smothering air of this Unit.

Instead, *she* reaches for *me*, clamps her hands onto the tops of my arms, holds me very firmly. 'Caddy, Caddy, listen to me, listen to me, *look* at me.'

And I do. I look into her eyes: *Look at me* means *Look into my eyes*. Rather than watching the slipping of cotton around and around the summit of her shoulder, as I have been doing in my panic, or noting the comma in the skin at the corner of her mouth. From a distance, even the smallest distance, Mrs Fox's eyes would seem to be anything but hypnotic; but now, I cannot look away. They are the colour of a mirror. How can a mirror have a colour of its own if it is nothing but reflection? Yet it is true, everyone knows that mirrors are silvery.

I look into her eyes and she whispers, 'She's *not* going to die, she *is not* going to *die*.'

It occurs to me that she will regret asking me to come here, and will send me away. So, holding her gaze obediently with my own, I swallow deeply, and still myself. I must show her that I can behave responsibly. Not that I am responsible for anything, anyone, here. Except myself. So I calm myself down and immediately she is reassured, because she relinquishes her grip and turns, and turns me with her. We are going to go to the bedside.

'What happened?' I ask, in a careful whisper. 'Has she had an accident?'

Mrs Fox flicks a glance over her rustling shoulder and says, dryly, 'I wish,' but now falters, slows, turns. 'Overdose,' she explains.

If *Overdose* is any explanation at all.

'*Overdose*?' I hiss. *Zoe?* 'Why?'

She shrugs sulkily and mutters, 'When have I ever known the first thing about Zoe? You're more likely to know.'

She strikes a forefinger softly and soundlessly on her suddenly swollen lips—a silent *Sshhh*—because we have reached the bedside.

Zoe's closed eyes are two huge pearls. The sole clue to the darkness at the cores is the soft black wing on each lid. Her strange short-long hair is simply short now, around her face, on the pillow, because it is denied its slick swing. The small plastic mouthpiece to the tube is baby blue. Mrs Fox is frowning intently down on Zoe, although presumably she has seen her face, and nothing but her face, for some considerable time. She seems to be thinking; but thinking what? The mirrory sheen of her eyes knocks my own gaze away, and I look back down again on Zoe.

I reach very gently towards the tube, stop short.

'This thing..?'

'She can't breathe on her own,' Mrs Fox confirms flatly.

To what is the tube connected? It disappears behind the bed, behind the stack of switches and dials. I listen: close to us, beneath the nurses' distant radio, I hear the regular sharp sighs of the machine, surprisingly unobtrusive.

'Will she ever breathe on her own?'

'Yes, when she wakes.'

I look up, nudge Mrs Fox's eyes to my own.

'And she will wake?' I ask gently; with more gentleness, even, than the gentleness which comes with a whisper.

'Yes,' she replies, matter-of-fact. 'It was sleeping pills, she took sleeping pills.'

Zoe's machinery reminds me of the black and white films about spaceships which are sometimes on television: not modern; an old-fashioned idea of modern. These machines were not here when Evie was here, yet already they seem antiquated. I glance around the other beds. Each one is a mess of plugs, mostly unplugged. I see now that one of them is empty, pinned with a note, *Brakes broken*.

I return to Zoe, flutter my fingers at the edge of her bed. Wires and tubes are held with dull white tape onto her forearm. Her forefinger is held inside a long steel clip which trails another wire. Beside me, placed on top of the machine of switches and dials, is something the size of a clock-radio, but with a black screen on which green building blocks shuffle from one pile to another. Next to the green columns is a green number, sometimes changing: 94, 95. I peer at the big square screen above the bed. It has several different sections, with different colours, red as well as green.

Mrs Fox says confidently, 'Everything that they want to know about Zoe is on these screens.'

I turn momentarily to the other two occupied beds, to their screens: one is blank, the other is less busy than Zoe's screen. But what does this mean for Zoe? Good or bad? I return my attention to Zoe.

'Can she hear?' I sub-whisper, below the sighs of the ventilator.

Mrs Fox shrugs, wide-eyed.

'Well, I suppose she could do with hearing a few things.'

Mrs Fox's eyes spark on my own.

'No,' I mumble, 'I didn't mean . . . I didn't mean anything.' I meant *voices*, simply voices, she could do with hearing voices.

'And when she wakes,' I start again, but whispering more than ever, 'Will she be all right?' I mean *brain damage,* I want to ask about brain damage. Because surely these machines mean brain damage. In the corner of my eye, Zoe is shining, spectacularly undamaged: clean skin, marked only by two tiny tracks of dark moss on her brow above her cleanly shut eyes.

'Yes, she'll wake fine.' Mrs Fox is looking woozily down on Zoe. 'Because they were sleeping pills, which don't kill and don't poison.' The balls of tin foil shudder in their sockets. 'They make sure of that,' she says darkly. 'Stands to reason.'

Now she explains crisply, 'If she had stopped breathing before she had been found, then there would have been a risk of brain damage.'

Stands to reason. So I nod.

'Lack of oxygen,' she explains unnecessarily.

And I keep nodding.

She glances back over Zoe, and swipes at Zoe's dense forelock.

'The problem is simply that the pills are slowing her down and down, and they have slowed her breathing down until it has stopped.' She folds her arms, slings them to each other. 'She can't breathe for herself, so the machine has taken over. But the pills will wear off and she'll start to wake.' She heaves the folded arms into her shrug. 'Things-can-only-get-better. Unlike for some of the other poor buggers in here, believe me.'

I do, I do.

And now I notice the bag of blood, crimson satin, strung low on the side of one of the other beds. The sleek red tube rising from it to nestle beneath the soft white blanket. I glance to the neighbouring bed: in place of the red bag, there is a yellow one. Musty yellow. The old woman in the yellow-bag-bed has no tube in her mouth but she is wearing nose clips. Her eyes are opening and closing, and she is shifting to and fro on the pillows. On the broad window sill alongside her bed there are lots of pink cards and two bouquets of flowers. Zoe's bed has no window sill. Nowhere for cards and flowers? Suddenly Mrs Fox sighs more noisily than the ventilator.

'But for now she is down there at the bottom, and we are waiting.' When she says *We*, I know somehow from the tone that she means us, and I begin to breathe easier, because she wants me here, if only for now.

After a moment I venture, 'Someone found her?'

Mrs Fox's gaze comes slow, sticky-slow, from Zoe to me. 'Her friend, Jane,' she says blankly.

I prompt: 'Found her?'

'Oh I don't know,' she says dismissively, 'I don't know the whole story.' But because I do not speak or nod or look away, she adds reluctantly, 'It seems that Jane came around during the day, I don't know why, she said she wanted to borrow a book, I don't know if that's true . . .' she shrugs with her mouth. 'I was out all day,' she adds, more wearily.

'And?' I try gently.

She indicates a chair. 'And, it seems that Zoe was able to tell Jane what she had done.'

Gratefully, I slide the chair across the tiles towards me. Mrs Fox continues, 'And Jane rang for an ambulance.' As I sit, she frowns at me, yet not at me: through me? 'I've never rung for an ambulance,' she ponders. 'Blue lights, apparently. Like a film.'

I nod towards Zoe, and the tube. 'How long will we be waiting?' And, 'Don't you want a chair?'

She shakes off the latter question, instantly, but ponders the former: her chin in a shrug, crinkled up and draped with her mouth. My mother would have warned, *If the wind changes . . .* It has never occurred to me until now that Mrs Fox, with her small surface-watery eyes, has an expressive face.

She is telling me, 'It's important to get her off the machine as soon as possible, wean her off, the doctor said.'

'Did he?'

Focus swills into her eyes. '*She*. It's a *she*,' another, apologetic, correction, '*she's* a she.'

And, underneath, the hum of my own apologies: *Yes, Of course, How silly.*

'She's an anaesthetist,' Mrs Fox is saying now.

'Anaesthetist? Aren't they pain?'

The focus, in return, is needle-sharp, needle-bright. 'Consciousness.'

Consciousness? 'Oh,' I bellow knowingly over the muddle which is puffing and falling inside me: air, pain, brain, machine, sleep. I know about *un*consciousness. *Unconsciously*: we are so conscious that we do not know our own minds. And we are *knocked unconscious*: but why not knocked conscious? (Knock, knock, who's there?) Was Evie unconscious when she died? Or just dying? Is there any difference between unconsciousness and sleep? I suppose the doctors have the answers. Zoe's doctor: I suppose *she* knows.

I say, 'Why did she do this?' A whisper of despair rather than a question, but I cringe in case it is taken wrongly, as an accusation.

But in reply, Mrs Fox stirs an eyelid over one weary eye. 'I don't know. The friend says she was depressed.'

'Well, yes, she would have to have been depressed to do this to herself.'

'Not necessarily,' says Mrs Fox, archly. 'It could have been an accident.'

'Where did she get the pills?'

'From my bedside table.' Immediately she flares, 'She's not a toddler, I didn't expect to have to keep them under lock and key.'

A male nurse – there are several male nurses here – passes us to go to the old woman. He is wearing gauzy white gloves rolled very low on his wrists.

I whisper to Mrs Fox, 'What if there's a power cut?'

She says, 'They have a generator. I've already asked.'

'A generator,' I echo, wondering where, and what like, and how often is it used?

'And, anyway,' she explains, 'They can do it themselves.'

'Do it themselves?'

'By hand.' She brings her hands demurely together and mimes a series of squeezes. Then she says softly, quickly, conclusively, 'Don't worry about power cuts.'

Meaning, I suspect, that power cuts should be the least of our worries.

I am grabbing the other questions which have been just below the surface since I arrived: 'How long have you been here? Where's her father?'

'Since yesterday evening. And I sent him home.'

I look at Zoe: tethered, afloat, stable; not breathing yet breathing. Being breathed?

'I didn't *want* to go home,' Mrs Fox replies, having read my mind. A small sigh drops from her. 'Quite honestly, I reckoned that I'd have more rest if I stayed here. My husband was quite emotional' – a direct, low, heavy glance at me – 'and I could see that there would be no rest for me at home: *my* pills . . . *my* daughter . . .' She stops abruptly, shrugs rigidly. 'He threatened to hit the doctor. Over something or other.' A flick of the fair, feathery eyebrows. Men are so emotional. They're a liability.'

'And he agreed to go?'

'Had to. I'd rung Danny and he was coming home, borrowing a friend's car and driving home, and I wanted someone to be there for him.'

'So, has Danny been here?' I ask her.

'Yes, yesterday evening, and this morning.' Swiftly she nips a fingernail with her teeth. Then, 'They're close, you know.'

Momentarily I do not understand: they're close to *what? who* is close to what? Sounds like a clue: *Getting closer . . . WARM.* Then I realise: Danny and Zoe, brother and sister, close to each other. 'Oh, yes, I know.'

She says, 'I wish he were still living at home.' Her words are so sudden, tumbling so easily, that I am slow to start picking back through them. I am stunned by the sting of misery and hopelessness. She is continuing, 'What will I do with her, when she wakes, when she comes home?' Her eyes are slippery with dread: to Zoe, over Zoe, to me, to Zoe.

I open my mouth, simply to stop her.

She says, 'I'll *kill* her.'

'No . . .'

'How could she *do* this to me?' the whisper whoops; then dives: 'Just wait until I get my hands on her.' And she scans the bed.

'She didn't do it to you, she did it to herself.'

'What am I going to do?' Suddenly she is facing me again, and this time her eyes are wide open to receive my advice. She is listening to me, listening for me. No longer scared of me.

But I have no answer. What can I say? *Be-nice-to-her?* Sharp little Mrs Fox being suddenly *nice* to Zoe would be horribly false, unconvincing, unappreciated. But, *Carry-on-as-if-nothing-has-happened?* Impossible. Worse, a betrayal. Because something *has* happened, and Zoe *made* it happen. There is nothing much that Mrs Fox can do. Nor me. Neither of us will make much difference to Zoe. She has moved on from us; and when she comes round, she will have moved on further. And we should not hold her back. We should allow her to grow up.

Mrs Fox tries, 'Perhaps you can talk to her.' But she knows, she knows *not*: there is no trace of hope in her wide-open face. It is not hope, in her face; so wide awake in this chamber of sleep. It is sympathy, or something like sympathy. *Sympathy* is the word which is closest. Sympathy without pity, *proper* sympathy. She said, *Perhaps you can talk to her.* But what she meant was, *We're in this together.*

Utterly weary, she shuffles past me to fetch herself a chair. Settling, she pivots her elbows on one knee, which is thrown over the other, swinging, and then slots her chin down into her hands. She is all tough young stem and blown buds.

'Do you have any other family who can come and sit with you?' I ask.

'I have a mother and a sister,' she muses.

'Will they come?'

She stares at me, but her brow pushes down her eyelids over her eyes. 'No. And I couldn't stand it if they were here.'

'You asked them not to come?'

'I haven't told them.' She snaps with a sigh: 'They don't need to know. We don't get along. They'd make me feel bad, awful, worse.' She switches away from me to Zoe. After a moment or two she slides her eyes back to me. '*Actually*,' she adds, the spice of a smile in the word, 'my sister is a nurse.'

I am careful to respond in kind, to match the tone. 'Don't tell me: you can do without her expert advice, at a time like this.'

Inside her cupped hands, she smiles with her eyes. 'And that's exactly what it would be: expert advice.' A wrinkle of her nose. 'And, yes, I can do without it, there's no shortage around here.' She slides her head forward, down into her hands, lifts her long grassy yellow hair in her fingers. 'She trained late,' she says, 'Brought up her children very efficiently – no overdoses, of course – and then trained as a nurse.' She releases her head from her hands. 'You'd think she'd trained as a doctor, if you heard my mother's version.' She rolls her eyes away from mine: '*Antonia-this-Antonia-that.*'

After a moment, she says, 'None of it was for the sake of the health and happiness of the patients, I'm sure. She trained as a nurse so that she could spend her days towering over their beds and looking down her nose at them.' She reflects on this with a smirk. 'She's tall, my sister. Unlike me. She was – is – four years older than me, so she was four years taller, but I never caught up, we never evened out.' She sighs and straightens in

239

her chair. 'Even Antonia's *nostrils* are tall. Do you know what I mean?'

I nod. And smile. Because I do.

She swings a light lazy glance in my direction. 'I spent a lot of time on the end of that nose, on the end of that look-down-the-nose, believe me.'

She ponders, 'I used to think that our differences were due to the four years, the big age gap between us. But it's not true, is it? Because she could have doted on me and I could have looked up to her.' Suddenly she asks, 'Did you have brothers and sisters?'

'Yes.'

'We never liked each other,' Mrs Fox seems to be thinking aloud, 'not even for one moment, not even for one long-ago moment of conspiracy upstairs together in our bedrooms.' Her eyes, glossed with wonder, slide across mine. 'We never had any such moments.' Sharpening, she says firmly, 'I did always want Danny and Zoe to get along.'

'And they do.' With my eyes, I stroke Zoe's flinchless face beneath, around, the tubing.

Mrs Fox follows my eyes, rests her own on Zoe. Rests each of her own breaths on those of Zoe. 'Yes,' she sighs.

Then she says, 'I always felt that there was some of my sister in Zoe, you know.'

'Oh, no,' I reassure, but nervously: because what is she trying to say?

She wipes the frown from her forehead into her hair with the sweep of a hand. 'I suppose it's simply that they were both good at school,' she admits, 'both success stories. Antonia went to a Grammar. I didn't. I lay eyes on an exam paper and it's all over.' Her taut face splits into a rueful smile.

'I'm the same,' I am telling her. 'Hopeless. But my older sister, Connie, won a scholarship to secondary school. Hardly anyone went on to secondary school, in those days.' I shrug. 'But, anyway, my mother had Connie all cut out for service, she had been saving for Connie's uniform for years.'

Mrs Fox glimmers with interest. 'Did your sister want the scholarship?'

'She did very well in service,' I explain. 'For years and years: Lady's Maid, which was the best; wonderful family, wonderful house, houses. In London and then in the country, until well after the war. We went on visits, sometimes. She always came home on her day off each month, full of stories. In the early days, I remember, she was given Sunday afternoons off because the lady thought that she was going to church, but she was sneaking out for a few hours.' And now it occurs to me: 'Goodness, she can't have been older than Zoe.' I look at Zoe, *so young*, I have forgotten how *young*. And Connie, a *big* sister? I never knew how young, until now.

'But did she want the scholarship?'

'She wanted it *at the time*, yes,' I allow, reluctantly. 'Or, she *thought* she did.'

'And your mother didn't let her go?' Slightly squeaky, creaky, with incredulity.

I try to explain, 'School would have been no use to Connie.'

Mrs Fox says simply, 'How awful.'

I am carefully choosing my reply when she continues, 'My mother made sure that my sister had everything. Even violin lessons. I suppose the lodgers paid.'

'The lodgers paid for the lessons?'

She grins, and clarifies, '*Having* lodgers paid for the luxuries.'

'You didn't play the violin?'

'Oh *no*,' but instantly she is lighter again: 'I fancied the flute. I was terribly impressed when I first saw one, I could hardly believe that it existed, it was so different from all those other instruments. All silvery and sideways.'

'But you didn't . . . ?'

'Oh, no. Which was probably right. I would probably never have practised.'

After a moment, she concludes quietly, to the floor tiles, 'Antonia always made me feel small; my mother, too: together they made me feel that I made everything go wrong, just by being born.' But when she lifts her eyes to mine, she is smiling. Only for me, though. Smiling politely, self-consciously, for me. 'If you can believe that,' she says.

I reply with a nervous half-laugh. 'Oh, I can. Lots of people have made everything wrong just by being born.' But, more seriously, I tell her, 'It doesn't matter. In the end, it doesn't matter.'

She mutters cynically, 'Well, perhaps I'm not at the end.'

I try again. 'It doesn't matter, *ever*.' And before I realise what I am doing, I am telling her, not without sympathy, 'Everyone makes you feel small.' Which is strange because this is exactly her own effect on everyone, to make everyone else feel small. Even me, I realise, now; even me, until now. Even when it is quite unnecessary, even when it was Zoe, when Zoe was tiny.

'Yes, I suppose so,' she concedes, resting her gaze on Zoe. Is the faintness of her voice due to weariness, or disbelief?

'But nobody can really *make* you feel anything,' I suggest. '*You* do the feeling.'

Turned slightly from me, she shrugs this off, grumbles, 'But I believed what I was told.'

I cannot resist, 'That's not like you.'

Switching back to me, she smiles; I know that she smiles, even though, on her face, nothing moves.

'Do you want a drink?' she enquires, briskly. 'Something to eat?'

'No. Thank you. What I'd like is to sit here for a while.'

She stands. 'Okay.'

Dinah
··············

I did not know that Danny was here until the touch of fingertips on my shoulder, something between a tap and a squeeze which turned me around in my chair. It was not surprise which turned me, I was not surprised to be touched; everyone, here, touches me. They are in the business of touching; it is what they do for a living. I have been watching their gloved hands; the gloves rolled so low and tight on their wrists that the hands seem severed. Minimally gloved: a mere observance of protocol, a mere lip-service paid to precaution. My bleary eyes have followed the time-lapse trails which the white hands unwind around the ward. Working on bedridden bodies as if they are bed linen, turning people as if folding sheets: brisk, sometimes apparently slapdash, but I have watched for so long that I can see through the blur of gloved sterile actions to the precision and care, the reverence.

At the touch of the fingertips on my shoulder, I turned in my chair to find Danny. Come from nowhere. Crept up on me. He smiled, once, not a real smile, a stand-in for a smile, a wordless greeting. He was susceptible, like most new visitors, to hospital hush. Or, he was too tired to speak. And of course he was tired: a day at work and then the journey home, the visit here to the hospital and then home with his father, and now back again. Looking up into his face, I was struck by his tiredness; struck that he is old enough, now, for shadow to clot in the hollows beneath his eyes. *So, you, too, Danny; you, too, are not so young any more.*

Unlike most visitors, he has not looked over me to Zoe. Not this time. The smile was brief, but his eyes have not unhooked from mine. He has drawn up a chair, and now he sits down. His gaze pulls on me. Unasked questions. I stop myself saying, replying, *I thought I'd sent you home.* Because I did not send him home; I sent Derek home. And with him, I sent Danny. I had to send someone with him. Has Derek sent him back? He sits forward in his chair: bent forward, braced, over widely parted knees; his forearms taking his weight, his elbows splayed to form some type of triangle of arms, one of those strong shapes which are somehow stronger than the sum of their parts. He is attentive; he wants me to talk to him, to confide, to unburden myself to him.

Instead, I state the obvious: 'She's not awake, yet.' My breath is slow and hot in these words, my footholds from sleep. Until now, I did not know that I was sleepy. An open-eyed sleepiness to match this work-a-day, work-a-night ward. 'And she won't be, for a long time.' *So, go home; do yourself a favour and go home.*

'I know,' he says, with another approximation of a smile; the shape of a smile, but rueful. 'I haven't come to see her, I've come to see you.'

There is nothing to see. Nothing to see from Zoe, and nothing to see from me.

But he looks down intently onto, into, Zoe's face; into, onto, her closed eyes. I see that he does not look at the mouthpiece; he sees around, or through, the transparent blue mouthpiece. After a few moments he looks up and around the ward, the beds, the patients on display. Intensive care requires extensive vigilance, so we cannot avoid seeing whatever the staff need to see, although, of course, it means nothing, or little, or less, to us. Or means something different. Without tracking Danny's eyes, I know where they are going and I know what he feels when he sees. Likewise, the staff cannot avoid seeing us. Two different types of battle being fought in the same small space, and sometimes we are caught in each other's crossfire. Space? There is no space in here. Danny looks down again, but this time unfocused, vaguely, onto his shoes. He is settling in.

So I say, 'You can't stay here.' Other words come to mind: *This is no place for a child*. Which is absurd, because he is not a child. Or is he? He is my child. Still. Forever. No, this is no place for a mother. How have I ended up in Intensive Care with my children, waiting for one of them to live? This should not be happening to Zoe or to me; I cannot allow it to happen to Danny too.

He looks up and asks me, 'Do you want anything? I mean, a cup of tea or something?'

'Do *you*? There's a machine in the corridor, and I have some change.'

'No, thanks. But do *you*?'

'I've just had something.' When Caddy Dutton was here, I went for a cup of coffee and a sandwich. The staff buzz with caffeine. They drug the patients to prevent resistance to the piping of air down their throats. Not Zoe, though, of course, because she drugged herself.

He continues hopefully: 'A Twix or something?'

'There's a kiosk downstairs in the entrance hall; and if they don't have what you want, there's a newsagent across the road.'

'I'm *asking you*.'

Me? I am his mother: *I* should be feeding *him*. And a *Twix*? I smile, tickled by his regard for my sweet tooth and his assumption that my habits are no different from those of his sugar-happy friends. I shake my head and take this opportunity to check with him, 'Have you eaten?' He knows that I mean *a meal*.

A weary *Mmmm*, less strenuous than a clear *yes* or a nod of his head.

'You and your Dad?'

The same reply.

So, 'What?'

His eyes spring to mine, an echo: *What?*

'What did you eat?'

He stiffens, says, 'Is it important?' A rhetorical question, with a bolt-on answer: 'Surely it's not important, Mum.' *At a time like this.*

Which is where he is wrong. Because it is particularly important. At a time like this, everything is important. *So, let me ask.*

'Mum,' he is complaining, countering with a whine of embarrassment although there is no one near to hear us, 'I'm quite capable of feeding myself.'

'Okay,' I allow, 'so, what did you have?' *Just talk to me.* Because, if nothing else, I am hungry, in this wipe-clean ward, for detail. Detail makes the world go round.

Still sulking, it seems for a moment that he will not answer. But now, reluctantly, he grumbles, 'A take-away, Chinese.' Despite no comment from me, he counters, '*Well?* We didn't feel like cooking.' Because he thinks that I do not regard a take-away as a proper meal. Now he mutters more honestly, 'Or maybe we didn't feel like washing up.'

Ah, yes, the washing up, tell me about it. But I ask him, 'Was it nice?'

His eyes start to shine from their tarnished silver shadows. '*Was it nice?*' This echo is unsure, slightly whispery with wonder, before his surprise sinks into a shy smile. 'Yes, it was, thanks. Very.' Hastily, he checks, 'Are you sure you don't want anything?'

I turn away from him, hide myself, because, *what a question.* But what *do* I want? I want everything to be all right, to slip back into place, to return to how it was. *No.* What I want is for my whole life to have been different.

'I'm sure,' I tell him.

I shut my eyes for a moment, perhaps for longer than a moment, or for a long moment, because I hear the rustle of his breath before he speaks: a breath taken to stir the silence, to test the water, break the ice.

He asks, 'Where have you been, Mum?'

I whirl around to him in surprise. 'Nowhere,' I protest. 'The furthest I've been is to the door for my sandwich.'

The corners of his mouth wilt. 'That's not what I mean,' he says, but refrains from saying more; which is a way of insisting, however gently, that I know what he means.

I did not know, but now, suddenly, I do. He means, *lately, generally*. I did not know that I had been anywhere, but suddenly I do know. And, immediately, I prickle to have been discovered. Uncovered. Cornered. But only partially, because he does not know everything. It is worse than he knows. He knows that I have been gone, but he does not know where.

And where I have been is nowhere. How is it possible to have been nowhere, to have disappeared, without realising? Is this how it is to die, to have died? Except that if I had died, I would never have known. And I do know. Now I realise that, lately, I have been dragged around by my thoughts. That there has been nothing more to me than this: the thoughts and the dragging. *Thoughts?* Contents of my head: flimsy, wild and windy. Whatever they are, or are not, there has been no rest from them. Sleep has been no rest. Often, lately, I have woken with aches, my muscles imprinted with strain. But how do I answer Danny? Turning back to him from the black window, my heart shivers: *Look at you*; poor Danny, he expects me to tell him the truth. Given the chance. In his eyes there is a faint squint of apology because he thinks that, lately, he has not given me this chance; that my silence is his fault, that he has been preoccupied with the split from Claire, with the job, the move away from home. A squint of faint apology: *I am being as gentle as possible*. I can see that, for him, it was difficult to ask the question, physically difficult to find and force the moment, to say the words. But now it is asked and, apart from this puckering of the lights in his eyes, he is ready for my answer. For him, my answer is the easy part.

But I do not have an answer. I have been nowhere. I can tell him nothing. I have not been thinking about what I have been doing. I have not been thinking what I have been *thinking*. My thoughts have been nothing to do with me, running on without me. If I told anyone about Zoe and Mrs Dutton, whoever would understand? Not even Zoe understood. Especially not Zoe, hit full-force. Poor Zoe.

'You've been hard on Dad,' Danny suggests.

I turn from Zoe's whacked out face to Danny's sharp tenter-hooks. What does *Derek* have to do with this? Derek, worlds away. At home. Where I have always been. All my life. Always will be. Except now. For once. Yes, I have been hard on Derek, I know that I have been hard on him: Danny is right. But how right is he? Does he mean *recently*, or *for a long time*, or *always*?

I suppose there is a sense in which this started with Derek. Certainly it will finish with him: Derek, at home with me when these two have gone. They will go out into the world, and he will retire home. As ever, I will be there, I will see them come and go. How did I end up there? Or even start out there? I never chose to stay at home, I never *chose*. But, I suppose, Derek never chose any of this either. And Danny, and Zoe? None of us has ever chosen much at all. Perhaps there has never been much to choose. I watch Danny's gaze fidget wearily around the main desk, around a group of laughing nurses. I suspect that he has taken my silence as, *Yes, I have been hard on your Dad*. Which is fine. Because it is true. But I could tell him so much more. And, yes, I *could tell him*: he is young, but he is tough. He is young-tough, elastic: there is give in him. And, anyway, he is not so much younger than me, any more. There is nothing which he would not understand. But if I told, I would be telling him my life story; which, although it is part of his past, is not part of his future. Not really. My life story is for me to solve. Eventually I must go home and face Derek: not necessarily simultaneously, but eventually home, eventually to face him. I do not know what I will say to him; but whatever, I know that I will say it to him, not to Danny.

Derek and Danny: for two people who are so strikingly similar, they are very different. No, they are not different, it is me who is different, I behave differently to them. For me, there is less history to Danny: there have been fewer differences between us, so I am kinder to him. Although history is supposed to be something to share: *We have been through so much together*.

Danny slams a hand through his hair. 'Come home,' he mutters, his fuse frazzling in this heat.

Momentarily I am mildly curious: come home *for him*, or *for Derek*, or for my own sake? Are these his own words, or have they been sent via him from Derek? But in any case, I smile my apology.

He whirls with incredulity, his gaze wiping over Zoe as he whines, 'But nothing will happen.' *To Zoe, tonight.*

So I remain smiling, amused by the implication that we are running on normal time, here; that everything, including patients' recovery, will stop for the night. In fact, this is true of Zoe: I have been told that nothing will happen for a while. 'I know,' I concede, but steeped in unease. Because how do I explain?

'And, anyway, what can you do, by being here?' he soothes, flopping forward again to engage me.

All I know is that, 'I have to be here for her when she wakes.'

'But nothing will happen tonight.' This reassurance is relished, rhythmic: *noth*-ingwill-*happ*-ento-*night*.

But surely there is a chance, the tiniest chance, an outside chance that she will regain consciousness tonight, if only briefly or partially; and as long is there is a chance, I cannot leave.

He insists, 'She'll be fine,' smiling over her before cheerfully warning me, 'You've been here too long. You've done your best. Don't martyr yourself. Come home for a rest. You'll be more use to her if you've had some rest.'

But suddenly I know, and can try to explain: 'If no one's here when she wakes, then for that one moment she'll not know that we've been here at all.' I urge him to, '*Imagine*: imagine that moment, imagine waking here,' alone, in Intensive Care, 'and perhaps knowing nothing, remembering nothing . . .' But these words are superfluous, they fall away, tipping me into a shrug. Quite simply, 'She shouldn't feel, not even for a moment, that she has been abandoned.'

Slowly, he relinquishes his stance, stretches back in his chair. 'Do you really not want me here?' A genuine question, not a complaint: he is wide open for my reply; there is nothing in his expression, no wariness, no niggling, no watchfulness except for my answer.

And this disarms me: because, *not want him here?* How could this ever have been true? So I try to explain, 'I think that I thought that I ought . . .' *to not have you here.* 'Do you really want to stay?'

'With you,' he confirms: *Not without you.*

I give up, give in, shrug: *Fine-by-me.* More than fine: inside the shrug I turn warm.

He stands, and yawns, 'I will have that cup of coffee, though.' Composing himself, he tightens his gaze to a twinkle. '*Then* I'll tell you what Claire said to me,' he stage-whispers, openly conspiratorial, 'when she *deigned* to return my phone call yesterday.'

He turns away, and I am struck: is this what kindness is? We are so very different, in so many ways, yet he treats me as his own kind. I call quietly after him, 'I'll *share* a Twix.'

Zoe

....

Surely there is no woman who would let this man leave home each morning in these clothes. But there is a ring on his wedding-ring finger. Perhaps he is divorced. Or perhaps she hates him and relishes his daily unknowing humiliation. Perhaps she has less dress sense than him. Less? Impossible. Today he is wearing a striped shirt with an unstriped collar, neither section particularly suggestive of cotton: what is the term, *man-made fibre*? And I think that I can see a vest. Last week I definitely saw a vest. How old is he? Thirty? Forty? He is wearing a bow tie, of course; because if there is something that a psychiatrist loves, it is a bow tie. Why?

Can he see what I am thinking? He is looking at me, as usual, from behind his desk, which is quite a distance because he is slumped far back in his chair. Small bright brown eyes. I ripple with a desire to tell him, *I have a phobia about psychiatrists.* But I suppress this because he would act as if he had heard it before, and perhaps this is true, it is difficult to tell, because he always looks as if he has heard everything before. Perhaps psychiatrists are all trained to look like this. Perhaps there is a specific Diploma in Superior Knowingness. In fact, he knows nothing about me. Even if I wanted to tell him, I could not, because he would think I was mad. And I am not mad. I am not mad and I do not need to be here. When I first came here, I considered telling him that I was adopted and that there had been trouble with my adoptive mother. But then I wondered: if I had been adopted, would this be written somewhere on my records? I cannot afford to let him think of me as a liar. To him, lying is more serious than madness. He would keep me here even longer.

It is his job to find the truth, and a lie is half-way to the truth. If I lied, he would be on the scent, I would never be free of him. So I tell him nothing at all.

But unfortunately, thinking of my new phobia, I fail to suppress the sparkle of a grin.

'Something is amusing?' he drawls.

Amusement is yet another nervous tic, to him. I have noticed that psychiatrists do not joke. I suppose that it is their job *not* to joke. They can theorise about jokes, I suppose, but not make them. But do they joke off duty? Dr Wilson always looks so depressed. And no wonder, because it must be an utterly depressing job. But, then, why do it? What is his problem? And these sessions, one-to-one, are sheer cabaret compared with The Group. The Group meets twice each week in a side room off a ward. It is organised by Dr Wilson and Lindy, an occupational therapist, for the younger people who are staying on the ward plus those who have been recently released, and a few other outpatients. I have noticed that those who come from the ward tend to be wearing slippers.

Susie wears slippers. She is a tubby anorexic: once anorexic, now fat and back on the ward with depression. There is also a real anorexic, Lita, who left the ward a while ago but is on her way back, thinner, sinking beneath huge jumpers but unable to hide the wearing-thin of her face. Surely Lindy, the occupational therapist, cannot fail to be aware of the irony of her own position, sitting supposedly wise and happy but utterly huge, with people who talk about nothing but their weight. I am thankful that anorexia is not my problem because I would be unable to mention it in Lindy's presence. I suppose that she is determined to brazen it out; but, then, what else can she do? As well as the anorexics, there are the orphans: Jennifer, whose mother died years ago and whose father died recently of spinal cancer; Paul, who never had any parents, who came from care, who cuts himself. Jennifer is gradually washing away her hands. And then there is Colin. Colin is due to marry soon but the wedding will probably have to be postponed again because he is back in hospital. He mentions *My fiancée* constantly; and, in a sense, I am fascinated, because what woman would marry Colin? This is a very different issue from Dr Wilson's wife. Because Dr Wilson is a psychiatrist, which is vaguely interesting. More interesting than a Telecom engineer, although mechanically-minded Colin will have his uses around the house. I am not serious when I wonder about Dr Wilson's wife. But *Colin's fiancée?*

Not only does Colin mention *My fiancée* constantly, but he mentions everything else constantly, he talks constantly. His nose twitches rapidly to keep his (tinted) glasses in place. Tiny nose. Tiny eyes. Tiny crinkles in his hair. He looks around at us all when he is talking, but I am unsure that he sees us. Not *really* sees us, like the rest of us see each other. He insists that there is nothing wrong with him. I have a suspicion that Dr Wilson thinks that there is quite a lot wrong with him. But what? There are no tell-tale signs, no sloppy slippers, no slashes on his wrists, and he is the right size.

Last week in The Group, Lita happened to mutter that she was, 'So fucking fed up.'

Dr Wilson could barely contain his excitement. 'What did you say, Lita?' he asked slowly, swooning with significance.

She ignored him, said nothing more, curled up her little hands inside her woollen cuffs.

So she failed to win the Wilson-Lindy prize for the session – *You have worked very hard today, it must have been very difficult for you to say those things* – which went instead to Jennifer for revealing that she had felt angry with her father. I tend to avoid saying anything, until Dr Wilson demands, *I wonder how listening to that makes the rest of us feel, how does it make you feel, Zoe?* And this invariably ends with me telling him that I feel that I am in the wrong place, that there is nothing the matter with me, that I want to leave.

Which is what I am doing now.

He shifts grandly in his chair. 'What if you had a problem with your liver, and I let you walk out of here?'

'Dr Wilson,' I stress, 'I'm not ill, and you will not cure me.' Unsurprisingly, there is no reaction in his eyes, so I decide to speak more bluntly: 'But I suppose that it won't look good for you if I come back in.'

And briefly there is something in his eyes. 'Actually, it won't look too good for you, either.'

Reluctantly, I concede, with a hint of a smirk.

'Don't you want people to care about you?' he asks mildly. He stretches, places his hands behind his head, revealing his wristwatch, snappy steel strap.

'You don't care about me,' I explain. 'It's your job, your duty.' He is not so very different from Mum, whose sudden, intense involvement in my life was not motivated by care for me. And Mrs Dutton? I do not know, but surely there is a sense in which her efforts to reclaim me were not made on my behalf: she wanted something, regardless of me. Both of them wanted something *from* me, not *for* me.

He smiles his superior smile (copyright, Institute of Psychiatrists): 'And the two are mutually exclusive?'

Very clever. I change the subject: 'Look, Dr Wilson, I made a *mistake*, I was *wasn't well*.'

'But I thought you *weren't* ill.' He frowns, an impression of concern.

I half-throw my hands in front of me, both flappy and stiff with fury. 'Whatever, why-ever, I made a mistake and I'm not likely to do it again.' I goad: 'Or don't you allow mistakes?'

'Not if there is no possibility of learning from them.'

'I'm *learning*, I'm *learning*, watch me.'

He inhales noisily, swings forward, 'You intended to kill yourself,' he reminds me, solemnly, urgently.

And I hate him to remind me, which, of course, he does during every session. It is his job to remind me.

I ask him, 'And you haven't ever felt like going to sleep and never waking again?'

He raises his unruly eyebrows, pretends to consider. Then

replies, 'I've never taken the entire contents of a bottle of sleeping pills, no.'

'Well, you haven't lived,' I snap, before tightening all over in terror, realising that I have gone too far.

But he says simply, 'I don't think that you're taking this very seriously.'

I sigh, suddenly weary. 'And I think that you're taking it too seriously.'

He sits back, folds his arms. 'You did a very serious thing.'

I shrug. 'It just happened.'

'But if this can *just happen* to you, then it seems to me that you're very vulnerable.'

No, it was not me who was vulnerable: it was Mum. She *was* vulnerable: now, somehow, she is different. The other day, when she was different, when she surprised me again by not turning on me, I half-snapped, half-laughed, *What's up with you?* She shrugged, said gloomily, *Live and let live.*

I tell Dr Wilson, 'It's my life, luckily I still *have* my life, and I want to go and *live* my life.' I know now that this is what I have been trying to say to him for some time. I lean so far forward that if I look down, I will be able to read the notes on his desk. But instead I look into his eyes and say, 'And I can't do any of that if I'm stuck here.' Does he revise the notes before I come to see him? Because surely he cannot remember the details of so many people. Would he know me if he saw me in Sainsbury's?

He is taking another deep breath (is he sleepy, after his lunch?). 'Okay,' he says sceptically. 'If you walk out of here, if you walk back into your life, what do you find? What is priority, for you, at the moment?'

Easy: 'Exams.'

A twitch of the eyebrows. 'A lot to cope with, don't you think?' *If you're vulnerable.*

'No, I'm good at exams. Weren't you?'

He looks down onto his desk, sits still and silent for a while. I wait, because I know what he is doing. I have learned that whenever he looks down, he is casting stillness and silence around the room, vital preparations for dispensing wisdom. If he was looking at me, then he would be waiting for me to speak. Eventually he indicates with one of his big sharp inward breaths that he is going to speak again.

'Zoe. You have been very close to death.' And he looks at me.

And, of course, he is right. And I remember how it felt, when I was breathless but somehow full of air, no, it was emptiness, I was full of emptiness.

I find that I am looking beyond him to the venetian blinds, the pot plant on the window sill.

'It felt inevitable,' I tell him, tell the plant. Tell myself.

'Which must have been very frightening,' he says distantly.

'No.' Curiously, no. 'Comforting. Reassuring.' Despite myself, I glance at him, check with him. His face says nothing to me. 'Nothing bad could happen.' I try harder to explain: 'If I was going to die, then nothing else, bad, could happen. If I stayed alive, I didn't know what was going to happen.'

He says softly, reminds me, 'It didn't happen, you didn't die.'

'No.'

I hear his chair creak, I know that he is leaning forward. After a moment, he asks, 'So how does *that* feel?'

'Fine.' And now I cannot stop myself looking up, insolent, eager to impress upon him, '*Fine*. I've told you before. I'm telling you now. That's my point.' My gaze falls away again to the pot plant, and I shrug nonchalantly. 'Change of heart.' I shrug again, perplexed. 'Change of mind.' I look again at him. 'To be honest, I can't remember why I took the pills.' Or why I felt that there was no future.

'Which must make life easier for you,' he replies caustically.

'Not at this particular moment,' I snap back. Because I would love to be able to remember something juicy to satisfy him.

Desperately, I challenge him, 'Surely life is all about starting anew?' How can I make him see? Small brown eyes. Flat white light, NHS light, all around this tiny room.

He says, 'I think it's about not letting the past cause the future.'

As if we can stop the past.

'Not letting the past blindly dictate the future.'

As if the past has no eyes. But my past has eyes. 'The past comes from everywhere,' I tell him. 'It doesn't belong to one person.'

But the present is mine. I look at the clock on the wall, very white, beaming, wide open. It is standard issue, of course, a reminder of every classroom and waiting room in which I have ever been, in which I have ever been held.

'Our time's up,' I prompt him. *YOUR time's up*.

He is startled, seeks his wristwatch. 'Oh. Yes.'

For a psychiatrist, he is a surprisingly bad timekeeper.

'Right,' he is saying. Or something like it. I am lifting my coat from the back of my chair. Whatever he says, I can go from here now, and never come back and no one can make me do otherwise.

Caddy

I know that Zoe has an appointment here, with a doctor, every Tuesday afternoon. This is all I know; I do not know the time, or the purpose. I know because Dinah Fox told me. She said, 'She seems fine, they have her up at the hospital for two mornings each week, some discussions or something, with some others; and then she sees one of the doctors every Tuesday afternoon.' Then she added, 'Very time-consuming; I think she's eager to move on now.'

This afternoon I am waiting for her, just this once, because I have something to say. I came at noon, sat on this bench, watched; and a few minutes before three o'clock, I saw her going into the building. She was moving very fast. The doors opened automatically for her, which struck me as odd, because why should this hospital require automatic doors? In an ordinary hospital, yes, for stretchers and wheelchairs; but a psychiatric hospital? Do psychiatric patients become too fearful or depressed to manage doors? The doors were slightly slower than Zoe, they slowed her down.

When Dinah Fox told me about Zoe's appointments, she was in my house. It was not the first time that we had spoken since our afternoon together in Intensive Care. I rang to ask after Zoe, and eventually Dinah called to tell me that Zoe had come home from the hospital. Then she came to my house to give me some old photos of Zoe, which I refused to accept.

'Why?' she challenged, determinedly cheerful. 'They're copies.'

I considered this for a moment but decided, 'Maybe you should give them to Zoe – they're hers really.'

Now, through the rosebushes, I see Zoe. She is walking away from the main doors, striding, tiny in the distance; but, I know, tall in reality. She is shrugging her coat onto her shoulders, she has not even paused to put on her coat. This pace, this impatience, is new; she was a slow, careful child. I leave my bench, stiff from too much sitting, and anticipate her route to the road. I stand on the pavement and she flies closer and closer: coat flapping, flashing a silky black lining; hair flying too. Her expression is a knot of concentration, determination. She sweeps effortlessly along the pavement and does not see me until she almost bumps into me.

'God,' she yelps, pulling up sharp, 'It's you. What are you doing here?'

'I want to talk to you,' I say mildly, deliberately unthreatening.

'You and the rest of the world,' she mutters crossly. She has been upset by something, or someone. Not by me, I sense. Her clean soft face is streaky with the steam of her anger. I sense that she wants no questions from me.

We start to walk together. She walks slowly, for me. Although nothing, no one, is slow enough, for me, nowadays.

'I want to apologise,' I start, undeterred by her downcast scowl, 'for saying the things that I used to say to you.'

Without altering her expression she replies, 'What things?' No note of curiosity in her voice: either she knows *What things*; or, if she does not know, she does not care.

But she asked, so I have to reply. 'When you were little.' I stop, start, 'I didn't give you an easy time.'

'Forget it,' she says immediately, in the same tone. And now she halts, because I am noisily breathless behind her.

Before I reach her, I stop. She waits, feet fidgeting. But I am not going in her direction. Almost instantly, she realises: 'Are you coming?' she asks, doubtfully, nodding down the road in the direction of the town centre.

'No, I'm going home.'

'Oh. Will you be all right, to go back by yourself?'

'Well, of course.'

She bites her lower lip and knocks a sweep of hair behind an ear. 'Is that it, then?' Upbeat, but a note of puzzlement.

'No.'

Her expression hardens and sinks: *I thought not.*

And I thought I knew what I wanted to say. But I know the feeling, not the words. I try, 'What you did was wrong.'

'You mean morally wrong,' she accuses, breathtakingly quick, viciously dismissive.

'No, no . . .' I shake my head, my hands, desperate to stop her, to correct her, to correct myself. But how? How to say what I mean? In her glare, I start again: 'What you did . . . was the wrong thing to do.' Try again: 'It wasn't the *right* thing to do.' Yes, this is closer.

She is still staring, but now she looks fairly serene, by comparison.

Much more lightly, I add, 'But I expect that you know that by now.'

'Yes,' is all that she says.

'Which means that you're . . .' and I cannot bring myself to say *Not going to do it again*, 'safe for the future?'

'Yes,' she repeats.

The relief sings silently in the chambers of my heart. 'That's all.' I smile, to seal this. 'I'll be off now.'

She responds with a spasm of a smile, a thanks. 'See you, then.'

But as I turn away, she returns to her frown. What is she thinking? Suddenly she surprises me by calling, 'Third time lucky, eh?'

I glance over my shoulder but she is already quite a distance away from me, too far away for me to see her clearly any more.

Suzannah Dunn

Blood Sugar

'Suzannah Dunn is a new writer with a brilliant touch . . . A real writer for the nineties.'   Malcolm Bradbury

Constantly crabbed at by her mother, her style cramped by her many siblings, Lalie longs for independence and love. But can she ever escape her roots? Caught up in the lives of her friends – fascinating, talented Deborah; pouting, well-preened Roz; eccentric, madcap Lucy; and Ali, calm, dependable, yet enigmatic Ali – Lalie wonders what will become of them all, and what mysteries the future holds . . .

Suffused with sharp, witty dialogue and affording startling insights into the absurd and arbitrary nature of everyday life, *Blood Sugar* is a vivid and evocative portrayal of a generation's coming-of-age.

'Her writing is loaded with vibrant, visual images of so strongly evocative, so poetic a quality that they seem about to burst and to yield up a weight of hidden meaning.'   *Literary Review*

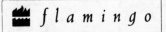

Maggie Gee

Lost Children

Alma wakes one ordinary morning to find her world has fallen apart. Her beloved teenage daughter Zoe has run away from home. On the landing is a curt note that explains nothing.

In the face of this catastrophe, Alma radically reconstructs her life – rejecting her husband, ignoring her son, plunging herself into a new job. But, insistent, inescapable, the same questions haunt her – what can she have done to Zoe to make her leave? Will she ever come home?

Beautifully written, *Lost Children* is the work of one of Britain's finest and most original novelists. Maggie Gee paints a searingly honest portrait of contemporary life, engaging in its humour, uncompromising in its intelligence and insight. A testament to the joys and pains of parenthood, *Lost Children* is also a poignant examination of what the process of growing up means to us all.

'The sheer quality of her writing borders on the sublime.'

Financial Times

A FLAMINGO HARDBACK

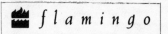

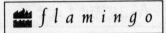
flamingo

Flamingo is a quality imprint publishing both fiction and non-fiction. Below are some recent literary fiction titles.

- ☐ No Other Life *Brian Moore* £5.99
- ☐ Working Men *Michael Dorris* £5.99
- ☐ A Thousand Acres *Jane Smiley* £5.99
- ☐ In the Lake of the Woods *Tim O'Brien* £5.99
- ☐ Dancing In Limbo *Edward Toman* £5.99
- ☐ Split Skirt *Agnes Rossi* £5.99
- ☐ The Great Longing *Marcel Möring* £5.99
- ☐ The Sandbeetle *Zina Rohan* £5.99
- ☐ Miss Smilla's Feeling for Snow *Peter Høeg* £5.99
- ☐ Postcards *E. Annie Proulx* £5.99
- ☐ Happenstance *Carol Shields* £5.99
- ☐ Desperadoes *Joseph O'Connor* £5.99
- ☐ The Bingo Palace *Louise Erdrich* £5.99
- ☐ The Bishop of San Fernando *David McLaurin* £5.99
- ☐ A Very Long Engagement *Sebastien Japrisot* £5.99
- ☐ Involved *Kate O'Riordan* £5.99
- ☐ Lost Children *Maggie Gee* £5.99
- ☐ The Kitchen God's Wife *Amy Tan* £5.99
- ☐ A Goat's Song *Dermot Healy* £5.99

You can buy Flamingo paperbacks at your local bookshop or newsagent. Or you can order them from HarperCollins Mail Order, Dept. 8, HarperCollins *Publishers*, Westerhill Road, Bishopbriggs, Glasgow G64 2QT. Please enclose a cheque or postal order, to the order of the cover price plus add £1.00 for the first and 25p for additional books ordered within the UK.

NAME (Block letters) _____

ADDRESS _____

_____